OPERATION MEDINA
THE JIHAD

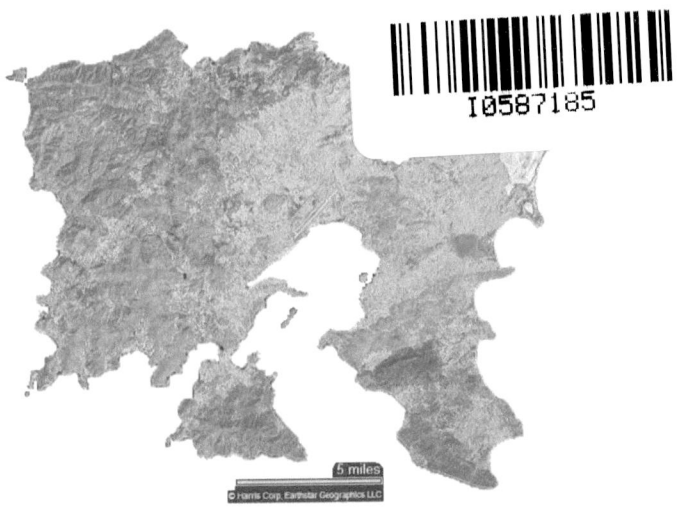

I0587185

George Mavro

TotalRecallPress.com
www.totalrecallpress.com

TotalRecall Publications, Inc..
1103 Middlecreek
Friendswood, Texas 77546
281-992-3131   281-482-5390 Fax
www.totalrecallpress.com

ISBN   978-1-59095-748-6
UPC   6-43977-27482-3

Printed in the United States of America with simultaneous
printings in Australia, Canada, and United Kingdom.

FIRST EDITION
1   2   3   4   5   6   7   8   9   10

To the air force security force members who have given their lives for their comrades and to the call of duty.

About the Author

George Mavro is a 24 year Air Force, security force veteran. He served over 22 years stationed in Europe, eight of those in Greece. He holds degrees in Government and International Relations. He presently lives in Florida with his wife and two sons.

About the Book

The Balkans and Mideast, a region very much in the news today, is the setting for this action novel which takes place in the not too distant future. The secular pro-western government of Turkey has been overthrown in a violent revolution and replaced by an Islamic fundamentalist regime. Her fanatical leader, General Muhammad Kemal, has contrived a devious plan to restore the Ottoman Empire in the Balkans and unite the Islamic world under his evil rule. To accomplish this, Kemal will launch a devastating war with all the tools in his arsenal including Islamic Jihadist terrorists and WMDs. His first targets are US ally Greece and the few remaining American forces stationed in the region.

Chapter 1

D-Minus 14, Istanbul Turkey

4 May, 0830hrs

General Muhammad Kemal, president of the Islamic Republic of Turkey, a middle-aged man of stocky build, gazed out of his downtown office window at the distant gleaming domes of the great Byzantine cathedral of Aghia Sophia. The majestic structure built by the great Byzantine emperor Justinian in the 6th century, prominently stood out in the early morning smog filled skyline of the bustling new Turkish Capitol. It had seen many a great empire rise and fall through the millennia. It was now witnessing the birth of another. Kemal's office located on the top floor of the ministry of defense building also served as his unofficial residence when he was away from the presidential palace. The office was outfitted with the latest in computer and telecommunication gear. With the press of a button, he could communicate with any of his military commanders in the field.

The General's desk was cluttered with empty coffee cups; he had spent most of the night working on the final details of his plan. The draft was ready to be presented to the Revolutionary Committee for approval, not that any one of them had the courage or the power to defy him. He would though ask for their rubber stamp of approval, to make them feel that they still had some vestige of power left. Kemal was looking forward to seeing the look on the committee members' faces when he revealed his ambitious plan to them. A knock on the door quickly brought the General back to the present.

"Enter!"

It was his aid, Colonel Ahmet Azoglou. "Sir, the meeting with the Revolutionary Committee is in twenty minutes. Oh and by the way, there has been another protest filed by the Greek Foreign Ministry, concerning alleged violations of their sea and air space by our air and naval units."

"They can go to hell! We will soon deal with the Greeks. When we are finally finished with them, they will beg us for mercy."

"That isn't all, sir. The Americans and the Germans are complaining about our financial aid, to what they allege to be radical Islamic fundamentalist groups located in Germany. Our Foreign Ministry has assured them, our aid is going toward the building of Mosques and Madrasas schools, so that we can better educate our youth in their Islamic heritage."

"I can always count on you, Ahmet, better to keep the infidel believing that they are safe and have nothing to fear from us. All these years the Germans have been growing rich from the sweat and labors of their Turkish guest workers. Their lack of gratitude has been displayed many times by the desecration of our Mosques and the murder of our women and children by

Neo-Nazi hate groups, with the local authorities doing little to stop these atrocities. Let them keep thinking, my friend, that we are nothing but stupid rag heads, as they refer to us."

"Of course, sir."

"Now go. I must pray."

The General knelt and began his morning prayers by asking the prophet to give him the strength and wisdom to carry out his bold plan. He also uttered a small prayer for the soul of his long departed father, the man who instilled in him the values of Islam and taught him of the past glories of the great Ottoman Empire. It was his father who insisted naming him Muhammad, using the Arab purist form of the prophet's name instead of the Turkish version Mehmet. His father and his grandfather had both been career soldiers. He had never met his grandfather who had been killed fighting the Greeks in Anatolia in the early 1920s. This was one of the reasons he had chosen the military as a career.

While attending the Military academy, Muhammad met Ahmet Azoglou, the son of a poor but pious Imam. The two young men found a lot in common, especially on matters of religion, and had become inseparable friends. It was Ahmet who later introduced Muhammad to the Brotherhood, a secret underground Islamic fundamentalist organization, dedicated to overthrowing the corrupt pro-western government and transforming Turkey into an Islamic republic. His struggle for power had been a long and hard uphill battle. The Brotherhood had been his tool, but he now controlled the future destiny of Turkey. There was a knock at the door. It was Colonel Azoglou again.

"Sir, I am sorry that I have interrupted your prayers. Major Bankasi is here."

"Send him in."

Major Nevzat Bankasi, Kemal's chief operative in Germany, entered the General's office, snapped to attention and rendered a sharp salute. Kemal motioned for him to take a seat.

"I only have a few minutes before I must meet with the Revolutionary Council, so make this quick."

"Yes, sir. I have selected Ramstein Air Base as our target. It's the only base containing USAF fighter assets on the continent that could pose a problem for us."

Kemal smiled. "Excellent, Major. I know the base. It's headquarters for the U.S. air forces in Europe. A strike there would not only cripple their air power, but also severely damage their morale and prestige."

"That is exactly what I had in mind, sir. I will have the finished operational plan for you by tomorrow morning."

"Thank you major, I will be looking forward to reviewing it. That will be all then. I will see you tomorrow."

As Major Bankasi turned to leave, the General's aid entered the room.

"Sir, it's time for your meeting with the Revolutionary Committee. They are awaiting your presence."

"Thank you Ahmet. Now help me with my uniform, I must hurry."

A few minutes later, General Muhammad Kemal, President of the Islamic Republic of Turkey, leader of the Revolutionary Committee and Commander and Chief of the Turkish Armed Forces, entered the smoke filled meeting chamber in full military regalia. Everyone in the windowless room which was purposely constructed this way for added security, stood up as a sign of respect.

"Good morning my brothers, please take your seats. I have something of great importance to reveal to all of you. What I am about to say to you is Top Secret and is not to be revealed to anyone outside this room under pain of death. As you are all aware, our consolidation of power has been complete for over three years. Our sacrifices have been great."

The General paused for a moment, as he looked around at the faces of all those present and remembered all the others who had given their lives for the revolution. He thought back to those early days of the revolution, when his forces had been attacked and severely battered on several instances by American F-16 fighters that were flying air cover for the western backed secular government. Had it not been for the outcry and threat of open military intervention by other Islamic states, notably Iran and Pakistan, the revolution might have faltered. Once the Islamic revolutionaries had established complete control of the Turkish armed forces, the rest of the country was quickly brought under the reign of the Islamic revolution. This was now all in the past, the revolution had triumphed and the Americans were quickly forced to withdraw from Turkey. The new Turkish Islamic Republic, as it was called, had been quickly recognized by most of the Islamic world, except for Saudi Arabia and Kuwait, whose rulers were western puppets. Nevertheless, he Muhammad Kemal would soon to be the most powerful man in all of Islam.

The General continued with his speech, "But the blood and sacrifice was not in vain my brothers. We are now ready to export our neo Ottoman Islamic revolution and render a decisive blow to the enemies of the prophet. I have named this great undertaking, Operation Medina, in honor of the holy city where the Prophet Muhammad began the Hijra, the beginning of the new era. So, as was for him, it will be for us. We will first begin our great Jihad by crushing our age-old enemies, the Greeks. If we succeed in this endeavor, we will have regained much of the territory lost to us during the Balkan wars of 1912-13 and we will have virtual hegemony over the Balkans. The Aegean Sea will once again become an Ottoman Turkish lake. This is the reason I have called you all here. I must have the council's total support for this great undertaking."

"Are you mad?" shouted Imam Ibrahim Karhan, a short frail man in his early seventies. "Your wild scheme will ruin us all and that which we have fought for. The Europeans and the Americans will not sit idly by and watch us destroy one of their allies."

General Kemal turned and stared for a moment at the Imam. Intimidated by the General's piercing glare, the old man took his seat and said no more. Kemal then turned his gaze for only a couple of seconds at the other skeptical faces in the room, before he began to unfold his bold plan.

"I know all of you have your doubts but please first hear me out. Our armed forces are prepared to deliver several crushing blows on to the Greeks. In two weeks, our military will begin their annual maneuvers in Eastern Thrace and in the Aegean Sea. Under the guise of these maneuvers, we will strike and we will strike the infidels hard with no mercy." There was now total silence in the room. He knew that he had captured their attention.

"During the opening phase of our offensive, we will launch non-persistent chemical attacks at Greek military installations and units on the island of Limnos as well as border defense units facing the Evros River in Western Thrace. These strikes will be delivered both by aircraft and by our Saladin long range missiles. The chemical attacks will be immediately followed up with coordinated air strikes on enemy air, land and naval bases, including telecommunications and government ministries throughout the country," said the General.

"The second phase of the operation will consist of airborne and naval landings, with the objective of capturing the island of Limnos. Enemy opposition should be limited. I'm positive our chemical attack will catch them in their sleep. Once Limnos is secured and fortified with Harpoon and other anti-ship missiles, control of the sea lanes in the Aegean, to the Black Sea and to the Mediterranean, will belong to us. While all this is taking place on Limnos, other airborne units will assault the city of Alexandroupolis in Western Thrace. Their objective will be to secure and hold the port facilities until the arrival of our armored columns."

A silence had fallen over the room. General Kemal looked at all of them. Their initial doubt was now slowly being replaced with one of optimism, as he continued to unravel his bold plan.

"Not only will the Greeks in Thrace have to face our army, but they will also have to deal with a civil insurrection in Thrace. I have instructed our agents in Kommotini, a town approximately one hundred kilometers from the border, to incite a rebellion amongst the local Muslim population, a few hours before our attack. This will be another thorn in the side of the Greeks which they will have to deal with. My brothers, we will not be alone in this great undertaking," stressed Kemal. "As an additional guarantee toward our success, I've enlisted the aid of our Muslim brothers and allies in Albania and Macedonia. Their armies will launch limited harassing attacks in Epirus and northern Greece. The Greeks will be attacked on all sides. It will be too much for them to handle at one time. Within ten days, our tanks will be in Thessaloniki and victory will be ours."

The room erupted in a clamor of shouts. Brigadier General Tanik Aturk, a dark, short and slightly overweight middle aged man and commander of the elite military police, stood and motioned for the others in the room to be quiet. He was a man not easily intimidated by General Kemal.

"This is a very bold plan brother Kemal. What of their allies, the Europeans and the Americans? What of the Bulgarians? Do we have enough fuel and supplies for such a vast undertaking?"

Kemal smiled. He had expected these questions. "Yes, these are valid concerns and I will try to answer them. The initial attack will be swift. By the time the Europeans debate and decide to come up with a plan calling for military intervention, our operation will be successfully completed. NATO today, is but a shell of its former self. In regards to the Americans, with their draw down of forces and the closing of bases in Europe, they have very few resources that could immediately intervene against us. Besides, I have a few surprises in store for the Americans which I will reveal to you in due time. I am positive they will more than equalize the odds toward our favor. As for our Bulgarian neighbors, they have promised to remain neutral, in exchange for free access to the port city of Thessaloniki. Believe me, there is no love lost between the Greeks and the Bulgarians, in this, rest assured. Besides, their military is in no shape to do anything." The General could see some of the members of the Revolutionary committee, looking at each other and nodding their heads at his last comment.

"Now as to the status of our supply situation, thanks to American stupidity, our forces possess some of the most advanced weapons systems in the West's inventory. Our seizures of huge amounts of weapons and material, which the Americans had stockpiled in our country after the Iraq war and the modernization programs of the previous governments, guarantee our military superiority over the Greeks. Our recent annexation of Mosul from the corrupt Iraqi Infidel regime which we helped our Shiite and Kurdish brothers overthrow will provide us with an unlimited fuel supply for our war machine. My brothers, by the grace of Allah we will succeed. Give me your support for this great Jihad and "Operation Medina" will be put into operation in fourteen days! Allah is great!"

Kemal overwhelmed by his own emotions, began shouting, "Allah is great! Allah Akbar! Death to the infidel!" Immediately the room erupted in pandemonium, as everyone present joined in praise to God. General Kemal knew he had the needed support to put his ambitious plan into action.

Chapter 2

Ramstein Air Base, Germany
11 May, 1326hrs

Lieutenant Colonel Jack Logan throttled back as he lined up his F-16 Falcon for final approach to Ramstein air base. Logan glanced out of his cockpit's right side and admired the aerial view of Landstuhl castle which overlooked the base from its perch, high atop a tree covered hill. It had stood there for centuries and had seen many great armies come and go, the latest being the American in 1945 with the collapse of Nazi Germany. This morning's training flight had been initially uneventful, until he and his wing man were ambushed by two Luftwaffe Mig-29 Fulcrums. The Migs, which had been the property of the former East German People's air force, had been added to the inventory of the German Luftwaffe upon unification of the two Germanys. The Mig was an excellent dog fighter and in the proper hands a dangerous adversary for even the F-16. However, the two Americans highly experienced F-16 pilots, veterans of the Iraqi wars and the Turkish civil war, quickly got the upper hand and successfully ended the engagement. The final score USAF two, Luftwaffe zero. With all the morning's excitement, Logan was looking forward to landing and having a couple of cold Bitburgers at the officer's club.

After touching down, Logan taxied his fighter and parked it in its hardened aircraft shelter, located in the 526th squadron area on the south side of Ramstein air base. Once the plane had been properly parked, he shut of the engine, opened the canopy and was helped out of the cockpit by his crew chief, a slim and very attractive brunette staff sergeant.

"How was your flight sir?"

"Had a great time, Cindy. We had a run in with a couple of German Mig-29s. But we smoked them. Make sure you give her a real good check out. I really put her through the loops today."

"I'll make sure to give her a good going over, sir," she said, with a bit of sarcasm in her voice. The inspection would take most of the evening.

"You're one hell of a crew chief. Take tomorrow off and go out and have some fun with your boyfriend."

"Gee, thanks a lot for screwing me again, sir," Cindy mumbled under her breath as Logan walked out of the Tab Vee structure. Colonel Logan wasn't your normal operations officer who usually spent more time flying a desk than an airplane. If he had exceeded the allowed Gs, it would be the second time in a month that he managed to exceed the G-stress load on his plane's air frame.

Officers Club, Ramstein Air Base Germany
1610hrs, 11 May

After his debriefing at squadron Ops, Logan jumped into his red Porsche and drove over to the officer's club on the north side of Ramstein air base. During the early 1980s, the Ramstein officers club had been the subject of a lengthy congressional inquiry over the misappropriation of $20 million dollars of the tax payer's money. The money had been spent during the club's construction, on such lavish items as a $200,000, handmade crystal chandelier. No one had gone to jail over it, but a couple of Generals had to opt for early retirement. Parking his car in front of the O-club, he walked inside to the bar, where he ordered a cold bottle of Bitburger beer and sat down at one of the tables to savor his drink. It wasn't too long before he was joined by his wing man, Major Tom Sutter and his squadron commander, Colonel Joe Hanson.

"Waitress, three beers, please", said Hanson.

"I heard you guys had a run in with a couple of Migs."

"It was a little touchy for a while, sir," said Logan

"Those Fulcrums can really turn. But the Falcon's lighter weight, superior avionics and our training, paid off at the end. The F-16's a top rate fighter plane. Deadly in the proper hands, as those two Luftwaffe fighter jocks found out."

"I didn't expect anything less from you two guys," said Hanson "Just to let you know, I got a call from the commander of those two Fulcrum pilots. They're sending the 526th two kegs of beer and would like a rematch. Next time, it will be against two experienced former East German pilots who will be flying the Migs."

"Sure sir, anytime, as long as they keep the beers coming." Logan's comments raised a laugh amongst the small crowd of fighter pilots that had gathered around their table.

"We got to be careful; I hear the Germans are using beer as their secret weapon."

"Yeah, maybe they figure they can beat us if we're flying with a hangover," said Sutter.

"Well, I'll see you guys later. I am going home for a long hot shower and some rest. It's been a long day," Logan said as he got up from his seat.

Walking into the lobby, he spotted Captain Wendy Barnes, walking out of the rest room. She was one of the few female fighter pilots in the USAF. Barnes had only been in country for about a month. He didn't yet know what kind of pilot she was, but he noticed that she did fill her baggy air force flight suit quite well.

"Hi sir,"

"Hey Captain. I was just about to leave when I saw you. I was wondering how you're coming along. Is there anything I can assist you with?"

"Thank you, sir. Everything's going along as well as can be expected."

The guys must be giving her the cold shoulder, thought Logan. "Can I buy you a drink, Captain?"

"Sure, why not?"

A few minutes later, they were sitting in the club's cocktail lounge which was frequented mostly by couples.   The atmosphere in the lounge was a lot cozier than the casual bar normally occupied by the rowdier fighter pilots. Logan looked around to see if he recognized anyone inside. He hoped he hadn't been seen by any of the guys. They would immediately interpret it, as him wanting to get into the new pilot's pants. Well let them think what they wanted. He was just being nice, more than anyone else had been so far to her.

"Well Captain, why did you want to be a fighter pilot?"

She looked at Logan, and then burst out laughing. "Please don't be offended, sir. What I am usually asked by most men first, is do I have a boyfriend or am I married. Well to answer your question, sir. My dad was a fighter pilot. He was one of the last shot down over Iraq. His mission was to take out a heavily defended power station. His plane was damaged by triple A on his first pass. Instead of jettisoning his munitions and returning to base, he continued with his bomb run and took out the target. As he was leaving, a surface to air missile blew him out of the sky. They awarded him, posthumously, the Distinguished Flying Cross for his actions. I was young and barely remember him. My mom never remarried. I grew up looking at his pictures and other memorabilia."

My, she's beautiful, he thought. Her high cheek bones and full lips gave her an exotic look. Logan caught himself staring at her.

"I'm sorry to hear that about your dad. Flying is a dangerous profession, especially during war time. Yet, it also offers a thrill no other profession does."

"I know. That's why I chose it. I hope I never have to use the skills I learned to kill others. But if I have to, I want to be the best."

Logan thought of the two enemy pilots he had blown out of the sky that cold winter morning over eastern Turkey. They hadn't even turned to fight. They had been running for their lives. But it had been war.

"Don't worry, if the time ever comes, you'll do great. Besides, that's what we train for."

She looked at her watch, and rose to leave. "Thanks for the drink, sir. I must be going; I have a lot of reading to do. I'm going to take my Stan Evil check ride tomorrow and I want to brush up on a few things."

"It was my pleasure, Captain. I wish you luck for tomorrow."

"Thanks, sir. I'll be seeing you." He watched her as she walked out of the bar.

D-Minus 7, Southeastern Aegean firing range
11 May, 0800hrs

Lieutenant Yiannis Vassiliou, commander of the Hellenic Navy warship Hydra, gave the order for flank speed. With columns of spray shooting up from her bow the French built, Combattante II missile boat, rapidly accelerated over the calm deep blue waters of the Aegean Sea. Armed with four Exocet surface to surface sea skimming missiles, two torpedo tubes and two light 35mm antiaircraft guns, the small but deadly craft, embodied the spirit of the ancient Athenian Peltest. The Hydra's mission during a battle would be to proceed to the front of the fleet and sling her missiles at the advancing enemy and like the lightly armed ancient Peltest, she would quickly retreat to the rear.

While the small nimble warship knifed through the water at 36kts, Lieutenant Vassiliou, a handsome man of medium build, dressed in a well-worn utility uniform, stood by his weapons officer, Kostas Georgiou, who was presently glued to the radar screen. Assured that everything was in order, Yiannis stole a quick glance around the rest of the cramped bridge and nodded his head, satisfied with what he saw. His well-trained bridge crew operated with a fine tuned precision at their battle stations, monitoring the functions of the boat as well as the air and sea space around them, just as they would in an actual engagement.

"Mr. Georgiou, what is our position?"

Kostas Georgiou ran his hand through his graying hair before replying. "Fifteen nautical miles from the target Captain," replied Ensign Georgiou, as he fed the latest target data to the missile's fire director computer. Satisfied with what he observed, Yiannis finally gave the order to shoot.

"We're well within range, Kostas. Prepare to launch."

"I have a positive lock on the target, sir".

"Fire!"

Even at the high speed that the Hydra was traveling, the boat shuddered as the Exocet anti-ship missile left its launch tube, smoke and fire trailing behind it. The missile accelerated rapidly and disappeared from view over the horizon. Flying at over 500 Knots, it had taken only a couple of minutes, before the Exocet's radar had found and locked on to the target, an old decommissioned destroyer. When the Exocet's radar indicated that the old ship was only a mile away, the missile's targeting computer gave the final course correction to its flight controls. The missile climbed to fifty meters and then dived into the target. The ensuing flash lit up the early morning sky. Pieces of the old ship were blown almost 100 feet into the air.

"A direct hit, sir." Georgiou informed his commander, after the Exocet had disappeared off the radar screen. Not that they hadn't already figured it out. Yiannis and the rest of the crew had seen the bright flash of the missile's detonation off on the horizon.

"Good shooting Kostas, you are the best weapons officer in the fleet."

"Thank you, sir, I 'm really flattered getting compliments from one of the finest skippers in the Hellenic navy," provoking a laugh from everyone on the bridge.

"The BS is getting too deep in here gentlemen. Let's get back to work. Helmsman, take us to the target. I want to see what our little rocket did,"

Twenty minutes later, the Hydra was drifting with the gentle Aegean swell, several hundred meters from the smoking hulk. Yiannis was amazed at the missile's destructive power. The Exocet had penetrated deep inside the hull before detonating. All that was left of the once proud ship was a smoking twisted wreck.

"I think the explosion has probably sprung some of her seams, she's beginning to slowly settle in the water. Let's finish her off. Prepare to fire a torpedo."

"Aye, aye, sir."

Warrant officer Panos, the helmsman, gave power to the engines and the Hydra pulled back to a safe distance of a fifteen hundred meters.

"Fire one," commanded Yiannis.

There was a hiss of air and a splash as the torpedo leaped from its launch tube and hit the water.

"Torpedo off and running, sir."

Fifty seconds later, there was a loud explosion followed by a tall plume of water. The torpedo had struck the smoking hulk amidships, breaking her back and quickly sending her to her watery grave. As she slipped beneath the waves, the crew of the Hydra cheered. She had served the Hellenic navy well and some of the Hydra's crew had even served on her. Everyone agreed this was a more fitting end for a proud old warship than the dock yard cutting torch.

"Captain, there's a message for you from the air force Albatross seaplane that's orbiting overhead monitoring the exercise."

"What do they have to say Sparks?"

"The message says: Good shooting, got great photos of the missile hit. See you back in Salamis for a drink. It's from Lieutenant Takis Mavridis, sir."

Yiannis smiled as he thought of Takis, his old academy classmate and friend, who was assigned as a naval support coordinator on the old refurbished Albatross seaplanes that were brought back into service to face the ever growing threat from the east. Takis dreaded flying, but he had volunteered for one of the few slots the air force allotted to the navy to fly as a navigator and naval reconnaissance coordinator.

"Makis, give me the mike and headphones."

"Here sir, we are on the Albatross's frequency," said the signal man.

"Thanks. Missile boat Hydra to Albatross, put Takis on please." A few seconds later his friend was on the radio.

"Hi Yiannis, what's up?"

"Hey buddy, just wanted to ask if you've soiled your pants yet," replied Yiannis.

"Come on, give me a break. It's a calm day with no turbulence. Besides, I can't wait till this old crate gets back to Elefsis. I got a real hot date that's waiting for me back in town."

"What about our drink?"

"Don't worry. By the time you dock and finish your debriefing, I'll drive over and meet you at the Salamis naval base snack bar. I also just remembered that she has a real hot friend."

"You never quit," said Yiannis laughing.

"How many times have I told you that there is just one girl in my life?"

"I know, Eleni, but you can't knock me for trying to set you up. Besides, what are friends for?"

Yiannis laughed. "Don't catch anything. Remember to use a rain coat."

"I'll keep your advice in mind. You better enjoy Eleni's company while you can. I hear that our friendly neighbors, the Turks, are coming out in force, real soon."

"I heard that too. They'll be on their annual spring maneuvers."

"That still means both you and I will be busy monitoring their movements. You will be away on patrol for at least two weeks," said Takis.

"Thanks for all that good news. See you in a few hours for that drink, Hydra out." *That was really bad news, thought Yiannis.* He had planned to take leave next week and go to the islands with his fiancée Eleni for a well-deserved holiday. Since the Turkish fleet would be coming out in to the Aegean for maneuvers in the next few days, all leaves would most likely be canceled. Eleni would be disappointed, but she would have to get used to the military way of life, if she was going to become his wife. Naval command would want to have most of its personnel available, in case the Turkish maneuvers escalated into armed hostilities. He considered a war between the two countries improbable, but he couldn't fault naval command's concern. Ever since the Islamic Fundamentalists had seized power, relations between the two countries had become severely strained. But since when have they not been strained? Even during the pre-revolution days, when Turkey had been a member of NATO, there had been a sort of cold war going on between the two nations.

"Mr. Panou, set a course for home."

"Already done, sir. Helmsman, steer compass heading 310 degrees, ahead two thirds."

"Aye, aye Mr. Panou," acknowledged the helmsman, as he pointed the Hydra's sleek bow toward the direction that would take them home to the island of Salamis, home to Greece's main naval base.

A few hours later, the Hydra had reached the island of

Salamis located less than a mile from the mainland and only a few miles from Athens. The island was home port for most of the Hellenic navy. Once the boat had secured to the dock side, Yiannis jumped into a waiting jeep and drove to division headquarters for his mission debriefing. The jeep stopped by a one story building that served as the missile boat squadron headquarters. It, like most of the buildings on the installation, was painted white. Yiannis dismounted the jeep and headed straight inside, where he was ushered in to the squadron commanders office, Captain Georgios Tassiou.

"Sir, Lieutenant Vassiliou reporting as ordered."

"Sit down Yiannis," said the short heavy set man. Would you like a cigarette?

"No thank you, sir. I quit last month."

"Wish I could. Anyway, I see that your missile test fire went off without a hitch," said the older man.

"Yes sir, everything went off very smoothly. The boat and the crew performed flawlessly."

"I only expect the best from you and your crew. The nation depends on us for its survival in these troubled times. We must show the taxpayers that the billions spent on the fleet have not been wasted. But most of all, we must demonstrate to any potential aggressor that we are prepared to meet and defeat any hostile threat."

"Sir, my crew and I will always do our best. That, you can be assured of."

"I know I can, Yiannis. The Turks are beginning their annual spring maneuvers in the next few days."

"I know sir, I already heard the news."

"Then you must know Lieutenant, all leaves of key personnel as of 2400hrs tonight, will be canceled for the duration of the Turkish maneuvers. I' m sorry but I have to disapprove your leave. I know that you were looking forward to it."

"Yes sir, I wanted to take a small vacation with my fiancée, but she'll understand."

"I'll tell you what Yiannis leave your second in command in charge and take the next two days off. Just make sure that your boat and crew will be ready for deployment to Limnos in three days time. Your patrol area will be the northern Aegean. I will have written orders prepared for you in the next couple of days detailing your responsibilities."

Yiannis was surprised at the Captain's offer. "Thank you, sir."

"You deserve some time off. You have worked hard getting your boat and crew in shape. Oh, and give my regards to your fiancée. You are a very lucky guy. Eleni is a wonderful girl. That will be all, Lieutenant. You are dismissed."

"Thank you very much sir," said Yiannis, as he saluted and departed the office.

"It's time for that well earned Ouzo with Takis," he mumbled to himself, as he left the headquarters building and headed for the base snack bar.

Chapter 3

Athens, Greece
1800hrs, 13 May

Stuck in a huge traffic jam near the parliament building, Yiannis glanced at the digital clock on his Toyota's dashboard for the tenth time and became even more frustrated. He'd be late in picking up Eleni. Usually he avoided downtown Athens, but today, he had business at naval headquarters which was situated in the heart of the city. With traffic finally beginning to move, he drove past Adrian's arch, an ancient Roman marble monument crumbling from the air pollution that was eating away at the marble. The Athenian smog had done more damage to the city's ancient monuments in the last thirty years, than two thousand years of wars and natural disasters. Yiannis wondered what the ancient Athenians would say, if they could see the concrete jungle their once beautiful city had become. After spending another twenty minutes crawling through traffic, Yiannis finally arrived at Eleni's home and parked the car in front of the house. He walked to the door of the two story residence and rang the bell, which was answered a few seconds later by a handsome dark haired youth, Eleni's younger teenage brother, Tassos.

"Hi Yiannis, Come on in. Eleni has waiting for you to arrive for the last forty five minutes."

"I hope she's not angry that I'm late, but traffic was horrendous." Yiannis said, as he entered into the living room.

Eleni came into the room. She was dressed in tight fitting jeans and a low cut blouse that accented her attractive five foot eight figure. Her long chestnut brown hair was rolled back in a bun. She came over and gave him a kiss.

"What time are we meeting Takis?"

"We have to hurry. Takis has reserved a table for us at the Tourkolimano marina. You know the restaurant. I told him that we would be there around eight."

"Oh, that's great. The food there is superb and you know how much I love fish. Let's go I'm famished.

"Okay, but first let me say hello to your parents."

"They're not here, dear. Mom has gone shopping and dad is at the caffeneon (coffee house) playing cards with his friends."

"Let's go then."

"Sure, let me grab my purse."

They said their goodbye to Tassos, jumped into Yiannis' car and drove toward Piraeus where the Tourkolimano marina was located. With traffic moderate on the coastal highway, the drive took almost thirty minutes. When they arrived at Tourkolimano Yacht Marina, he pulled into the crowded restaurant parking lot where they were supposed to meet Takis and parked the car. Making their way inside, they were met by the manager who recognized Yiannis, a frequent customer, and showed them to their table which overlooked the marina that was filled with many luxurious yachts. Upon seeing his friends, Takis got up and greeted them, giving Eleni a hug and a kiss on the cheek. Almost a head taller than Yiannis, the polo shirt he was wearing accented his slender but muscular body.

"You are looking prettier every time I see you."

"Thank you, Takis. You're not looking bad yourself."

"Be careful. He says that line to all the pretty girls." Yiannis said, jokingly, evoking a laugh from both Takis and Eleni.

Yiannis motioned to get the waiter's attention. "Bring us a carafe of Ouzo and mezedes."

A few minutes later the Ouzo, a clear licorice tasting aperitif had arrived. Along with the drinks, the waiter had brought a plate of mezedes, which consisted of bite size portions of various cheeses, sardines, boiled Octopus, sliced tomato and cucumber. After everyone had their fill of the Ouzo and mezedes, their main meal arrived. The main course was broiled red snapper, deep-fried baby squid, a couple of types of salads topped with a bottle of Boutari Imyglikos red wine.

"That was really delicious," said Eleni.

"How about we all go for a drink", said Yiannis.

A few minutes later they found themselves in a smoke filled room at one of the many nearby pubs. After the first round of drinks was finished, Takis went to order another. "Don't order another one for me. It looks like I will be driving Yiannis home tonight, 'said Eleni.

"Don't worry love, I can handle it. This is only my second

drink. Don't forget I'm leaving for Limnos in two days. This is the only chance we'll have to enjoy ourselves for the next couple of weeks."

"I know both you men will be very busy defending the country. We had made plans to go on a trip, but the navy never fails to ruin everything."

"Come on, I know you are pissed about my canceled leave, but it's not the navy's fault the Turks decided to hold maneuvers now. Anyway, I've been thinking, our vacation might still be salvageable."

"How's that?" she asked.

"You can meet me on Limnos. I have a friend, Petros, who runs a Pension there with his wife. It's near Mirina, the main port. We used to be shipmates. He retired from the navy last year. You might remember him."

"Yeah, I remember Petros. He's a really nice guy."

"So what do you say? Do you want to join me on Limnos?

"I don't know. It sounds kind of crazy."

"Come on, say yes. After the Turkish exercises are over, I will arrange to take my leave on Limnos. My second in command can take the Hydra back to Salamina."

"I think you should go. You'll have a great time there," said Takis.

"Okay, since you both insist. I'll go."

Yiannis gave her a peck on the cheek. "You won't regret it. I promise we'll have a great time. I'll swing by the Aegean

Airways ticket counter in the morning and book a seat for you on an afternoon flight." Yiannis glanced at his watch.

"It's still early; I'll give Petros a call and have him reserve a room for us."

"You know I envy you two. Maybe I should find someone to settle down with."

"Why, I didn't think you had it in you. Takis finally settling down, I'd like to see that," said Eleni.

"Maybe after the tourist season is over," Takis said jokingly.

Chanakale Turkey
13 May. 2125hrs

General Muhammad Kemal briskly stepped out of his personal UH1 helicopter while the rotors were still turning. The noxious odors of the engine exhausts were quickly replaced by the fresh smell of salt air brought in by a gentle breeze blowing off the Aegean Sea less than a kilometer away. At the base of the landing pad, he was greeted by a military honor guard and by an older officer dressed in battle fatigues. Kemal immediately recognized him as Lieutenant General Enver Guven, the commander of the Fourth Army Corps or as it was popularly called, the Army of the Aegean.

"Sir, it is both an honor and a pleasure to have you here," said General Guven, as he rendered a sharp salute and then shook his commander's hand.

"Thank you. Your honor guard looks very sharp; I can only hope the rest of your command is this impressive."

"You can rest assured, sir,"

"Take me to your headquarters. We have much to discuss in very little time."

"As you wish, sir."

Both officers entered a waiting staff car and were whisked to the headquarters building, only a short distance from the helicopter pad. When they arrived, General Kemal was shown into the staff conference room which had an armed guard posted at the door. The walls of the room were adorned with several large maps of western Turkey, northern Greece and the Aegean islands. On these maps were different colored markers that represented both Greek and Turkish troop dispositions and other strategic data. In the corner of the room was a small TV set and a laptop connected to it.

"Sir, would you like something to drink?"

"I would like some Raki, if you have it. After my long flight I need something to warm my tired old bones."

General Guven gave his commander a puzzled look. "Raki, sir?"

General Kemal smiled, as he spoke to his subordinate. "Enver, the prophet never officially forbade the use of alcohol. He knew that man could never fully free himself of his earthly vices. As good Muslims, we must strive to really know ourselves. We must know our limits. One must always indulge in moderation, whether it is in eating, drinking or fornication."

"The prophet was indeed a wise man, sir."

General Guven called to his orderly. "Sergeant Major, bring us a flask of Raki and something to drink it with."

"But sir, there is no alcohol on this base."

"Sergeant, I'm sure that you possess the resourcefulness to procure some Raki for your commander and chief."

"Of course sir," said the sergeant with a sly grin on his face as he rendered a salute and departed the room. As soon as the orderly shut the door, General Guven locked it.

"Sir, the room is now secure. We can speak freely."

"Excellent. Now, as you may have already guessed, I'm here to check on the readiness level of your forces and their staging areas. We begin Operation Medina in five days. You're one of the few people that know of its existence. Every officer's complete devotion and loyalty to duty is essential if this operation is to succeed. The future of our nation depends on it."

"Sir, I swear by Allah, that my men and I will fight to the last in this Jihad against our sworn enemies."

"I know that I can count on you. That's why I chose you. Now I would like to see your operations plan."

"Of course, Sir,"

Guven walked toward a medium sized safe located under one of the maps of the northern Aegean and began dialing the combination.

"I had instructed my staff to draw up plans for a fictitious invasion of Limnos, using all the previous data and guidance that you had provided me. Our official maneuvers are set to begin in thirty-six hours. All exercises have been tailored to accurately simulate the future operating conditions that the men would face in an actual invasion," said General Guven while the last combination number clicked in place.

Opening the safe, he removed a small thumb drive and a large manila envelope which had a TOP SECRET label stenciled across its cover and handed it to his commander.

"Sir, in these plans, you will find a detailed description of our exercise scenarios leading up to the commencement of hostilities. Also, you'll find the actual invasion plan which my staff drew up. I have included a unit order of battle and tables of proposed munitions expenditures. Securing the island should take no more than five days. I do savor the moment when I announce to my staff that their battle plans will actually be implemented," he said excited at the prospect of finally getting the chance to deal with his nation's eternal enemy.

"Hmm, this looks very good," muttered Kemal as he read over the plans.

"Briefly tell me about your exercise scenarios," said General Kemal.

General Guven walked to the corner of the room, turned on the TV and plugged the thumb drive into the laptop's USB port.

"Sir I had my executive officer record this file for you. I believe pictures are better than words."

The TV screen quickly came to life depicting scenes of large transport helicopters off loading men and material on a beach. The soldiers in the video quickly took up defensive positions several hundred meters inland. The short recording concluded with the arrival of naval landing craft unloading more men and heavier material. What impressed Kemal was that all the men were wearing their chemical protective gear and were going about their duties without any hindrance.

"It looks to me your troops will be very busy for the next few days,"

"As you noticed in the video sir, I have instructed that all the men receive intensive training in chemical warfare operations. Several exercises of this nature will be conducted to condition them."

"Excellent!"

"Sir, I have given additional orders to the air force and my army aviation commanders to conduct flight operations near Limnos, throughout the next several days, until termination of the exercise. This should get the Greek radar operators used to seeing our aircraft on their screens. Optimistically, by D-day, the enemy air controllers should be lulled into believing that our helicopters carrying the nerve gas are just part of the ongoing exercises. Hopefully, this will buy our air crews some time before the enemy air defenses are alerted. The attack will commence five days from today, at 0500hrs, on the 18th of May, as per your instructions."

General Kemal nodded. "How is security and what are the men thinking, Enver?"

"Our operations security has been excellent so far, sir. My key staff members still believe that this is just another war game. No one will be briefed on the actual war plan until all the troops and equipment is loaded up and under way. You can rest assured. Everything is proceeding according to plan."

"Your plan is brilliant," remarked Kemal, as he handed back the TOP SECRET folder.

"Thank you, sir."

There was a knock at the door. "Just a minute," said General Guven putting the USB drive and battle plans back inside the safe and slamming the door shut. With the safe secured, he unlocked the door. It was his orderly with the Raki and two glasses.

"Sergeant, just leave everything on the table. You are dismissed for now."

"Yes, sir," replied the NCO closing the door behind him, glad to be finished with the two senior officers. General Kemal took the flask of Raki and poured a round for both of them. He handed one of the glasses to General Guven and proposed a toast.

"May Allah grant us victory!" Both men quickly downed the harsh liqueur.

"Train your men hard Enver, especially in chemical operations. Remember, timing is everything! Your troops must secure the beaches and the airport before the Greeks recover from the chemical attacks."

"Sir, we will defeat them. That I swear."

"Do you have any questions for me, Enver?"

"What about the Americans. Will they sit by and let their allies be defeated?"

"Don't worry. I have a surprise in store for the Americans. By the time they recover, our army will be in Thessaloniki and Limnos will be ours."

"And the local civilian population? How are they to be treated?"

"Deal with them as you see fit. Any civilian caught with a weapon or committing sabotage, should be executed."

"The world will condemn us," said General Guven.

"Damn the world!" Kemal slammed his glass on the table.

"What did the world do to stop the Serbs from murdering tens of thousands of our Muslim brothers in Bosnia? Except for a little lip service in the U.N. and a worthless piece of paper called the Dayton Peace Accords, the world did nothing at the time."

"Look what happened in Kuwait, sir."

"That was different. Saddam Hussein was a fool. He thought he could get away with seizing 25 percent of the world's oil supply. The economies of the west need that oil for their survival. They would never tolerate a man like Saddam holding the West by the balls. Greece is not vital for their economic survival. It has no great oil or mineral deposits that the greedy western capitalists need. And besides, that was a different time. The Americans don't have the military capability to massively intervene anymore. They have drawn down their military forces throughout the world."

"You're right, sir. I never looked at it that way."

"The opportunity to rid ourselves of the hated Greeks is now. We will destroy them before anyone can intervene. Turkey will once again reign supreme in the Balkans and the Mid East and regain her place as the leader of the Islamic world! Now take me to my helicopter. I still have to inspect some more units and it's getting late."

General Kemal was escorted to a waiting staff car by General Guven and driven to his helicopter. Both officers got out of the car flanked by Military Police and walked toward the waiting helicopter. Stopping just a few feet from the aircraft, Kemal turned toward the other officer.

"Good luck. Remember, you must not fail the nation. Train your men well."

"I will not fail, sir. You can count on me." said Guven raising his arm in a salute. General Kemal returned the salute, climbed into his helicopter and departed for Eastern Thrace.

Eastern Thrace, Turkey
2347hrs, 13 May

The night was cool and the surrounding air was heavy from a combination of dust and diesel fumes churned up from the tracks of dozens of armored vehicles. General Kemal pulled the zipper of his battle dress jacket up to the collar for added warmth. He had chosen to attend these night maneuvers staged by the elite Suilliman armored division which belonged to the First Army corps. The exercise was being conducted near the town of Ouzoun Kioprou, only a few kilometers east of the Evros River, which served as the geographical border between Greece and Turkey. The General, sitting in an open jeep, had just observed a live fire exercise with the unit's commander.

"Colonel Karakoglou, your men have performed most splendidly," said General Kemal.

"Thank you, sir. My tankers are always ready to crush the enemies of the faith."

"Your regiment's chance to prove itself may come sooner than you think," remarked Kemal to the younger officer who was slightly shorter and impeccably dressed in a tailor-made tanker suit.

"I don't understand, sir."

"During the revolution you displayed exemplary loyalty to the Brotherhood and to the Islamic ideals for which we stand. What I will tell you is Top Secret and is not be divulged to anyone. Do you understand this Colonel?"

"Of course, sir."

"In five days, what you and your men have been practicing here will become a reality."

"We are to attack the Greeks?"

"Yes. Your tank division will be the first spearhead which will be thrust into the heart of the infidel. You will lead your armor across the Evros River. It will be the instrument which will liberate our enslaved Muslim brothers living in western Thrace."

"Sir, I have dreamt of this day my entire career. I swear by the prophet that I will do my best to crush the enemy."

"I have no doubt that you will. Your tank division is one of my best."

The Colonel gave the General a somewhat confused look, his face barely visible in the dim moon light. "What is it Colonel?

"Sir, you keep saying my division. I'm only but a lowly Colonel and only a regimental commander."

The General looking at the Colonel, smiled and said, "As of 2400hrs tonight, you are promoted to Brigadier General. I brought you my old set of epaulets. You have been appointed commander of the Suilliman armored division. The order is official as of 2400hrs tonight."

The Colonel was surprised and caught off guard by the General's statement.

"I don't know what to say. Thank you, sir. I am truly

honored."

"I know you will wear them proudly and do your duty."

General Kemal looked at his watch. "It's almost midnight, I must be going."

"As you wish, sir."

"For the next few days you must push your men extra hard, especially in chemical warfare operations. Our offensive against the Greeks will open with a chemical attack. With the element of surprise in our favor, our tank divisions should quickly smash through the enemy front line defenses with minimal losses. Our ultimate objective is Thessaloniki."

"Praised be the prophet! That is over 300 kilometers."

"Don't worry," said General Kemal. "We'll have assistance in this great Jihad. Our Muslim brothers in Thrace, Macedonia and Albania will join us in a great alliance. Islam will triumph once again!"

A squadron of Leopard I main battle tanks passed by, momentarily drowning out Kemal. The tank commanders standing in their turrets raised their arms in salute as they drove by. "Your troops look superb! Keep up your good work. Train them well.

"Rest assured, sir. The men will be ready."

"That's what I want to hear. Everything will be explained in the secret orders you will be receiving soon. Remember; speak of this to no one. The orders will specify when to brief your subordinate commanders. I think we're done here. I must say

I'm more than satisfied with what I have seen. Now, please take me back to my helicopter. I must return to the capital."

Chapter 4

D-Minus 3, the Northwestern Aegean
1307hrs, 15 May

While the Hydra sped toward its rendezvous with the island of Limnos, Yiannis gazed out over the crystal blue Aegean waters. Seagulls were diving into the peaceful waters in an effort to catch their daily lunch. In the far distance, he could make out the hazy outline of the rocky shores of the small but strategic island. Hopefully within the hour, they would be dropping anchor in Mirina, the island's main port. He had received his orders yesterday, officially deploying the Hydra to the island to monitor the Turkish naval maneuvers. After taking on a full combat load of munitions and supplies, they departed Salamina naval base just before daybreak.

"Mr. Faniou," Yiannis called out to his communications officer.

"Sir?"

"Send a message to naval headquarters Limnos, advising them that we'll be arriving in roughly forty minutes. Have them arrange for fuel, supplies and transportation to meet us there."

"I'll send it immediately, sir."

The closer they got to Limnos, Yiannis thought of Eleni. She had caught the early morning flight and would be waiting for him at his friend's pension. He planned to spend as much time as possible with her, but he knew that wouldn't be much until the Turks finished their exercise. Hopefully, they'd be done by the following week, and he could then enjoy the rest of his time on the island.

"Sir, I'm picking up multiple surface contacts on the radar. Distance twenty-eight miles, bearing 150 degrees, speed fourteen knots. Most probably Turkish."

"Which way are they headed?"

"North, sir. Radar indicates five large contacts and five smaller ones".

"Keep on an eye on them. Mr. Faniou. Notify headquarters of their position. I'm sure we will be seeing a lot of the Turks in the next few days."

"Sir, I'm also picking up contacts on the ground to air radar, two unidentified aircraft inbound at four hundred knots. They're ten miles out at an altitude of five hundred meters."

"Sound general quarters. It's better to be safe than sorry." As the Hydra's klaxon blared, the crew quickly grabbed their steel helmets, emergency flotation gear and assumed their assigned combat posts. This included the manning of the Hydras' two 35mm antiaircraft cannon, which everyone knew was virtually useless against a high speed jet, unless the gunner was extremely lucky.

"Helmsman, increase to flank speed, zig zag course."

"Aye, aye, sir."

"Aircraft two miles out, altitude two hundred meters, speed 350 knots," said Mr. Georgiou.

The approaching aircraft could clearly be heard over the roar of the Hydra's powerful diesel engines which were operating at full power.

"Don't fire, unless fired upon first. Remember, we're supposed to be at peace with our neighbors." He thought of what he had just said to the gunner and laughed. There would be no second chance to fire. If the fighters shot first, they would probably all be killed. But he wasn't willing to start a war.

An ear splitting roar of jet engines rocked the boat. Everyone looked up and saw the two F-4E Phantom fighter bombers, bearing Turkish markings, pass low overhead.

"Those bastards are well inside our air space," said Yiannis. Less than a minute later, another ear splitting roar rocked the Hydra, as two Hellenic air force Mirage 2000 fighters, coming from the direction of Limnos, flew past, chasing the Turkish planes back into their own air space.

"It's a cat and mouse game out here. One of these days, somebody is going to do something stupid and the shit will hit the fan."

"You are right, sir. It almost happened back in 87, when one of their oil exploration ships came out to search for oil in disputed waters and also in 96, over the Imia isle dispute. Fortunately cooler heads prevailed," said Ensign Georgiou.

"Things have changed considerably since then. Ever since

those Islamist fanatics took power they have wanted to resurrect the old Ottoman empire. They wouldn't need much of a provocation to start a shooting war. Secure from general quarters," said Yiannis, visibly relieved that the encounter ended peacefully.

"Yes, sir."

Thirty minutes later, the Hydra dropped anchor in the picturesque port of Mirina, which was filled with dozens of fishing and pleasure boats. After securing the Hydra to the wharf and shutting down her engines, Yiannis turned her over to Ensign Georgiou.

"Mr. Georgiou, make sure that the crew gets properly fed and bedded down for the night. Set up a rotation schedule so the men can go ashore to shop or get something to eat if they like. I want everyone back by midnight."

"Will do, sir."

"Have the chief order supplies for tomorrow and when the civilian fuel truck arrives, one of you should supervise the refueling to make sure they don't rip us off. Then get some rest yourself. Here's the address and phone number of the pension where I'll be staying. I'll try to drop by or call you later this evening to see how things are going. Just make sure we are ready to sail by 0500hrs."

Naval Headquarters, Mirina Limnos
1416hrs, 15 May

Lieutenant Commander Theodorou, a middle aged man, with a slightly receding hair line, looked up from the stack of administrative papers that awaited him each morning.

"Can I help you, Lieutenant?"

"I am Lieutenant Vassiliou, commander of the missile boat Hydra. We just dropped anchor."

A smile appeared on the executive officer's face. "Welcome to Limnos, Lieutenant. We have been expecting you. I'll tell the Captain that you're here. Have a seat; it might be a few minutes."

While Yiannis sat there waiting, he glanced around the room. The walls had been freshly painted white and decorated with several pictures depicting famous historical naval battles. The office furniture was the standard type government issue that one could find in any other administrative office in the Hellenic Navy. What impressed him the most was that he could not see a speck of dust on any of it. Even the old wooden floors were spotless and highly polished. The only thing that looked out of place was an old typewriter, on the exec's desk. Yiannis would have expected a computer. The Captain must run a tight ship, he thought to himself.

A few minutes later, Yiannis was ushered into the commander's office. He stood at attention and rendered a salute. "Sir, Lieutenant Vassiliou, commander of the missile boat Hydra, reporting as ordered."

Captain Nikos Thomopoulos, a tall slender man of about fifty, the island's senior naval officer and acting commander of all naval units temporarily assigned to Limnos, returned the salute and motioned for Yiannis to have a seat.

"Welcome to Limnos, Lieutenant. Sorry to have kept you waiting. I was on the phone with Athens concerning the latest violations by the Turkish military."

"We were buzzed by two of their fighters near the island. Two of our Mirages were hot on their tails, chasing them back into their airspace, sir"

"Well Lieutenant, that's one of the reasons you're here. Your job will be to monitor the movements and whereabouts of the Turkish naval units taking part in their exercise. Your presence should ensure that they stay on their side of the line. If for any reason they decide to cross it, you will immediately radio headquarters for further instructions. The missile boat Batsis should be arriving in port shortly. It will be assigned similar patrol duties. Do you have any questions, Lieutenant?"

"Sir, will the Batsis be patrolling with us?"

"No. You will have the first patrol, starting at 0500hrs tomorrow. The Batsis will relieve you at 1700hrs. I realize that it will be a long patrol, but it's only for a day. We just got word that the gunboat Preveza will also be arriving tomorrow. I expect the three of you to work out an equitable rotating patrol schedule amongst yourselves."

"Yes, sir."

"I don't expect that you'll have any problems from the Turks. They know the rules out here. They've been following them for years. I don't want to keep you any longer Lieutenant, you need to get settled in and get some rest. Are you staying at officers billeting?"

"No, sir. My fiancée arrived yesterday from Athens and has a room in town. I was planning to take ten days leave on Limnos after the Turks finish their games and go home. If it's all right with you sir, I would like to stay there."

"As long as you leave an address and phone number where you can be reached with my executive officer. I'll have a vehicle assigned to you for the duration of your stay. That should make it easier for you to get around."

"Thank you sir, that's very kind of you." Captain Thomopoulos stared at Yiannis for a moment.

"Lieutenant, are you by any chance related to an Admiral Spiro Vassiliou?"

"Admiral Vassiliou is my father."

"Well, like father like son," the Captain said smiling.

"He and I were shipmates on the old Themistocles back in 1986. He was the ship's executive officer. I was just a young Ensign, fresh out of the academy. Good man your father, strict but fair. How is retirement treating him?"

"He is enjoying it, but he still misses the sea. He has a small boat and spends much of his time fishing."

"Well your father should be proud of you following in his footsteps."

"He is, sir."

"As the son of an old friend, let me give you some advice. There are many soldiers stationed here on the island, especially around the coastal areas. Limnos is the key to the Aegean. Whoever controls her, controls the approaches to the Dardanelles and to the Mediterranean. So we must always keep this island well fortified. There will be three companies of Special Forces troops arriving here in the next couple of days. They'll be conducting exercises with various units throughout the island. Advise your fiancée not to wander around alone after dark."

"I will, sir. Thanks for the advice."

"You know Lieutenant, when I first visited this island almost twenty years ago, it was just another backwater Aegean island, which no one even cared to visit. But after the Turks invaded Cyprus back in 1974, we have poured in thousands of troops and spent billions to fortify all of these little, out of the way, islands. With the collapse of the former Soviet Union, everyone has managed to save billions in defense cuts, except Greece. While everyone else continues to save from the so called peace dividend, we continue to spend billions on defense."

The Captain got up and escorted Yiannis to the door. "I don't want to bore you any longer, Lieutenant. I know you want to see your fiancée. Enjoy your stay on Limnos. If you need anything, please let me know. And give my regards to your father."

"I will, sir. Thanks for your help." Upon leaving, the Captain's exec handed him a sealed manila envelope which contained his patrol orders and a set of vehicle keys

"You can borrow my jeep. I don't really use it much. I only live a few blocks away. It's parked outside in front of the building," said Commander Theodorou. Yiannis thanked him for the use of the vehicle and departed the headquarters building. Yiannis found the jeep right where the exec said it would be parked. It was an old Willy's jeep, probably over forty years old, but looked well maintained.

"Well I hope it runs as well as it looks," he said to himself as he hopped into the driver's seat. After about the third try, the old jeep started.

Mirina Beach Hotel
1500hrs, 18 May

"Excuse me, got a room?" Yiannis shouted across the small lobby which was decorated with local pottery and handicraft depicting an island theme.

Petros turned around and saw his old friend and former shipmate.

"Yiannis, you old sea dog. How are you?" he shouted, as he rushed out from behind the desk and gave him a bear hug.

"Welcome to Limnos."

Yiannis embraced his friend. "I see that civilian life is treating you well, Petros."

"You look good yourself. You can't imagine how surprised and happy we were, when we received your phone call that you and Eleni were coming to visit. She arrived here yesterday. She is a real beauty. But I should have expected nothing less; you always were a lady's man. I'll go get Anna and tell her you are here." Petros went back to the kitchen area.

"Anna, come here. Yiannis has arrived." Anna came out from the kitchen. Her dark hair was attractively streaked with gray and her brown eyes were clear and alert. She greeted Yiannis with a kiss on the cheek.

"You haven't changed a bit since I last saw you. Still as handsome as ever. Your fiancée is a lucky girl, but so are you. She seems to be a wonderful girl. She's been patiently waiting for you to arrive since yesterday. She is upstairs in room 212."

"Thanks Anna. You are getting more attractive every time I see you. I wish I could say the same for Petros." Petros roared with laughter at his friend's joke.

"Still the same Yiannis."

"I'll go upstairs and let Eleni know I am here. We will see you guys later."

"Sure, how about dinner?"

"That sounds great, Petros. It has to be early because the

Hydra has the morning Patrol."

"That's fine."

Leaving his friends down in the lobby, he went upstairs and found room 212. He knocked on the door.

"Who is it?"

"It's me!"

"Yiannis!" Eleni quickly opened the door and jumped into his arms. He noticed that she was wearing a revealing, light, summer night gown.

Anna and I did some shopping this morning. When I got back I was tired so I decided to take a nap."

"How was your trip over?"

"The flight over was okay. Anna was waiting for me at the airport. I found her next to the information desk where you said she would be waiting. I recognized her by the picture you showed me. They are both very nice people. They took me out to lunch and Petros told me about some of your wild escapades, while you two were serving together on the Destroyer Sachtouris. I never knew you were so mischievous." Yiannis grinned, as he remembered some of his earlier escapades.

"I probably would still be an Ensign if Petros hadn't taken me under his wing and kept me out of trouble. Anyway dear, I am going to take a quick shower and change into something more comfortable. Then, if you want, we can go down and meet Petros and Anna. They both invited us out for dinner," he added.

"That's fine with me, Yiannis."

"We can't stay out too late tonight. I have to get up very early. The boat sails at 0500hrs."

"Why so early?"

"We have to be on station by 0600hrs, to relieve the Batsis.

"That means I will have to sleep here all alone when you are on night patrol."

"I am sure that you will survive for a couple of nights alone. Besides, consider this small sacrifice a patriotic duty," Yiannis said jokingly as he removed his clothes and stepped into the shower.

As the warm water sprayed onto his tired body bringing a sense of relaxation, he suddenly felt the smooth touch of feminine hands running down his back. He turned around and saw Eleni standing naked in the shower, the water cascading like a waterfall off her voluptuous breasts.

"I thought since you looked so tired, I would soap your back for you," she said mischievously.

"UMM that feels good," said Yiannis as Eleni's sensuous hands slowly lathered his back and moved downwards.

"Oh, what do we have here, my good Captain?" she said as she began to work her way lower.

"I see you're not so tired after all." Yiannis, who by this point was beginning to lose all his self control, turned around, pulled her toward him and their two bodies became one as the water poured over them.

"That was fun," said Eleni, as they were both lying naked and still wet on the large king size bed.

"You know the old saying," said Yiannis teasingly. "We sailors have a girl in every port. So we do get a lot of practice," he said laughing at his own joke.

"Well, this sailor better keep it in one port, or he will lose what he has got!" said Eleni, making him laugh even harder.

"Yes, Ma'am!"

"I am glad that you understand that", she added, as she also burst out laughing.

Ramstein AB, 526TH Black Night's Squadron 1554hrs, 15 May

Logan heard a faint knock on the door. "Come in!"

Captain Wendy Barnes entered the office, rendered a salute, "Captain Barnes reporting as ordered, sir".

Due to Colonel Hanson's short notice departure for emergency leave to the States the day before, Logan had taken over as acting squadron commander. He wasn't looking forward to this meeting with her. Anyone who was anybody on Ramstein had heard that wing Stan Eval had flunked her on her initial check ride. Afterwards, she had accused the instructor of unfairness, failing her just because she was a woman. It had only been two years since Ramstein had been reactivated as a fighter base giving him the opportunity in an ever shrinking air force to become a squadron commander and make colonel. Hopefully, he'd try to solve this before it got all blown out of proportion.

"Have a seat Captain."

"I prefer to stand, sir," she said while standing at attention and eyes fixed straight ahead at the picture of a B-2 bomber that hung on the ceiling behind Logan.

This is the wrong way to start things off, he thought. "As you prefer, Captain, but please stand at ease," he said, trying to keep a neutral attitude toward her. "I see here in your rebuttal letter, that you have made a few serious accusations about Major Kerns concerning your Stan Eval check ride the other day. I hope you realize Captain that you are not the first or will be the last pilot to flunk a check ride. It isn't the end of the world."

"I didn't fail, sir. I was railroaded".

"What exactly do you mean?"

"Major Kerns stated that the reason he failed me was sloppy flying and that's not true, sir. Every procedure was carried out by the book and well within set tolerances."

"That's your opinion, Captain."

"That's the damn facts, sir! He made me do more than he ever made any other male pilot ever do! Oh, he told me that I would probably pass next time with a little more practice. I know he failed me because I'm a woman!"

Logan did not immediately reply and thought about what she had just said. It was the general opinion of everyone around including Kerns that women should stay out of the cockpit. What best to prove that point by failing the first woman fighter pilot assigned to USAFE.

"Well Captain, I will take what you have just told me under consideration. I will let you know of my decision to let you retest or let the present Stan Eval score stand. And let me tell you this. I will not give you any preferential treatment because of your sex. You will be treated just like any other pilot in this squadron."

"Thank you, sir. That's all I ask." With that she gave Logan a salute, rendered an about face and walked out of the office.

"I wish I were still a Captain, with no responsibilities to the world except for my own ass. I'd better give that idiot Kerns a call in the morning and get to the bottom of this, before this totally gets out of control," thought Logan.

Limnos
1720hrs, 15 May

Eleni glanced at her watch. "We'd better get out of bed and get dressed. Petros and Anna will be waiting for us."

"I am really tired, but you're right, Eleni," complained Yiannis, as he got out of bed and half-heartedly got dressed. Fifteen minutes later, both Yiannis and Eleni had gone down to the lobby to meet Petros and his wife

"Is everybody ready?" asked Petros.

"Yes, and I am famished, " replied Yiannis.

"Good. I know an excellent taverna on the other side of Mirina, about twenty minutes from here. It serves the best kokoretsi and lamb chops on the island."

"That sounds delicious," said Eleni.

"Let's go then," said Petros. "My car is out front." Thirty minutes, later they were all sitting around a table at Petros' favorite taverna and savoring kokoretsi, a Greek delicacy of cut up lamb kidneys, liver and lungs, heavily spiced and wrapped in lamb intestines and roasted over a slow fire.

"Petros you were right, this is the best kokoretsi I've ever had," said Yiannis. I wish I can say as much for the appearance of this joint. I wonder when the last time was this place had a paint job. Man it really looks like a dive," added Yiannis.

"Looks can sometimes be deceiving, my friend."

"You can say that again," said Yiannis.

"Eat up, Yiannis; we want you to enjoy your stay on our island. Here, try some of this local wine," said Anna filling Yiannis' small wine glass.

"Thanks, I'll try some wine. I can't drink too much though. I have a morning appointment to keep with the Turkish navy."

"Those damn Turks! When will they ever leave us in peace?" said Petros.

"My friend, I am sure that our ancestors in Byzantium probably asked the same question, almost eight hundred years ago" replied Yiannis.

"You know I am really worried about those Islamic fanatics that are in power over there. They constantly make outrageous demands, they want our islands," said Petros' wife.

"That's the very reason that the navy is here, Anna."

"I know Yiannis, but there are so many of them and so few of us. If you remember, after they annexed Mosul, the United Nations slapped an arms embargo on them. It doesn't seem to be stopping them from building and acquiring more military equipment every day."

"That's true, Anna, their Muslim brothers from the former Soviet Union and Iran are providing them with weapons and moral support."

"So who is going to help us if something happens? The European Union, Nato?"

"Anna, we Greeks have been a seafaring people for thousands of years. Our ancestors, twenty-five hundred years ago, also faced a threat from the east, the Persian Empire. The Athenian navy stopped them. We will stop the invader from the east again if we have to."

"Come on you guys, change the subject. This talk of war is getting me depressed."

"You are right, Eleni. Let's all have some more wine," said Petros, as he refilled everyone's glasses.

Yiannis proposed a toast. "Here's to an excellent tourist season and lots of business."

"And to a happy wedding and lots of healthy children,"

added Petros.

"So how is the tourist business anyway?" Yiannis asked.

"We expect this summer to be one of the best tourist seasons we have had in a while, "Petros answered his friend.

"We should have many Germans over this summer. The Germans love the sea and sun and fortunately we have lots of both."

"Ah, here's dinner," said Eleni smacking her lips.

The waiter had finally arrived with the main course of charcoal broiled lamb chops.

"Mmm, they look delicious, I am famished," said Anna.

"You're always hungry." Petros said to his wife.

"Look who's talking. Have you looked in the mirror lately my dear?" Anna said to her husband. That's not exactly baby fat that you have around your waist," her comment bringing laughter to everyone including Petros.

"Petros, that was an excellent dinner," Yiannis commented after everyone had finished eating.

"I told you the food here is the best on the island."

"That you did. Well everybody, the company is great but I have to get to bed. Waiter, the bill please!"

"No Yiannis, it's on me! You're both our guests tonight."

"Okay Petros, but next time, dinner will be on me."

"That's fair enough." Twenty minutes later they had returned to the pension. Eleni and Yiannis said goodnight to their friends, went upstairs to their room, undressed and went to bed. Within a few minutes, much to Eleni's dismay, Yiannis was fast asleep.

Kommotini, Greece
1907hrs, 15 May

Warrant officer Mihalis Manakos of the Hellenic police sat inside the bus, puffing on his last cigarette while watching the progress of the demonstration. He and his riot squad had spent most of the day parked in a residential area, a few blocks from Kommotini's main square, waiting to respond in case the demonstration got out of hand.

"I'm bored. Let's go home. My wife's got dinner waiting," complained one of Mihalis' men. *A home cooked meal would be nice, thought Mihalis.* He had never married. Though of only medium height and build and in his late thirties, he could still be considered handsome, despite recent weight gains that put on slight bulge around his mid waist. He had never had a problem finding women, his real problem had been staying in one location long enough to develop any meaningful relationship. Throughout his career his outspokenness had gotten him in trouble with his superiors, which had usually resulted in his transfer to other less desirable locations. *Kommotini had to be the shittiest assignment of his sixteen year career in the Greek police, he thought to himself.* There was nothing here but Muslim troublemakers and sheep fuckers and he couldn't figure out who was worse.

For the past couple of days, many of Kommotini's Muslim residents had been protesting over alleged human rights violations. These types of demonstrations had been going on since the early 1980s, but they never amounted to much. Lately though, the number of participants had increased dramatically and the demonstrations were getting violent. This could be attributed to the rise of Islamic fundamentalism in Greece's Muslim population, obviously instigated by Turkey's militant Islamic government.

During the last few months, their demands had been getting bolder. They were now asking that an Islamic council be established that would try any offenses committed by Greek Muslims. They'd even gone as far as to demand the appointment of a Muslim deputy mayor of Kommotini. Mihalis could not understand why Athens tolerated these people. They should have the ringleaders arrested and tried as subversives or deported to Turkey. The more he thought about them, the angrier he got. For the past ninety years, the Muslim community had prospered in Greece. Their population now numbered over 120,000. They could own property, freely worship their religion, appoint their own clergy and run their own schools which taught Turkish to their children. They had even elected their own representatives to parliament, who spoke out openly in favor of Turkish policies and against Greece herself. If that wasn't treason, then what was? As for the

Greeks living in Turkey today, they probably numbered less than a thousand from a community that had once numbered in the millions. The Greeks had lived and prospered in Anatolia for twenty-five hundred years. Through wars, programs of ethnic cleansing, religious prosecution and discriminating laws, the Greek community had been forced to leave their homes in Turkey. Sometimes they were lucky enough to sell their property for a fraction of its worth to a Turkish friend or neighbor. More often they just abandoned their homes with only the clothes on their backs, lucky to have escaped with their lives. His grandfather who had come from a very wealthy merchant family had been one of these Greeks. When he was a boy, he had witnessed his father butchered and his mother and sister raped after the Turkish army retook the city of Smyrna (now called Izmir) from the Greek army in 1922 which had occupied it as part of the peace treaty ending WWI. The Greeks today would never commit such atrocities against their Muslim citizens, Mihalis was sure of that. The Muslims must now understand that they would have to obey the same laws just like any other Greek citizen.

"Mr. Manakos," Mihalis was suddenly jolted from his train of thought.

"What is it Christos?"

"How much longer do we have to put up with their shit? It's been two days since they erected those barricades in the square."

"We will stay here as long as we have to. They haven't destroyed any property or hurt anyone. Athens wants to keep this low key. They don't want us using any force unless it becomes necessary. We don't want the propaganda boys in Istanbul to have a field day at our expense."

"I guess you're right, sir,"

"I know this is starting to get on everybody's nerves, but that's just what they want. The Muslims would love it if we lost our cool and broke up their little show here. They would cry to the world that we violated their human rights by using force against them while they were peacefully protesting. We're not stupid to fall for their ploy. They'll eventually get tired and go home," said Mihalis, trying to build his men's' flagging moral.

"I hope so sir, they're really starting to piss us off, but I see your point. We'll wait them out," shouted one of his men from the rear of the bus.

Kommotini, at the Grand Mufti's home
1917hrs, 15 May

Several blocks from the demonstration, General Kemal's two intelligence agents had decided that it was time to pay the Grand Mufti of Kommotini and spiritual leader of Greece's Muslim community a visit. The two men entered the Mufti's study which was adorned with several Islamic inscriptions from the Koran. The Mufti, a frail bearded man in his late sixties, offered his hand to the two men. The shorter and somewhat younger man, who went by the name of Osman, spoke to the Grand Mufti.

"What may I do for you, gentlemen?"

"Your holiness, General Kemal sends you his most humble respects."

"That is very kind of the General," the Mufti replied with some distain.

"Your holiness, the General has a very important request."

"And what is this request that the almighty General and savior of Turkey asks from a simple clergyman such as I?"

"The General wants the world to gain more attention on the plight of Greece's Turkish Muslim community. Our people face daily harassment and have their human rights trampled on by the Greek authorities.

"How would this be accomplished?"

"We will orchestrate an incident during a demonstration. When the Greek authorities respond with violence, we will capture all of this on film for the world to see"

"If you don't mind me asking, where will this demonstration take place?"

"It will begin at the mosque. The demonstrators will march from there to the city police station and surround it. No one will be let in or out. This will most likely cause the Greek police to panic and force them to clear the crowd with riot batons and tear gas. We will capture all of this on film."

"I see," replied the Grand Mufti, now visibly angry.

"Will you help us, your holiness?" asked Osman.

The Mufti stood up angrily from his chair. "Tell your General that I will not be part of his political schemes. Nor will I have my people endangered on his behalf. Yes we have our differences, but we've lived with the Greeks all these years and have peacefully worked out most of our problems with them. Ever since you rabble rousers came to power we've had nothing but trouble with the Greeks, much of it, orchestrated by Kemal. I'll have no part in instigating a riot."

"Your holiness, you don't seem to understand," said Muhammad, the older of the two agents, rather abruptly.

"It is to your benefit that you cooperate with us in this matter."

"How dare you threaten me in my own house! I will have you turned over to the Greeks as spies and provocateurs!" shouted the Mufti, his face red with anger.

"Your holiness, we are by no means threatening you," said Osman. "We are just reminding you that your true loyalties must lie with the Turkish nation."

"My loyalties lie with the faithful here in western Thrace."

"Forgive me for my assumptions," said Muhammad. "We would like to compliment you on what a fine son you have raised. And I believe your only son, such a bright young man and a devout Muslim. He is a model student of Islamic studies at the University of Istanbul. I'm sure you will be proud to have him one day assume your place as the Grand Mufti of Thrace. But alas, our glorious army is in constant need of soldiers and I believe his university deferment has expired. What a pity that he will have to interrupt his studies. But I am sure you will be so proud of him serving against the enemies of Islam in the mountains of northern Iraq."

"Get out of my house you bastards. Tell your General that you will have your demonstration. I hope Allah will forgive me and have pity on my soul," the Mufti said to the two men.

"Now, please get out."

"As you wish," said Osman. "We'll be back in two days. Come Muhammad, let's go." They bowed to the Mufti and departed.

"Osman, I can't wait to see the look on the old traitorous fool's face when he finally figures out that he will be the cause that will set off the riot!"

"Yeah and I would like to see what his cunt of a daughter looks like under all those robes she wears," replied Osman, as he thought of just how much pleasure he would have with her.

"We will soon find out my friend," said Muhammad, both men began laughing as they made their way to one of their safe houses in Kommotini, satisfied with what they had just accomplished.

Northeastern Aegean
1942hrs, 15 May

The island of Skyros swiftly faded from view as the Albatross seaplane winged its way at a steady 120kts toward its assigned patrol sector. The plane and its crew had departed Elefsis air base, with a full load of fuel and orders to monitor units of the Turkish navy that had ventured into the Aegean to conduct maneuvers. Lieutenant Takis Mavridis sat in the navigator's seat monitoring their course and checking his radar screen for potential targets.

"How much longer to our patrol zone Takis?" asked the aircraft commander.

"Since we picked up this tail wind, I would say about another fifteen minutes."

"Anything on the radar?"

"I've been monitoring a fairly large convoy of ships heading north for the past few minutes.

"Well don't just sit there, Takis. Tell us how many ships there are and give me an intercept heading," said the pilot.

"I have ten surface contacts, distance twenty-five miles."

"Turn to a heading of 105 degrees to intercept."

Slowly the lumbering sea plane turned toward its new heading. Several minutes later, the crew of the Albatross could make out the haze of smoke on the horizon indicating the presence of ships.

"There they are." The aircraft commander pointed to the growing visible smudge of smoke in the distance. "I am taking us lower so we can get a better view."

"You're the pilot," said Takis. A little while later, they could clearly make out the ships of the Turkish naval flotilla.

"I can make out three escort destroyers, four landing craft, two Dogan missile patrol boats and a landing ship tank," said Takis while peering through a pair of binoculars. "Two of the escorts are MEKO 200t class frigates and the other is an older Fram I destroyer. Why it's D 347, the old Antitepe!" said Takis evidently surprised. "I thought they had scrapped her," he said peering through his binoculars.

"Ah hum, interesting, she looks like she's been overhauled and had her front 127mm gun removed and replaced with missile launchers, most likely, Exocets. I'll take a few pictures for the Intel boys. Antoni, take us closer, I also want to shoot a few photos of the troops in the landing craft before it gets too dark," Takis said to the pilot.

As the plane neared the landing craft, they could distinguish the individual soldiers on board. "Good, I got enough pictures of them, now fly closer to the LST. I want to get some shots of the armored vehicles on board she's carrying."

"Takis, you're crazy! That ship is smack in the middle of their flotilla. They have already broadcast warnings not to approach any closer than two miles and we have already disregarded those warnings."

"Come on, Antoni. Intelligence could really use those photos."

"Okay, but I must be just as crazy as you are to be doing this. I hope you got enough memory in your camera."

Changing course, they headed for the LST. The escort closest to the LST veered out of formation and into the path of the approaching plane, its guns turning toward them. The pilot who had slowed the plane to almost stall speed so Takis would have sufficient time to take his pictures on the first pass, yelled in terror.

"Jesus, they're going to blow us out of the sky, we are sitting ducks!" He had barely finished his sentence when the frigate fired one of its main guns. The shell exploded three hundred meters in front of the plane. The ensuing shock wave nearly caused the pilot to lose control of the aircraft which would have spelled disaster, since they were flying less than fifty meters above the wave tops.

"That's all the warning I need," said the pilot, as he rammed the throttles to their stops and turned to a heading that took them away from the Turkish flotilla.

"I got the pictures!"

"Good for you, Takis! I hope they were worth it. Your curiosity almost got us killed!" said the co-pilot.

"Come on, they wouldn't dare shoot us down, that's an act of war."

"Yeah, Takis, tell that to the Turks," said Kostas, the flight engineer.

"Shit!" We have company, aircraft at one o'clock," yelled the co-pilot.

"We've stirred up a hornets' nest. Hold on, I am taking her lower," said the pilot pushing both throttles forward to full power once again. While the lumbering seaplane began a slow descending bank to the left, it was buzzed by two Turkish F-16 fighters, the bright flame from their tail pipes clearly seen in the darkening evening sky. "The bastards!" shouted the pilot struggling to keep control, as the jet wash from the two fighters severely rocked the aircraft.

"I think we're no longer welcome around here."

"No, shit Takis," replied the co-pilot.

"I am calling Skyros for help. Damn it! Here they come again," shouted the pilot. But the two fighters had to abort their pass because of the seaplane's low altitude and disappeared toward the east. Ten minutes later, two F-16s bearing the blue and white roundels of the Hellenic air force, had arrived to escort the Albatross home.

"I don't like this one bit, Takis," said the visibly shaken pilot.

"Back there was just too close for my liking. It's beginning to heat up around here. Our former NATO allies have never acted like this before."

"I don't know why, but you're right. They are acting really strange. Somebody is going to get hurt and probably very soon. Let's hope that it won't be us. Well anyway guys, it's my turn to buy the booze when we land," said Takis changing the subject.

"I think we could all use a stiff drink after this," replied the flight engineer

"It won't be long before we land. There are the lights of Athens on the horizon," said the pilot.

After they landed, Takis handed his camera over to the wing intelligence boys who had been patiently awaiting the return of the scout plane. They, in turn, rushed the camera to the lab to download and analyze the photos.

Elefsis Air Base Greece
2301hrs, 15 May

When the photos that Takis had taken of the Turkish flotilla were processed late that evening, Major Stavropoulos, the Wing intelligence analyst noticed something unusual. Even though shot in very poor light, the photos showed the infantry troops on the landing craft having something besides the usual equipment strapped to their side. Some of the soldiers were even wearing a garment that covered their whole body. The Major quickly surmised this could only be chemical protective ensembles and the items strapped to their side had to be gas masks. This was verified once the photos were digitally enhanced. That was very odd. Never before, had Turkish troops on an exercise in the Aegean theater of operations, used any type of chemical equipment. Neither had they ever fired on a Greek patrol plane before. The only explanation that he could come up with for the shooting incident was that they were trying to prevent the patrol plane from getting too close to take pictures of the troops and their equipment. He decided to brief headquarters. Picking up the STU 3 secure voice phone that was in his office, he rang Colonel Papalexis, the duty officer at the Hellenic Intelligence Agency. Normally, by this late hour in the evening, everybody would be long gone. But since the initiation of the Turkish exercises, everyone in the intelligence community had been working overtime.

"Hello Colonel Papalexis, this is Major Stavropoulos at Elefsis."

"How are you Pavlos? What can I do for you? I was just about to go home for the evening."

"Would you please activate your secure voice line, sir."

"Just a minute, I'll get my key." said Colonel Papalexis as he pulled out the key from his desk drawer and activated his STU 3 phone. "Okay Pavlos, we can speak freely now."

"One of our Albatross patrol planes that had been keeping tabs on the Turks, just returned with some very unusual photos."

"Tell me what you have."

"Well sir, the photos were taken of a ten ship flotilla, southwest of the isle of Imbros. The flotilla consisted of two Dogan missile boats, two destroyers, a frigate, four landing craft loaded with infantry and an LST carrying light armor. The infantry on the landing craft was carrying what appeared to be gas masks and some of them were wearing full chemical suits. I find this very peculiar. They've never carried this type of equipment before in the Aegean theater, and that's not all sir. One of their ships fired a warning shot at the Albatross to chase it off."

"That is rather unusual, Pavlos. They have never shot at one of our planes before. But, with those fanatics in power over there, it doesn't surprise me.

"As for the chemical gear, I believe that one of their army commanders must have a wild hair up his ass and wants to impress the boys in Istanbul. I wouldn't worry about it."

"But sir, the chemical gear, I . . . "

"Major," the Colonel interrupted before he could finish. "I told, you don't worry about it." Colonel Papalexis hesitated for a few seconds before speaking. "Okay Pavlos, since you are so worked up over this, have the pictures and your analysis report delivered to me first thing in the morning by courier and I'll take a look at them."

"I will do that, sir and thanks for your time."

"That's what I am here for. If you come up with anything else, don't hesitate to call. Pass on to your air crews that their doing a great job, good bye." Even after his talk with the colonel, Major Stavropoulos still could not shake the premonition that something was very wrong. Little did he know how right he was and that his hunch would shortly have far reaching consequences.

Mediterranean Sea, Ten Miles North of Benghazi
2356hrs, 15 May

The seven hundred ton, Lebanese registered motor ship Shatila, was slowly working its way northwest through the gentle Mediterranean swells at a leisurely ten knots. It had departed Benghazi, Libya, with Athens, Greece as its destination. The ship had been named in commemoration of the hundreds of Palestinians that had been massacred at the Shatila refugee camp in Beirut, by the Lebanese Christian militia in 1982. The ship's crew had just finished applying the final touches of camouflage on the missile canisters which contained two deadly Exocet sea-skimming, anti-ship missiles. The camouflage job was so expertly done that the missile launchers blended in perfectly with the ship's superstructure. In two days, they would reach their launch position, ten miles southwest of Athens, to deliver their deadly cargo.

Saleem Hadaad, a handsome young man with a thin mustache, tanned face and a pair of dark intelligent eyes was sitting in the Captain's seat monitoring the actions of his crew. Looking out the window at the lights of Benghazi which were slowly fading in the distance, he thought of his family and of the impending operation. The last couple of weeks had been very hectic for him, but in two days, his opportunity to pay back those that had brought pain and suffering to both his family and the Palestinian people would arrive.

Saleem, the older of the two sons of a west bank Palestinian dirt farmer, had been born and raised in poverty under the guns of Israeli occupation. From the early years of his childhood, he and his brother had been taught to hate the Israelis and the United States. Israel was seen as the direct oppressor of the Palestinians and the Jew loving United States as her moral and material supporter. So when the new Palestinian intifada erupted in the west bank against the Israelis, Saleem and his brother were amongst the first Palestinian youths to follow the calling. They had both participated in numerous violent demonstrations against the Zionist occupation, until an Israeli bullet splattered his fifteen year old brother's brains all over him. As if this tragedy was not enough, Saleem's family home was blown up by the Israelis as punishment for his participation in the demonstrations.

His brother's murder by the Zionists and subsequent destruction of his family's home was a major turning point in his life. He decided that the only way the Palestinians would ever free themselves from Israel was by armed force. So one day, Saleem crossed the border into Lebanon and joined the Palestinian Liberation Organization and was inducted into their military wing, the El Fatah. After a couple of years of serving in Lebanon with the El Fatah, Saleem became discouraged at the PLO's lack of action against the enemy. Furthermore, he felt betrayed at their acceptance to take part in the American peace talk proposals and their eventual agreement of a new

Palestinian autonomy plan that was proposed by Israel.

One day, while Saleem was passing through Beirut, he visited a popular Palestinian coffee house in the Muslim district of the city. While having a coffee, he struck up a conversation with two other fellow Palestinians who were sitting at the adjacent table. During the course of the conversation, the subject of the discussion eventually turned to politics and the Palestinian authority's acceptance of the new Middle East peace talks. Saleem's vehement disdain for the Palestinian authority due to their betrayal of the Palestinian cause impressed the two men. Unknown to Saleem, these two men were high ranking officers in the pro-Iranian Shiite Hezbollah terrorist organization. Even though he was a Sunni Muslim, the two men saw promise in Saleem. They politely introduced themselves and offered him membership in the armed wing of Hezbollah, if he was willing to continue the armed struggle against the Zionists and their supporters. Saleem, who found their offer a godsend, immediately accepted, seeing it as his chance to finally strike back at Zionism.

After undergoing rigorous training in the arts of explosive making and sabotage, Saleem was sent on several missions to conduct terrorist bombings and assassinations of Palestinian collaborators in the west bank and Gaza. After several successful missions, Saleem was noticed by the Hezbollah hierarchy and the Iranian Revolutionary Guard intelligence chief in Beirut. It was after the daring and brutal assassination of a prominent Palestinian west bank mayor, from right under the nose of Israeli and PLO security that Saleem was elevated to Lieutenant in the organization.

One day, Saleem was summoned by his commander and asked if he would like to volunteer to lead an extremely important, but dangerous mission. The mission would strike right at the heart of the American Jew lovers and enemies of Islam. Saleem not only jumped at the opportunity, but thanked his commander for selecting him. All that Saleem was told about the mission was that he would be leaving for Libya immediately.

The next morning Saleem boarded a Libyan Airways flight from Beirut to Benghazi. On arrival, he was met by two burley security men who transported him downtown to military headquarters where he was introduced to Major Hussein, the director of Special Operations. The Major briefed Saleem on the details of the upcoming mission. He was told that he would strike a devastating blow to Israel's main supporters, the Americans. The plan called for a missile attack against a U.S. aircraft carrier while it was in port. The ship, crew, weapons and the training would be provided by the "Brothers of Islam," a mysterious Turkish terrorist group. Hezbollah's participation in the operation was requested by the Turks to cement the cause of Islamic solidarity.

Saleem had been flabbergasted at the sheer audacity of the plan. His function would be to lead the mission and to make sure that tight security was maintained to prevent compromise. This he could understand.   There were Zionist spies everywhere, even at the highest levels of some Arab governments. When the meeting was over, he was taken to his hotel which overlooked the bustling waterfront and was not far from where he'd be working.   The next day, Saleem immediately went to work supervising the Shatila's outfitting. After many weeks of preparations and training, most of the work being done at night for security reasons, the ship was finally ready to sail. Once Benghazi's lights had finally faded from view, Saleem wished everyone a good night and left for his cabin. When he was outside the bridge, he looked up at the stars and thanked the prophet for finally giving him the chance to avenge his brother's death. Little did he know that he was, but a pawn, in the greater game that was about to be played out.

Chapter 5

D-Minus 2400hrs, Ten kilometers North of Lake Doiranis, Macedonia, 0900hrs, 17 May

The sentry guarding the unit command post of the 3rd Macedonian Mountain Regiment snapped to attention when he recognized the short stocky officer with the shiny square face and broad nose approaching. Lieutenant Colonel Ali Mihalovic, commander of the Macedonian 3rd light mountain regiment, nodded and continued toward his tent. He had just completed his first post checks upon returning from Skopje and was satisfied with what he had seen. His intuition had told him that something was aloof ever since the unit had been ordered to the border and his recall to the capital had confirmed his suspicions. Never in his wildest dreams had he ever envisioned that the Turkish dictator, General Kemal, would be in Skopje chairing a meeting of his nation's armed forces defense committee.

The Colonel stopped for a moment and looked over the calm waters of the lake. He could see in the distance a few fishermen in small boats setting their nets to earn their meager living. Everything was so quiet and peaceful he thought, as he took off his hat and ran his hand through his thinning black hair. Unfortunately, that would all change very soon.

Since its secession and independence from the Yugoslav

Federation in 1992, the new Macedonian Republic had run afoul with its powerful southern neighbor, Greece. The decision of the tiny Slavic and Muslim populated Balkan state to name itself Macedonia, had not sat very well with the Greeks. Greece which had its own province named Macedonia had used the name even before Alexander the Great in the 4th century BC. Tito, the former Yugoslav leader, had given the province the name in support of the Greek communists during that nation's civil war in the late 1940s.

To counter Macedonia, Greece had hoped her membership in the European Community and NATO would give her the diplomatic leverage not to have the new republic recognized until it changed its name. Macedonia had steadfastly refused to bow under this intense pressure. Eventually, every major European power had officially recognized the new republic under the name Macedonia. This had infuriated the Greeks to the point of closing all their border crossings with the new state resulting in a virtual cut off of all of Macedonia's trade routes to the south. Thanks in part to her large Muslim population, Macedonia turned to her Muslim neighbors, Albania and Turkey for help. Thus, when the opportunity for revenge against Greece presented itself, Macedonia quickly jumped on the band wagon.

Mihalovic, himself a Macedonian Muslim of Slavic ancestry, had been a young Lieutenant in the former Yugoslavian army. When the Yugoslav Federation disintegrated in 1991-92, he left the Serbian dominated federal army and joined the new Macedonian force which had been established right after their independence. The Macedonian army had been conceived as a lightly armed defense force, trained mostly in mountain warfare and hit and run guerrilla tactics. Its armaments consisted mainly of light infantry weapons such as rifles, machine guns, RPGs, mortars, mountain howitzers and some light armored vehicles left by the former Yugoslav army. As for an air force, it was virtually non-existent, except for a few small ex Soviet helicopters which doubled as transports and attack choppers. It was common knowledge in most military circles that this lightly armed force could not hold off an attack by a heavily armed aggressor for long. Nor did it have the capability to carry out offensive operations against a superior foe.

Mihalovic had been aghast, after he left the meeting and received his Top Secret orders instructing him to prepare his unit for hostilities against Greece. He still wondered if the leadership in Skopje had lost their minds when they decided to join Kemal. The mere thought of contemplating such a suicidal undertaking was insane. His unit was to participate in a coordinated attack with other Macedonian forces against Greece. The army's overall objective would be to seize and hold a fifteen kilometer border buffer zone. His regiment would enter Greek territory on the southern end of Lake Doiranis and advance through the rugged Mavrovouni mountain range. They were supposed to proceed to a point fifteen kilometers inside Greek territory and establish a defensive line and hold it until relieved.

The cool fresh morning breeze sent a shiver through his body and put his hands in his pocket for added warmth. No matter how hard he tried to justify his country's reasoning in joining Turkey in the impending war against the Greeks, he could not find one cause that did not defy logic. A premonition of impending catastrophe looming over all of them had haunted him all morning. The last courier from Skopje had brought word that hostilities would begin once the word "Medina" was broadcast over the command net. How appropriate a name, he thought. Medina was where Islam, the true faith was born, the city from where the prophet began his great mission to spread the faith throughout the world. He wondered if the name Medina would, in the future, be identified with the destruction of his nation. Only Allah himself could answer that question.

Mihalovic spotted his top NCO Sergeant Major Bakier sitting outside the command tent savoring a cup of hot tea.

"Sergeant Major!" When the old burley sergeant heard his commander's summons, he put down his cup of tea and hurried to the command tent.

"You called, sir," said Sergeant Bakier as he stood at attention in front of the Colonel. A full head and two shoulders broader than his commander, the old NCO had been in Michlovic's old federal army unit and had deserted with him to join their nation's new army.

"Sergeant, have all the officers report to the command tent in twenty minutes."

"I will notify them immediately," said the senior NCO. "Oh by the way, sir, would you like a hot cup of Tsai?" asked the Sergeant Major, calling the tea by its Turkish name. "I just brewed it."

"Certainly my old friend, anything to warm these tired old bones. But first go notify the officers, my Tsai can wait a few minutes."

"As you wish, sir."

Twenty minutes later, the regiment's officers had arrived and were seated in the command tent. When Mihalovic entered the tent, everyone present rose to attention.

"Gentlemen, take your seats. As of this moment on, we are on war footing. Every man is restricted to camp and armed guards will be posted to ensure this order is not violated." They all looked at their commander in awe and disbelief.

"Once I have read the contents of these two messages to all of you, maybe things will become a little clearer." After the Colonel had finished reading the two Top Secret documents, he paused for a moment to let it all sink in. Everyone was shocked at this news. One of the junior officers, Lieutenant Pavlovik, was the first to speak.

"Sir, is this some kind of joke or test?"

Colonel Mihalovic gave the young officer a sympathetic look. "No son, this is as real as life and death." The Colonel paused for a moment to clear his throat and continued with the briefing.

"From this moment, I expect all officers and non-commissioned officers to know the location of their men at all times. Proper communications security will be adhered to. All outgoing message traffic will be encrypted until further notice. After this meeting, all company commanders will pick up their code books from the G2 officer." The Colonel turned toward his executive officer, Major Zaid, a middle sized man in his late thirties, with a soft mouth, small nose and dark eyes behind rimless glasses.

"Major, what is our current ammunition and supply status?" The Major peeked at his notes.

"Well sir, once we begin issuing gear, each soldier will receive his three day supply of field rations, three hundred and sixty rounds of 7.62mm ammunition and four HE fragmentation grenades. Before we left base, each company had been issued a hundred rounds of 81mm bombs for its M-31 heavy mortars and one hundred fifty rounds of 61mm bombs for each of their lighter M-57 mortars. Additionally, ten SA-7A Grail antiaircraft missiles had been allotted to each company and thirty RPG7s had been distributed to each platoon. As for machine gun ammunition, we have one hundred thousand rounds, that's five thousand rounds per gun, Sir"

"Oh, I almost forgot, we have fifty rounds of 105mm ammo, for each of our two Italian-made Otto MELARA Pak howitzers and about a hundred mines ranging in size from antipersonnel to antitank."

"You have been very thorough, major. Now tell me in what shape the pack mules are in. It's vital to this operation that they are in perfect health. They will be carrying extreme loads over some very rough terrain."

"They're healthy, sir. Each mule will also carry a three day supply of fodder. There are plenty of running streams in the mountains for drinking water this time of the year.

"Excellent, Major. Thanks for the information," said the Colonel.

"Gentlemen, we must be ready to move out by 2400hrs tonight and be in position to cross the border by 0600hrs, unless, we are told otherwise. You will brief your men on the operation and what will be expected of them." The Colonel moved to the side of the tent and uncovered a map of northern Greece hanging from a tent pole.

"Once we cross the border, consider everyone you meet as hostile. We should initially not meet any significant opposition. The Greeks have never considered us a real military threat, so the border was never fully militarized. Our first objective will be the town of Doirani," he said pointing to the map.

"There are only a few policemen stationed in the town. Most of them live at the police station." Lieutenant Kosovich, this is where you come in." The younger man looked up from his note taking, his light blue eyes registering surprise.

"You will be in charge of the advance reconnaissance squad. Your job will be to cut the town's communications and neutralize the police station." Kosovich nodded his head acknowledging what he had just been told.

"After Doirani is secured, the regiment will move into the Mavrovouni mountain range and establish a defensive line in these foothills just north of Kilkis," the Colonel pointed to the map.

"Sir, what about the city of Kilkis?" asked Captain Slovik, a tall lanky man in his late twenties and a Muslim by religion but whose Slavic ancestry was apparent by the thick crop of blond hair sprouting from his head.

"What about it, Captain?"

"Sir, Kilkis has a large garrison and it's the training center for their artillery school. If we are counter attacked in strength by the city's garrison, we will be wiped out. Please don't get me wrong. I do not mean any disrespect, nor am I afraid to die for my country and its cause, but committing suicide is another matter."

Sounds of mumbling in agreement with Captain Slovik's comments could be heard coming from several other officers present in the tent. "My dear Captain, I also share your concern, and in no way do I doubt your patriotism," said Mihalovic.

"Don't forget gentlemen, the Greeks will be attacked on several fronts. We will be operating in terrain that is very favorable for defense. The whole objective of this operation is to divert and tie up as many Greek units as possible and take some of the pressure off our allies, not to conquer the country. Besides, if things get too rough, we can always fall back into the mountain and establish another defense line." He looked at his men. They were now beginning to nod their heads in agreement to what he had just told them.

"Are there any other questions?" No one raised their hand. The Colonel's explanation seemed to have satisfied everyone's anxieties for the time being. "Remember gentlemen, I expect every man to do his duty to the utmost of his ability. I don't have to tell you that the future of Macedonia depends on our army's success." The Colonel looked at the faces of the officers that would be leading his soldiers into combat. If there were any doubts, he did not see any showing. "Before I dismiss you, I want all of you to know that I think very highly of each and every one of you. You are all very competent and professional officers. If you weren't, you would not have remained in my regiment. It will be up to you to motivate your soldiers and pull them through. Now go back to your respective companies and platoons and take charge. You are dismissed."

"May I have everyone's attention for a moment," said Major Ziad. "I need all company commanders including Lieutenant Kosovich to report back here at 1300hrs for an intelligence brief. That's all I have, thank you."

After all the officers had departed for their respective commands to carry out their instructions, Major Zaid stayed behind. "Sir, may I speak frankly?"

"Why of course, Ali."

"Sir, we have been friends for many years and I have always respected and valued your judgment."

"What is troubling you, my friend?"

"Sir, it's about this whole operation. What Captain Slovik said is very true. They're setting us up to be slaughtered. Our leadership must have gone mad to follow the Turks."

"I've had the same thoughts, Ali. I have done a lot of soul searching, more than the time we both decided to desert from the old Federal army."

"That was different, sir. We did it because we had lost the belief in the ideals we served for. They were also murdering our fellow brothers in Bosnia."

"Have you lost your faith in our cause, Ali?"

"It's been definitely shaken, but I have not lost my belief in Macedonia."

"Good, my friend. Then as soldiers, we will all do our duty," said Mihalovic. "There is a slight chance we may pull this off. The Greeks will most likely contend with the more serious threats first. I don't intend to blindly sacrifice our men. We will hold as long as it's humanly possible and then withdraw into the mountains, link up with other units and hold a defensive position there."

"I will pray that all goes well, sir. Thank you for listening to me. Now I must go and check on how preparations are going."

"Go my friend and thank you for trusting in me. May Allah always watch over you."

Army Headquarters, Argyrokastron Albania
1026hrs, 17 May

Several hundred kilometers to the west, near the provincial city of Argyrokastron, in a bunker that had been built and used by the Italian army more than seven decades ago, General Kemal and General Omar Hoxa, Chief of the Albanian armed forces, reviewed the final battle plan operations for the Albanian army. Both officers were certain the Greeks would be caught with their pants down. Since the crisis with Serbia, over the Albanian military intervention in the mostly Albanian populated autonomous province of Kosovo, which General Hoxa had been the major architect, military alerts were commonplace in the region. The ethnic Albanians which made up almost 90% of the population of Kosovo, then a Serbian province, had voted in an internal referendum for union with Albania. This was too much for the Serbians who had tolerated a semi-independent Kosovo after the NATO intervention, but union with Albania was just too much for them to tolerate. The Serbians had immediately dispatched troops to the region to crush this union and bloody fighting had broken out. Prompt Albanian military intervention, along with the help of the local militia that had been secretly armed by Albania, thwarted the

Serbians. Not wanting the war to spread, the European powers had forced Serbia to back down.

The crisis ended in a political and military victory for Albania and especially so for General Hoxa who commanded the Albanian expeditionary forces. The only negative point of the almost totally successful outcome to the operation was northern Epirus. This territory which was now part of southern Albania, had in previous times in history belonged to Greece. It was home to a minority of over three hundred and fifty thousand ethnic Greeks. During the crisis with Serbia, this minority had openly come out in favor of succession and union with Greece. Quick intervention by Albanian security forces nipped this movement in the bud. The ruthless crack down drew protests and threats from Greece. Fearing possible military intervention by the Greeks, Albania had sent large numbers of troops and equipment to reinforce her frontier with Greece. The much feared intervention never happened.

Unfortunately for the people of Albania, victory came at a great cost, their freedom. The cost of the war and the continued maintenance of large numbers of men under arms virtually bankrupted the country and wrecked the fragile economy. The collapse of several pyramid investment schemes and subsequent food riots throughout the country had caused the government in panic, to call out the army to restore order. General Hoxa who was then chief of staff quickly restored order, but in the process, he also overthrew the government whom he deemed inept, corrupt and responsible for the whole affair.

Thus, having saved the country again, this time from internal anarchy, the people united around their hero. To legitimize his rule, he formed an alliance with the Islamic nationalist parties turning Albania into an Islamic Republic. With himself as president of the revolutionary council and commander and chief of the armed forces, he virtually assumed dictatorial powers. Soon, aid in the form of petro dollars and military hardware began to arrive from the other Islamic states which helped put Albania back on its feet.

"Well Omar, I think your plans will succeed if you don't try to exceed your force's military capabilities," said General Kemal.

"Yes, we know our limitations. I know my army still lacks much in modern equipment, but with the military aid you have provided, my soldiers will triumph by sheer will power. Besides, all we want is Igoumenitsa. The Greeks will be too preoccupied in Thrace. They can't do much more that a holding action against us." There was a knock on the door. "Come in," said General Hoxa.

"Gentlemen, I hope I am not too late, I was inspecting the troops," said Major General Hamid Alia, deputy chief of staff of Albanian forces.

"No, come in Hamid," said Hoxa. The General got up from his seat, went to a cabinet and pulled out a bottle of Johnny

Walker. At six feet and of medium build, General Hoxa towered over the shorter and skinnier man. He got three glasses and poured them all a drink.

"How are preparations going?" asked Hoxa.

"Excellent, sir. The Greeks will be caught completely by surprise. We have detected no movement on their side."

"That is very good to hear," added General Kemal.

"Yes indeed. We will need the element of surprise if we are to have any chance at succeeding. Our aircraft coming in from the sea, must hit their targets at Corfu, Igoumenitsa, and most of all, the NATO AWACS base at Aktion at precisely 0500hrs. This is the time that your forces and our Macedonian allies will begin their attacks. If our planes are late in reaching their targets, the Greek air defense networks will have been already alerted and the possibility of catching the AWACS plane on the ground will be greatly diminished."

"Sir, I have made this point perfectly clear to General Karras. He reassured me that his pilots will come through," said General Alia.

"Let's hope so, Hamid. Everything depends on his main strike force not getting detected by Italian radar, when they fly out into the Adriatic."

"They will be flying at wave top level, sir."

"That's another reason I am worried. Most of our aircraft are old and obsolete, but thanks to the recent aid from our Turkish brothers," said General Hoxa nodding at his Turkish guest, "we have acquired some modern SU-27 fighter bombers with state of the art terrain following avionics. It will be up to these pilots to guide the rest through. Our older planes will have to follow the newer fighter bombers navigation lights to keep them on course and at altitude. The most dangerous phase will be when they turn back toward land and each formation separates and flies to its intended target. Losses in this phase are inevitable," he added.

"Let's pray that these losses aren't crippling. We need all the air support that we can get to assist the army in capturing the port city of Igoumenitsa," General Alia remarked.

"Also, thanks to your brilliant handling of the Kosovo affair, your army was able to re-equip itself from the large amounts of equipment captured from the Serbians."

"You are too flattering, Muhammad. The credit must go to my soldiers and their commanders. I only hope that we are half as successful in this war as we were in the last."

"You must be. Your contribution is vital, if Turkey is to succeed. Your attack will draw a significant amount of Greek forces away from my army. Remember gentlemen. Turkey doesn't forget her friends and allies. Once victory is achieved, Albania will receive the Greek Province of Thesprotia for her contribution to the war."

"We will show the world that Albania is no longer just another backward third world nation," said General Hoxa raising his glass. "To victory."

"Yes, to victory," added Kemal, as he gulped the smooth scotch down.

"Well gentlemen. I must be going. I have some final preparations to see to."

"I will escort you to your plane," said General Hoxa.

First Army command bunker, Kesan Turkey
1255hrs, 17 May

The honor guard snapped to attention as General Kemal's vehicle pulled up to the entrance of the Kesan bunker. The bunker was located just a few kilometers from the town of Kesan which was only forty kilometers from the Greek border. The General had just finished an early luncheon at the Kesan officers' mess, where he had given a speech, commending everyone for the fine job they were doing in making the maneuvers so far a success. He was exhausted from all the traveling he had done in the last 24 hours. Peering out the window of his staff car, Kemal could barely discern the camouflaged entrance to the bunker which had been built into the side of a large hill. He noticed the manned machine gun guarding the entrance. *At least security was tight, he thought.* When the car came to a halt, he was greeted by Lieutenant General Hasan Imbrahim, First Army commander, who escorted him inside. Both men descended the two narrow flights of stairs and entered the air conditioned command center, which was situated thirty meters under the ground. Everyone inside the bunker came to attention when they saw the two General officers.

"As you were," blared out General Kemal, loud enough to be heard by everyone in the large room. "Please continue with your work, don't mind me." The General then continued with the tour of the underground complex and was very satisfied with what he saw.

"This is a very impressive facility that you operate here, Hasan."

"It certainly is sir, thirty meters underground, encased in tons of steel and cement, with the hill over us for added protection. The bunker is equipped for nuclear, chemical and biological warfare. Its entrance and air ducts are all camouflaged to confuse any aircraft attacking with smart weapons. The engineers that designed and built it, said that it is impervious to almost anything but a direct hit by a perfectly aimed smart weapon or a hit by a nuclear warhead."

"I wouldn't want to be in here to test that theory," Kemal said, jokingly. "Enough small talk. Now, tell me how your preparations for the upcoming operation are proceeding."

"Please sir, follow me to my conference room." Kemal followed his subordinate out of the main command center and down a long corridor till they came to a room that had an armed guard posted outside the door. The guard came to attention, opened the door and closed it behind them after they had entered the conference room. Kemal looked around the room which had a large conference table with several chairs around it and at the front of the room were several maps that had cover sheets over them marked TOP SECRET.

"I believe now we can get down to business," Kemal said as he took seat at the head of the table.

"Sir, everything is on schedule. My battle staff was put on war alert at 0400hrs this morning. My armored units have been brought up to peak strength and have been alerted to move out of their holding areas by 0400hrs tomorrow morning. So far, everyone still thinks that this is another part of the exercise."

"That's good, security is paramount. Our success depends on the enemy being taken by complete surprise."

"I will brief my divisional commanders on the operation during my 1800hrs staff meeting and swear them to secrecy. Sir, I realize that it is a very short time for them to prepare, but most of the units are already operating at peak war readiness levels. The commanders will be given their battle plans which have already been prepared by my staff."

"Excellent I have total confidence in you. By the way, what is the status of the Saladin missiles? The whole operation depends on them functioning properly."

General Imbrahim went to the front of the room and pulled the cover sheet off a map of northern Greece.

"Sir, all our re-engineered Scud-D missiles that were provided by our Pakistani brothers have been rechecked by our technicians. The missiles, except for a few with some minor mechanical problems that are being repaired as we speak, are ready for launching. The warheads containing the blood agent Hydrogen Cyanide have been loaded on the missiles which will be fueled at midnight. They have been all targeted to hit Greek front line defense positions, command and control centers, airfields and military installations. None have been targeted to hit near any major population centers. All the missiles are under heavy guard. No one is allowed near them without special passes."

"There will be enough international outcry due to our use of WMDs, we don't want the Scuds landing near any heavily populated centers. Especially in areas that are populated by Muslims," said Kemal.

"Fortunately for us, sir, most of the faithful Muslims live some distance away from the border zone."

"We must be seen by the Greek Muslims as their liberators, not their executioners. Our success will depend on the gas catching the Greeks by complete surprise. The blood agent is quick acting. One good whiff and you are incapacitated almost immediately with death soon following."

Kemal then added with special emphasis, "Remember General, Alexandroupolis must be taken no later than thirty six hours after the initiation of hostilities. That is all the time that our airborne forces can be expected to hold out without reinforcements. It's imperative we take the port intact, so we can use it to land reinforcements and supplies. Without it, we will be hard pressed to resume our offensive towards Kommotini."

"Sir, I can assure you that my men will not fail. They will do their duty."

General Kemal thought for a brief a moment before answering his subordinate. "You must never underestimate your enemy. The Greeks are a very proud and cunning race. They will fight us to the bitter end. But, we will not only match them in their cunning, we will surpass them and ultimately defeat them!" Looking around the room, Kemal glanced at a map of northern Greece that was filled with colored pins indicating various units.

"It is over three hundred and fifty kilometers to Thessaloniki. We must reach our objective in no later than fourteen days. Any longer than a fortnight and we risk European and American military intervention. Praised be the prophet, that we are not totally alone in this grand venture. Our Albanian and Macedonian allies will be hard pressed. If they follow the battle plans that my staff developed for them and not get greedy and careless, all will go well."

"But sir, will the Americans stay out of the fight? The Greeks are a major ally of theirs in this region."

"Don't worry about them. I have a few surprises in store for the American dogs that will keep them occupied with their own problems for a while. If all goes as planned, by the time the

Americans have recovered enough to be able to intervene in strength, we should have achieved most of our major objectives. By then, it will be too late to save the Greeks without heavy losses in American lives and material and no American president will be willing to pay that price and face his electorate."

"They were in Kuwait and Iraq, sir."

"Yes, but Greece doesn't have the huge oil reserves that Kuwait and Iraq have. As for the Europeans, if their conduct and actions, or should I say, inaction during the Yugoslavian civil war have anything to say about them, their response will either be too weak or too late."

General Imbrahim, still having reservations about the operation, spoke openly to his superior."I pray that you are correct in all your assumptions, sir. If by any chance we do fail, the revolution would have been all for nothing and the blood of thousands would be on our hands."

"It seems to me that you are becoming too soft," said Kemal visibly irritated. "There is no room for failure." To make his point clearer, the General added, "Remember this, I will not tolerate failure. Those who fail me will pay the ultimate price. Is that clear?"

"Yes, sir!" Imbrahim said, regretting that he had even brought up the mere mention of failure.

"Now, take me back to my staff car, I must immediately return to Istanbul. Time is short."

After both men had exited the command bunker, General Imbrahim still appeared to be visibly shaken by his brief conversation with General Kemal. As Kemal was quickly let into his waiting staff car, he opened the car window and spoke to General Imbrahim.

"Our destiny is now in the hands of Allah. What will be, will be. Insh Allah, it is God's will."

Mackenbach Germany
1320hrs, 17 May

Major Bankasi and Lieutenant Olzum, a handsome young man in his early twenties, sat around the table in their safe house discussing the final details of their planned attack on Ramstein air base. The Lieutenant, his men and all their equipment had arrived several days ago, in two mini vans. Used to the cold rugged conditions of northern Turkey where his team had been training, Olzum had taken his shirt off in the warm environment of the house. Bankasi marveled at the Lieutenant's well trained body. Not an ounce of fat was noticeable on the younger man's muscular frame. Bankasi was in much better shape than most men his age, but the life he led had definitely taken its toll on him.

During the last couple of nights, the team had thoroughly scouted and familiarized themselves with the intended target area. The knowledge they gained from their forays into the area had greatly assisted Lieutenant Olzum in establishing his operations plan.

"You know Major, last night's reconnaissance in the area proved very rewarding," said the younger officer.

"How's that, Lieutenant?"

"The Americans are making things a lot easier for us. In the last two nights, we have found several structures that have been left open and others with the aircraft parked outside. They seem very lax.

"After tomorrow they will have second thoughts about their security," remarked Major Bankasi.

"Have you decided where you will position your security team?"

"Yes sir, during my reconnaissance of the area I found a good position to place the security detail. The area that we will hit is in the shape of a horse shoe. The detail will be positioned on top of a structure at each entrance to the area, in other words, at the tip of each end of the horse shoe. I believe sir, that is where you also suggested they be placed. There they can cover most of the area. Each man will be armed with two LAW rockets and a light machine gun. From their vantage points they will be able to easily take out any responding security patrol vehicles."

"I see that you have everything well planned. I have the utmost confidence in you. I'm sure the mission will be a success."

"Sir, my men and I know that this will probably be a one way mission. We have already made peace with ourselves and Allah. We are determined to sell our lives dearly and to send many of the infidels to hell. All that I ask of you is to buy us sufficient time, by delaying the follow on response force after the charges blow or in the case we are discovered."

"That, I promise you Lieutenant. The follow on force will be delayed," said Major Bankasi thinking of Layla and her crucial part in this mission.

Ramstein Air Base, Ramstein AB. Enlisted Club 1402hrs, 17 May

Nineteen year old Airman Mike Jones looked back at the events of the past few days. He could not believe his good fortune, as he looked across the table at his new girlfriend. He had only been in Germany three months, assigned as a security specialist to the 568th Security flight at Ramstein Air base. Most of his first month on the base had been real hectic. Base in processing and learning his new job on flight had taken most of his free time. Once he had passed his initial quality control exam everything had settled down and life had become rather routine.

After settling in, he had decided that it was time to venture off base to see Germany. He wanted to meet those beautiful German girls that all the guys in the barracks were talking about and hopefully get laid. Since he was only a poor underpaid airman, he couldn't afford a car. So he usually ended up bumming rides to the local GI hangouts from the guys that did have a set of wheels. One of these hangouts was the In Club, which happened to be located right off base, in Ramstein.

At the In club, he would frequently try to hit on the German girls, but always struck out. They would dance with him, but he could never get any to go out with him. That was until his luck took a turn for the better. Two nights ago, just when he had given up for the night and was about to leave, he met Layla, his dream girl. When he had first laid eyes on her, she was sitting at the bar sipping on a drink. With her dark complexion and her beautiful figure accented by the tight outfit she was wearing, she had to be the best looking girl at the club. He thought that she had given him a glance earlier when he had passed by, so he decided to ask her to dance. What did he have to lose? She could only say no. When he asked her, much to his amazement, she accepted.

After a few dances, he invited Layla to his table and bought her a drink. She had guessed correctly that he was a cop from the jacket he was wearing which was emblazoned with the 586th Security force logo. He obviously had made such an impression on her that they both talked till the club closed. Not having a car, he couldn't offer her a ride home. But she had her own and ended up giving him a ride back to the base. When they arrived at the barracks, he casually invited her up to his room for a drink. What surprised him even more was her spending the night. That was two days ago and now he was at the club having lunch, still in her company.

"A penny for your thoughts," said Layla.

"Sorry Layla, I was just day dreaming."

"About what?"

"About you, babe."

"Oh, really," she said in a very sensuous tone.

"Excuse me for a moment Layla, I need to go use the rest room."

"Sure, no problem Mike." After Mike had left for the rest room, Layla thought to herself how easy it had been to find the young fool. She had spent the last few days scouting the various dance clubs and pubs in the Ramstein area, looking for the right American to make her move. When she had first seen the skinny red headed kid at the In Club, she knew right away that he fit the profile that she was looking for. He was young, probably an airman, therefore without much money and best of all he was more than likely a security force member. She could tell the latter by the jacket he was wearing, it had USAF Security Force embroidered on it.

In the course of the conversation that she had with Mike she confirmed all of her earlier assumptions. The naive fool had spilled his guts to her about himself and his job, trying to impress her of the how important his particular job was to base security. Of course she acted very interested and awed and kept him going by asking innocent questions. When he told her that he didn't have a car and needed a ride home to the cops' barracks, she jumped at the opportunity. The small sacrifice that she had made of herself in spending the night in the barracks with Mike was well worth the information she acquired during the stay. If she had to buy time for Major Bankasi, she had found the way in the person of Mike Jones.

"I hope I didn't take too long?" said Mike sitting down beside her.

"No, you didn't dear. Let's go, I am finished eating."

"Sure, I've already paid the bill. Hey, by the way, do you want to go to Fred's lounge tonight? It's an all nighter."

"Sure, that sounds like fun. I'll meet you outside the west gate at the visitor control center at 10 p.m. tonight," said Layla, finding it a convenient opportunity to get herself and her vehicle onto the base.

"Okay, I'll be waiting for you at the visitor control when you get there."

They both got up, walked outside where he escorted Layla to her car. "I'll see you at 10.00 then." Before she got into her car, she gave him a long passionate kiss. He watched the car drive off.

"Wow, I can't wait till tonight," he said out loud as he turned to walk back to the barracks.

Ramstein Air Base south
1426hrs, 17 May

Jack Logan had left his office, in the 526th squadron headquarters building and drove to the 86th Wing headquarters. He was still filling in for Hansen, while the Colonel was back in the States on emergency leave. Logan had just finished reviewing the plans for the 526th's deployment to Italy to take part in a live fire exercise on the new NATO firing range. He had a meeting with the wing commander in fifteen minutes and he didn't want to be late.

After spending almost ten minutes looking for a parking spot, Logan finally found one across the street from wing headquarters. When he walked into the wing commander's office, he looked at the clock on the wall and saw that he was a few minutes late for his appointment. The General's executive officer, a young and very attractive female Captain was on the phone. "Excuse me sir, it will be a few minutes before the General will see you. He is on the phone with the CINC/USAFE."

"I can wait." Logan was thankful that the General who was a stickler for punctuality was preoccupied and wouldn't notice that he was late. A few minutes later, Brigadier General Tom Pope, the 86th fighter wing commander, opened the door and walked out of his office.

"I am glad you're here Jack, I was just briefing the four star on the deployment preparations. Let's go into my office." Both men entered the office, the General closing the door behind him.

"I have two things. The first thing concerns a Captain Wendy Barnes. I heard that she failed her Stan Eval. Some rumors that have been floating around say she feels that she was failed on purpose by Major Kerns. I don't need to emphasize that I don't need a sexual discrimination charge made against this command. Now is there any basis to her accusations?"

"Well, it's difficult to say, sir. I spoke with Kerns and he did admit that he rode her rather hard and put her through the wringer."

"Damn it! The liberals will eat us alive if they get a hold of this in Washington. So what is your recommendation, Colonel?"

"That she be given another Stan Eval by someone other than Kerns as soon as she gets back from a couple of days leave that she requested."

"Then see to it, Colonel."

"I have spoken to her sir, and I am personally looking into the matter."

"Good! Now, tell me Jack, how are preparations going for the 526th deployment to Italy?"

"Everything is moving right along according to schedule. All deploying aircraft have received any needed maintenance and we're looking at 100% operational status come departure day. All that is left to do is palletizing our support equipment. The folks over at AMC tell me that everything will be ready by tomorrow. We'll be ready to depart for Italy on the 20th as planned."

"Good work, Jack. I told the four star that the 526th would be ready to leave as scheduled. Our aircrews need the practice. Ever since we lost all our NATO bombing ranges in Turkey, live bombing practice is at a premium now."

"You're right, sir, our pilots do need the bombing practice. Simulators are good but they're not like the real thing. At least our pilots are getting adequate training in their air to air combat skills."

"Thank god for that," said General Pope. "Even with all the force cuts and budget reductions, we have strived to still maintain a quality force. But with only two fighter wings left in the European theater, we aren't much of a force anymore. God help us if we have to deploy and fight somewhere. Those so called self righteous bastards in Washington really did a fine job in emasculating us, especially here in Europe. The peace dividend, they called it. Well, enough of my rambling. Thanks for the update Colonel. Tell the troops they are doing a great job and I appreciate their efforts."

"I'll do that, sir," said Logan.

Athens, the Greek Pentagon
1500hrs, 17 May

After reviewing the report and photographs that Major Stavropoulos had sent over from Elefsis, taken by the surveillance Albatross, Colonel Papalexis had come to the same conclusion as the Major. Even though the lighting conditions had been poor when the photographs were taken, computer enhancement did reveal that some of the Turkish troops on board the ships were wearing what appeared to be chemical suits. Even Colonel Papalexis, who at first had been skeptical about the whole issue, was now himself concerned. The original assessment he had given to Stavropoulos about some field commander wanting to "gain points" by impressing his superiors in Istanbul with his aggressive training, was still very plausible. Though to be on the safe side, he would brief his superiors on this latest piece of intelligence. Picking up his phone, he called his boss, Brigadier General Stamatis.

After looking at the photos and reading the analysis report, General Stamatis was also convinced that the photos did reveal the presence of chemical gear. So he decided that the intelligence should be passed on to his superiors. Fifteen minutes later, both officers and the pictures were in the office of the deputy chief of Staff, Lieutenant General Pavlos Makarios.

The General, a medium sized man in his early fifties with dark intelligent eyes, examined the photos. After reading Major

Stavropoulos' analysis report, he too reached the same conclusion. "Well Colonel, what do you make out of this? Do you agree with Major Stavropoulos' original report?"

Colonel Papalexis not wanting to over commit himself, but still wanting to stress the importance of what the photos had revealed, took the middle of the road approach.

"Sir, it's very possible that one of their army field commanders is trying to make an impression as a "go getter" with the boys in Istanbul. It could also signify a major doctrine change by Turkey."

"Meaning, Colonel?"

"The possible first use of WMDs in any future military operations undertaken by their armed forces."

"I find that rather hard to believe."

"Sir, may I please continue?"

"By all means, Colonel. Please do."

"Sir, chemical weapons today have become the poor man's version of nuclear weapons. Chemical weapons do have certain advantages. They are just as lethal as nuclear weapons without the destruction that accompanies the use of a nuke. They don't require huge amounts of money or the advanced technological facilities to produce them. Any country that has even a simple chemical industry or fertilizer plant can quickly convert it to produce chemical weapons. Turkey, having a substantially sized chemical industry would have no trouble at all producing deadly chemical agents locally."

"This is all a very interesting assumption, Colonel. Let us say that the Turks do have chemical weapons. Do they have the delivery systems to successfully use these types of weapons?"

"I believe they do, sir. It's been suspected for some time in the western intelligence community that Pakistan may have sold them modified Scud C missiles."

"I've also heard of that rumor. But the Scud isn't an accurate weapon. We saw this during its use in the Gulf war."

"With North Korean modification kits, the missiles can be significantly enhanced to carry a 200-kilo payload to well over 500 kilometers and land well within a hundred meters of the target. Several of these missiles straddling a target, depending on the prevailing wind, can saturate it with poison gas. I am sure that the Turks have the ability to even modify them further. They also have the ability to deliver chemical attacks by using artillery, aircraft bombs and the aerosol spray method delivered by helicopter. The Iraqis used this method against the Kurds in the late 1980s, killing thousands, mainly women and children."

"I remember seeing pictures of the after effects of those attacks when I was stationed at SHAPE Belgium as a young Lieutenant, "said General Stamatis.

"Everybody knows that relations between Greece and Turkey have been deteriorating ever since those Islamic fundamentalist fanatics seized power. It would spell disaster for us if we were attacked and caught unprepared. You are the intelligence specialist colonel, what action or actions do you suggest that we take?"

Colonel Papalexis had not been caught unprepared by the General's question. Any intelligence specialist worth his salt would have expected this question. He had already formulated the safest possible answer in his mind, one that would protect the troops in the field and also safeguard his career if anything actually happened.

"Sir, I suggest for a short term solution, that you draft and send a message to all military units stationed on the Aegean islands and in Thrace ordering the immediate issue of gas masks. For the long term solution, we must re-examine our defense doctrine and amend it to incorporate the possible use of chemical weapons against us. We must develop better and more intensive chemical warfare training programs than the ones we have now to meet the threat."

"What do you think, General Stamatis?"

"I agree with the Colonel's overall assessment and suggestions, sir. We were extremely lucky that the Albatross was even there to take the photographs. I believe our discovery possibly explains why the Turks fired to warn the plane away. They didn't want us to see their troops training in chemical gear."

"I think you're right Harry."

"Well, Colonel, your briefing was most enlightening. I'll immediately have your first suggestion implemented and order the issuing of gas masks to the troops in the field. As for your other recommendation, I will pass it on to my staff and see what they can come up with. Please keep me informed of any other developments." With the meeting concluded, Colonel Papalexis departed the General's office convinced that he had said and done the right thing concerning the intelligence photos. At least now the staff was aware of the possible chemical weapons' threat posed by Turkey and something was going to be done about it.

After the two intelligence officers departed his office, General Makarios called his aid in and had him draft up a classified message for all military units stationed in the Aegean and Thrace. The message ordered the immediate issue of chemical protective gear to all personnel. Within an hour, it had been received by most of the effected units. Unfortunately it was a Friday and the last work day of the week when everyone likes to get off early. So when the message arrived many unit commanders left it pending till Monday while others gave it to junior officers or NCOs to implement. Only a few of the more conscientious commanders stayed overtime and implemented the order. These would be the lucky ones.

When the message reached Limnos, some commanders gave the chemical gear out the same day, but most did not. One of the units that did receive the masks was the air defense battery defending the island's airfield. The fortunes of war this time would be kind to the Greeks.

Faliron Bay, Athens
1514hrs, 17 May

Captain Samuel Taylor watched in admiration, as his bridge crew maneuvered the aircraft carrier Abraham Lincoln into its anchorage in Faliron bay. The ship was in Greece for a routine port call visit. In a time of budget and force cuts the navy's tradition of showing the flag in ports throughout the world was still alive and well.

After twenty-five years in the navy, most of them as a naval aviator, he now commanded one of the most powerful warships in the world. Known as a fast burner in most naval circles, the six foot, two hundred pound former all American football star and Annapolis graduate had been one of the youngest officers to receive command of such a powerful warship. The Abraham Lincoln was one of the latest in the line of nuclear powered Nimitz class carriers that had been built for the U.S. navy. It displaced almost a hundred-thousand tons, was over three and a half football fields long and carried eighty combat aircraft able to carry both conventional and nuclear weapons. Captain Taylor had in his command, the power to destroy the war making ability of a moderate military power.

Putting the pair of binoculars that hung about his neck to his eyes, Captain Taylor viewed the shore front. The last time he had visited Greece back in the early 1990s, the shore leave boats were greeted by hundreds of protesters yelling, "Yankee go home." Now there wasn't a soul out there and the date of the visit had been announced weeks in advance. It's a very different world. With a hostile Turkey next door, most Greeks were happy to see the Lincoln. He remembered when the US always had two battle groups in the Mediterranean and another only a few days away in the Gulf. Now it was just the Lincoln.

Looking out toward shore, Captain Taylor spotted a small boat approaching the carrier. It was probably the US Naval attaché and the Greeks coming to give him his security briefing.

Turning the ship over to his executive officer, he left the bridge to go meet the shore party.

Limnos

1940hrs, 17 May

Feeling hungry after an afternoon of fun and games, Yiannis and Eleni had driven into town and had had early dinner. Having little time to waste, they both jumped into the jeep and headed back toward the pension. Tonight would be the Hydra's first night patrol. Yiannis was really looking forward to the termination of the Turkish maneuvers so he could take his leave and be with Eleni. Driving along the coastal road, they came upon a column of soldiers.

"Yiannis, who are those soldiers and why are they dressed like that?" asked Eleni, pointing to the soldiers as they trudged by wearing battle dress uniforms and weighted down by their weapons and combat gear.

"They're Special Forces troops here to participate in field exercises with the island's garrison. Two companies, almost three hundred soldiers, arrived yesterday from the mainland."

"They look very tough, Yiannis."

"They're a mean bunch. They train for special operations such as infiltrating behind enemy lines to cause sabotage and mayhem. And they're also excellent mountain fighters. Those soldiers are another reason for you to stay inside at night."

"Oh Yiannis, you're treating me like a little girl. I can take care of myself."

"I didn't say you can't, but there are a lot of horny soldiers running around this island."

"Okay sweetheart, I will stay inside after it gets dark."

Ten minutes later, Yiannis had dropped Eleni off at the pension and drove to where the Hydra was moored. He was met at the gangplank by Ensign Georgiou. "Good evening, skipper. How was your day?"

"Just fine, Mr. Georgiou. How are preparations going?" Yiannis said as he looked around seeing many of the crew hauling boxes of supplies to the storage hold.

"We will be ready to sail, once refueling has been completed. That should be in about fifteen minutes, Captain. Oh and the boys have all had their dinner, fresh fish donated by one of the local fishermen."

"Very well. I see you have everything ship shape."

"Thanks Captain, but I hope the Turks finish these damn maneuvers soon. Everyone is getting tired."

"I know what you mean, Mr. Georgiou. I think they should be finished, at the most by Sunday."

"I guess we can make it for another two days."

Fifteen minutes later, the Hydra was passing the harbor breakwater and heading out into the Northwestern Aegean to relieve the Batsis and assume its patrol sector. Patrol reports had indicated that there had been little Turkish activity during the last twenty-four hours. Yiannis hoped that it would stay that way.

Chapter 6

Into the brink, Kommotini

2053hrs, 17 May

Mohamid Alia and Osman Gezeglou, General Kemal's agents in Kommotini had left the noisy demonstration that had been taking part in the town square, satisfied at the large turnout which the Mufti had arranged. The moment for them to go into action was fast approaching. "Osman, it's time that we paid the old fool a visit."

"You're right my friend, let's go see the old man."

Ten minutes later, after making sure that no one had followed or seen them, Osman knocked on the Mufti's door. They were answered by the Mufti's pretty daughter who was wearing traditional robes and a head scarf. She let them inside. They immediately proceeded into the study where they found the Mufti reading the Koran. The elderly Muslim cleric looked up at the two men visibly agitated for being disturbed. "What do you want here again? You got your demonstration," said the Mufti angrily.

"We have come here to thank you personally for your cooperation in arranging the demonstration."

"Leave my house! You are not welcome here any longer."

"But your holiness, we are only seeking your help against the infidel."

"I will not help you any longer. Please leave before I call the police."

"Shut up, you traitorous old fool!" shouted Osman, as he pulled out a silenced 9mm automatic pistol from under his jacket.

"How dare you bring a weapon into my house?"

"Did I not tell you old man that you would help us cause an incident that would result in violence?"

"You will get nothing more from me!"

"Yes we will. Your death! It will appear that it was perpetrated by Greek security agents and should get the results we want. Once the Muslim community finds out that you were murdered and is led to believe that it was committed by the Greeks, they will raise this town to the ground."

"No!" screamed the Mufti as he lunged for Osman's silenced gun. Before he could fully get out of his chair, he was shot twice in the chest. The old cleric collapsed, mortally wounded against the coffee table, tipping it over and causing the china to smash on the tile floor. Hearing the commotion, Fahtme came running into the room to see what happened. She screamed when she saw her father lying on the floor in a pool of blood.

"Shut up slut!" It's now your turn," said Osman as he pistol whipped her across her forehead knocking her unconscious. "Osman, what do you say that we have a little fun with this little whore before we kill her? Like I said before, I'm curious to see what this bitch is hiding under all her robes"

"Why not, brother? It will serve our purpose better. The Muslims will be even more incensed when they find out the Mufti's daughter was raped and murdered." They carried Fahtme into the bedroom and ripped her robes off.

"The little bitch does have a fine body after all," said Mohamid. "This will be a pleasure."

They tied her to a bed and the two of them took turns raping her. When they had satisfied themselves, Osman shot her in the head. Before leaving the house, they deposited a small gold crucifix on a broken chain at the foot of the bed. Anyone searching the scene would obviously find it. Once safely away, Osman made an anonymous telephone call to the Greek police and reported that he had heard screams coming from the Mufti's house.

When the Greek police arrived at the house fifteen minutes later, they were met there by a Muslim cleric. The Imam had received an anonymous phone call from someone speaking Turkish. The caller had informed him that he had heard screams and seen two men running from the Mufti's home. After repeated attempts at knocking at the door and getting no answer, the two responding policemen were at an impasse. Not wanting to provoke an incident with the Muslim community, they were hesitant to gain forced entry. Only at the insistence of the Muslim Clergy man did they force the door open.

Rushing inside with guns drawn, they found the house in total disarray. The floor was strewn with books and smashed

China and much of the furniture was overturned. Upon entering the Mufti's study, they were met by a gruesome sight. The room was splattered with blood and written on the wall in blood were the words, "Die Muslim Pigs." They found the Mufti's body hanging from the ceiling rafters. He had been shot and his genitals cut off and stuffed into his mouth. While one of the policemen cut down the body, the other one continued to search the house and found the Mufti's daughter. She was covered in blood, still tied naked to the bed where she had been raped and burned with cigarettes. The shocked policeman yelled out to his partner to inform him of the gruesome discovery. Quickly checking for vital signs, he thought he detected a slight pulse, he immediately radioed for an ambulance, cut the girl free and began administering first aid.

Once the ambulance finally arrived, the two cops helped lift the barely living girl from the blood soaked bed onto a stretcher. Only then did they notice a small crucifix attached to a chain at the foot of the bed. One of the policemen picked the crucifix up and staring at it considered its implications. The Muslim Imam who till now had remained silent, exploded in a fit of rage and hysteria. Swayed by this damming piece of evidence that this devious crime had been perpetrated by the Greeks, he began screaming obscenities at the police in both Turkish and Greek. The two policemen along with their shift commander and several other officials attempted to calm him down. They tried to explain that everything humanly possible would be done to find and punish the killers. However, the cleric was beyond reason. He was convinced that the Greeks had murdered the Mufti to silence him and frighten the Muslim community into submission. He ran screaming out of the house to go inform his people of this horrible crime. The first phase of Operation Medina had commenced.

Bellame Disco, Bad Homburg Germany
2145hrs, 17 May

Sitting at the front bar where he could monitor the club's entranceway, Logan took a swig of his beer and looked at his watch one more time. The loud music and thick noxious cloud of cigarette smoke was beginning to annoy him. Where the hell is she, he wondered. She was supposed to have met him here fifteen minutes ago. Well, it wouldn't be the first time he was stood up in his life. Helga had chosen this locale. He would have rather gone out for a nice dinner and afterwards gone back to her place and sipped some wine. *I must be getting old, he thought to himself.* Logan reflected back to all the good times he had through the years with numerous girlfriends and romances. There had been some women whom he could have settled down with, but flying had always come first in his life. He wondered how many years he had left in the cockpit before being grounded for medical reasons brought on by aging. Maybe it was getting time to settle down. His thoughts were suddenly interrupted by a pat on the back.

"Hey fly boy, buy me a drink." Logan turned around on the bar stool.

"Wie gehts, Helga. I thought you wouldn't show."

"You know us women. We can never be on time. It takes us forever to dress and put on our make up to look good for you boys."

"Well you certainly look good tonight," he said taking in her low cut dress which revealed her ample bosom.

"What are you drinking? The usual?" She nodded her head in agreement.

"Bitte ein Gin and Tonic," he said to the bar tender.

"So, when will you be leaving for Italy?"

"Probably in the next couple of days. What do you want me to bring you back for a souvenir?"

"Oh, a tall dark and handsome Italian to keep me company when you're gone"

Logan laughed. "No, really?"

"Just bring yourself back in one piece. You're not a young buck anymore."

"Don't worry about that. I'll be back. But you're right; I'm not getting any younger. I have given settling down some thought. How about you?"

"She smiled at him. If that was a proposal Jack, I'm flattered. But I told you I will never marry a pilot. And I don't think you are about to suddenly give up flying, are you?"

Logan thought a few seconds before answering. "No Helga. I'm not ready to give up flying just yet."

"I knew that would be your answer Jack. In spite of that, we can still be friends. Come on, how about a dance."

"Sure, I can keep up with all those young bucks out there," said Logan with a lecherous smile.

"I bet," she said as she pulled him toward the dance floor.

Sofia Bulgaria, Ministry of defense
2206hrs, 17 May

With less than seven hours remaining before the commencement of the Turkish attack on Greece, the Bulgarian ministry of defense was humming with activity. The Defense Minister, Georgi Zukov, was in conference with his military chiefs of staff.

"Gentlemen, you are all aware the Turkish attack will begin at 0500hrs, tomorrow morning. Our frontier forces have been on a heightened alert ever since the Turkish maneuvers began a few days ago. At 0200hrs, I am ordering that all our military forces be placed on war alert. I do not want any fighting spilling over to Bulgarian territory," said the Defense Minister.

"Remember, the President has stressed that our role will be humanitarian in nature. We will give any refugees entering Bulgaria, food, shelter and protection. Any Greek forces crossing into Bulgaria will be treated according to the international laws governing the relations between belligerents and neutrals. All heavy military equipment will be seized, but they will be allowed to keep their side arms. Under no circumstances, will Turkish military units be allowed to cross into Bulgarian territory. Even in hot pursuit. Are there any questions on this particular point?" he added.

"I have a question Mr. Minister," said General Petrov, the air force Chief of Staff.

"Yes, General Petrov?"

"What if Turkish aircraft violate our airspace and refuse to heed our warnings? Do my pilots have authorization to shoot them down?"

"Yes, the President has stipulated, any Turkish units which are violating Bulgarian territory and refuse to heed our warnings will be forcibly removed. That is to include the shooting down of the offending aircraft. Are there any other questions?" Since there were no other questions at the moment, the Defense Minister opened his brief case and pulled out a file stamped Top Secret. "General Gregov, the President has reviewed your plans and concurs with them. If our military intervention in this upcoming war is deemed necessary, we will be ready," said the Defense Minister.

"Gentlemen, the whole world will be watching and judging us from our actions. I do not trust the Turks. They promised us the use of the port of Thessaloniki if we remained neutral. If intervention proves necessary, this is what we will do," he said as he began briefing the plan.

Kommotini, the Central Square
2212hrs, 17 May

After the Imam had left the Mufti's house, he went immediately to the town square where many of the city's faithful were gathered to tell them of the murder of their religious leader. The organizers of the demonstration had built a wooden platform and had covered it with various banners displaying various anti Greek government slogans. The Muslim leadership was using this stage to give stirring speeches to the crowd that had swelled to several hundred. When the Muslim clergyman arrived, he was still in a semi hysterical state. He immediately informed the leadership of what had taken place at the Mufti's home. They, in turn, immediately broke the news of the murder to the demonstrators that were gathered in the square.

The news struck like a bombshell. When they heard that their Mufti had been murdered, the crowd had gone into a state of shock. For a few seconds, an eerie calm hung over the square. Osman and his partner who had infiltrated the demonstration after they had left the Mufti's home seized on the moment and went into action.

"Death to the infidel murderers, " screamed Osman.

"Death to the killers of our Mufti," shouted Mohamid. Soon

others in the crowd began to take up the chant.

"We must avenge our Mufti!" screamed Osman.

"Yes, we must avenge the Mufti!" shouted someone else.

"Everyone to police headquarters. Death to the infidel!" screamed Mohamid, in a feigned fit of passion to help incite the crowd.

The chant of: "To police headquarters and death to the infidel," soon swept up the now angry demonstrators. The chairman of the Islamic committee, who had been one of the co-organizers of the demonstration, immediately got on the microphone. A rational man, he attempted to calm the situation before things got out of hand. However, it was already too late. The crowd had become a mob now under the control and leadership of General Kemal's two agents. Fortunately, most of Greek owned businesses around the square had closed early so their employees could go home to avoid getting caught in any outbreak of violence which could have erupted from the demonstration. As a result, except for a few smashed car windshields and store fronts, there were no serious incidents of violence when the mob departed the square.

After the mob had left the area, undercover policemen who had been observing the demonstration radioed and updated headquarters of what had transpired in the square. Within minutes police vehicles began driving through the Greek section of the city advising residents via their loud speakers to go home and stay inside. With the possibility of serious violence imminent, the Greek inhabitants of the town bolted themselves in their homes.

Kommotini, Central Police Headquarters
2236hrs, 17 May

It had been almost an hour since the discovery of the gruesome crime at the Mufti's home. Colonel Sakis Makris, Kommotini's police chief, had no other leads as to who had perpetrated the crime, other than a gold crucifix. The Mufti's daughter, who was in a comma and not expected to live, was being air evacuated to Athens for immediate surgery. She was his only hope in finding out what had really occurred at the house. He had been notified of the murder while at home and immediately rushed to headquarters to supervise the investigation and call his superiors in Athens to brief them on the situation. Athens in turn, had instructed him to fully cooperate with the Muslim community and take whatever actions were necessary to help solve the crime and do nothing that would antagonize the Muslims and spark violence. One of the things that the Colonel did do after being notified of the incident was to initiate a recall of all off duty policemen. This was a precautionary measure, just in case there was any violence started by the Muslims.

All of the Colonel's hopes to a peaceful solution quickly faded when the message had come in over the radio that the

Muslim mob was heading toward police headquarters. Fearing violence, he ordered the sentries outside the building to be doubled and all standby personnel to be issued riot gear and tear gas grenades. In addition, the armory was put on standby in order to issue heavy weapons if the need arose. He would give it his best shot to avoid bloodshed. When the demonstrators would arrive outside, he would go out and meet them. Hopefully, his assurances that the Greek police would fully cooperate with the Muslim community and do everything humanly possible to find the perpetrators of the crime would avoid trouble.

Kommotini, five blocks north of Police Headquarters

2239hrs, 17 May

Warrant Officer Mihalis Manakos and his riot team had been parked just a few blocks from the town square monitoring the demonstration, which as a whole, had been peaceful. When the news of the Mufti's murder and the subsequent recall of all off duty personnel was broadcasted over the radio, Mihalis began to fear that violence was probably inevitable.

After the Muslims left the square for police headquarters, Mihalis was positive his riot team would now intervene, but instead, he received orders to remain out of sight and redeploy to a location a few blocks away from headquarters. His new instructions were to remain at their new location and do nothing to provoke the Muslim protesters. Now parked a few blocks north of the headquarters building, they could clearly hear the loud chants of "death to the Greek murderers," coming from the mob. Mihalis gave the order for his team to prepare for deployment.

Kommotini, Police Headquarters
2245hrs, 17 May

With the angry Muslim mob now only a few minutes away, Colonel Makris was on the phone with the ministry of public order in Athens updating them of the new situation.

"General, there are several hundred pissed off Muslims coming this way. I am sure you can hear them now too!" said Makris, holding the telephone receiver out the window for the General to hear.

"They're chanting, "death to the Greek murderers.""

"I can hear them, but you must avoid violence at all cost, Colonel," said General Pappas, the Commander of the Greek police. "I just got off the phone with the Prime Minister. He is on his way down here. His instructions were to defuse the situation, catch the killers and avoid violence."

"I am attempting to do that, General. But if there is any serious trouble, I do not have the manpower to handle it."

"You can handle it, Colonel! Go out and speak to them, they

are reasonable people. Tell them that we will do our best to catch the killers."

"I intend to do that, sir."

"Good. Keep me informed of any further developments. I will send you some additional men and investigators in the morning. Goodbye for now."

"Callous bastards. It's easy enough for them in Athens to issue orders, but they're not here facing a mob of pissed off Muslims," remarked a visibly agitated Colonel Makris to his deputy.

"What did they exactly say?" asked Major Costopoulos, his deputy commander.

"We are expected to avoid trouble at all costs. We are by ourselves on this one, Major."

A sense of approaching doom had gripped everyone in the building. The Colonel could see the fear growing on the faces of his men.

"Major, make sure that all the men stay off the streets and out of view for the time being. Stand by on issuing weapons. I want that done only as a last resort. I will go out to meet with them and see if we can diffuse this situation before it escalates out of control. The last thing we need is a blood bath"

"Sir, I am going with you," said Major Costopoulos.

"No Harry, stay here in case anything happens. Call the nearest army garrison post and tell them we might be requiring their assistance. They probably will not act unless directed by

Athens, but at least we can give them a heads up."

"Yes sir, good luck."

"Thanks, Harry. I'll need it."

A few minutes later, the mob whose numbers had now swelled to over five hundred, reached police headquarters and surrounded the old two story building, effectively isolating it from outside contact. Colonel Makris, unarmed and with a bullhorn in his hand, bravely walked out to speak with them. He could clearly see that some of the men in the crowd were carrying shotguns and clubs. When they saw the Colonel, they jeered him and their chants became even louder.

"Please, please, everyone listen to me!" he said speaking into the bullhorn. "Disperse and go to your homes. We are doing everything that's humanly possible to solve this horrible crime and bring those responsible to justice."

Osman, who was now clearly the leader and in control of the crowd, raised his hand calling for silence. "You tell us to go home. Will you find and bring the murderers to justice?"

"We are doing everything in our power to catch those responsible," said Makris.

"How can this be? You Greek dogs are the killers and the rapists! You Greeks murdered our Mufti to terrorize and silence us!"

The mob roared in approval to what Osman had said.

"No, that isn't true. We don't know who committed this terrible crime, yet. Please believe me. We are leaving no stone unturned to catch the ones responsible," said Colonel Makris.

"You lie!" yelled Osman. "We know a crucifix was found by his daughter's body which the infidel dogs had violated. Greek security agents murdered him because he fought for his peoples' rights! We demand you give us the murderers immediately. Death to the infidels!"

The mob began to chant in support of Osman. "Please everyone calm down," he pleaded with them. Unseen by anyone, Mohamid had disengaged himself from the main body of the crowd and had snuck between some of the parked cars in front of the building. Mohamid checked to make sure that no one was watching him, but that was unnecessary since everyone's attention was riveted on Osman and Colonel Makris. Seeing that all was clear, he pulled out a grenade from his jacket pocket. Pulling the pin, he tossed it toward Colonel Makris who was standing in front of the building's entrance, only fifteen meters away. The Colonel never saw the grenade which landed a couple of meters away from him and exploded. Like a giant scythe, the shrapnel cut down all those that were in its lethal kill radius including Colonel Makris and one of the sentries. If Mohamid and Osman had hoped for causing a panic with the grenade attack, they got more than they had ever bargained for.

Hearing the grenade explosion, the once obedient crowd became an unruly mob fleeing for their lives. One of the sentries who had survived the blast with only minor injuries, thinking they were under attack by the Muslims, panicked and opened fire with his MP5 sub machine gun. The 9mm slugs tore into the packed crowd with devastating effect, dropping many in their tracks. But the gunfire also had an immediate sobering effect on the mob. Once the shooting erupted, it caused those that had not been hit by the hail of bullets to stop running and dive for cover. Thus, with the panic temporarily halted by the shooting, Osman and Mohamid grasped the opportunity to reestablish their control over the mob. Having taken cover in the doorway of an adjacent building after tossing the grenade, Mohamid sprang into action. Jumping out of his hiding spot with an automatic pistol, he began shooting at the police station and screaming at the top of his lungs, "death to the infidel. Allah Akbar!" Witnessing his act of armed defiance, many of those in the mob who were armed with shotguns began shooting at the police. Others who had brought homemade Molotov cocktails, lit and tossed them at the building. The sentry who had opened fire had emptied his thirty round magazines into the crowd and was now out of ammo. Realizing this, he tried to run the few meters separating him from the building's entrance and safety. He got no further than a couple of steps before he was struck down by at least three rounds. The police inside the headquarters building were caught completely by surprise at the sudden turn of events. Finding themselves trapped, surrounded and shot at by hundreds of hostile Muslims, they began returning fire. The battle for Kommotini had begun.

Kommotini, five blocks north of Police HQ
2318hrs, 17 May

When the grenade explosion and the gunfire was heard, Mihalis worst fears had suddenly come to pass. With the frantic calls for help coming over the radio, Mihalis decided to attempt a rescue of his trapped comrades. But first he would have to sell the almost impossible task to his men.

"Listen up everybody. We all heard the blast and the shooting that is going on right now. I personally can't just sit here while our comrades are being killed," said Mihalis. As if to emphasize his point, another cry for help came over the police net.

"All of you heard that last request. I am game for a rescue attempt. Are you all with me?" Without the slightest hesitation, the decision for a rescue attempt was unanimous. Mihalis and his key NCOs quickly formulated a rescue plan.

Their plan was simple. He would divide his twenty-five man team into two groups. He with twelve other men would attempt to crash through the mob's barricades with their bus while the other group would set up a rear guard to help them in case they got stalled on the return trip. They would have to hurry. Time was running short for their trapped comrades at police headquarters. The last thing they heard over the radio before it went off the air was that the building was on fire.

Kommotini

2325hrs, 17 May

Having successfully achieved the goal of instigating a revolt, Osman put their next phase of their operation into execution. After the shooting had started, Osman had become the de-facto leader of the Muslims. Temporarily taking over an adjacent house after butchering its Greek inhabitants, Osman swiftly began to organize his followers. He knew that they didn't have much time. Within the hour, Athens would most likely dispatch troops from nearby garrisons to restore order. But this was exactly what he wanted. The more troops that he tied up in restoring order, the fewer troops would be in the field to fight the Turkish army once the attack on Greece began in the morning.

The first command that Osman had given to his followers, was to destroy the city's telephone exchange. This would effectively cut the city's communications with the outside world. He also sent runners to all the nearby Muslim communities to enlist their aid in the insurrection against the infidels. Before leaving for the Muslim section of town where he would set up his command post and from where he would direct the insurrection, he gave his final instructions to his new Lieutenants.

"Brothers, we must hurry to complete the destruction of police headquarters. There must be no survivors! Afterwards, take any weapons and ammunition that you can find and return with them to the mosque where we will set up our headquarters. The Greeks will most likely dispatch troops against us. We will barricade ourselves in our community and show the world how the faithful fight and die! Many infidels will burn in hell this night! Allah is great! Allah Akbar!"

The shout of Allah is great, momentarily drowned out the sounds of the gun battle that was still raging, only a few hundred feet from where they were standing.

"Now hurry my brothers. Time is running short!" As everyone began to depart to carry out his commands, Osman pulled Mohamid to the side, out of hearing distance from the rest of the Muslim community's leaders.

"You must go at once to where we have hidden the radio and transmit the code word "Mecca" to Istanbul. This will let them know that our mission was a success. Once you have accomplished that, join me at the mosque where we will direct the fight against the infidels."

"I understand, Osman."

"Be careful, and make sure no one sees you." After the two men parted, it was relatively easy for Mohamid with all the fighting that was taking place to slip away. Within twenty minutes, Generals Kemal's command post had received the message confirming that the first phase of operation Medina had so far been an overwhelming success.

Kommotini, six blocks north of the police station
2333hrs, 17 May

After the entire squad had been briefed on the rescue plan, they prepared the bus by smashing the windows in order to have a clear field of fire. Those who were going with Mihalis stayed on board while the rest got off the bus. Most of them were armed with .38 caliber revolvers. Mihalis knew that these weapons were useless against the shotguns that most of the Muslims were armed with. He was hoping that the elements of speed and surprise would help them overcome their handicap.

"Okay men, let's do it!" As the bus started to move through the deserted streets, some of the men uttered prayers while others donned their helmet and gas mask.

"When I give the word, start dispensing the tear gas," shouted Mihalis.

Nearing police headquarters, they could see that the upper level of the building was engulfed in flames and the outside area was strewn with bodies and numerous overturned cars. The gun battle between the cops trapped inside and their besiegers was still raging strong. It would only be a matter of time before their comrades were forced to flee and take their chances of being butchered outside, or roasting alive inside the burning building. Neither prospect held any chance for them. "Now," shouted Mihalis. With a loud thump, several tear gas canisters flew from the bus which was now only a hundred meters from the front of the building. All those that did not have dispensers, manually lobbed CS gas grenades out of the windows.

"We aren't going to make it," someone shouted.

"Hold on!" screamed the driver, as he slammed on the brakes and side swiped an overturned car which was blocking the road.

"This is as far as we go," yelled the driver so he could be heard through his gas mask. The bus came to a stop less than a hundred feet from the front of the building. The immediate area around headquarters was quickly blanketed by a thick, choking cloud of tear gas. The Muslim rioters who were totally engrossed in eliminating the surviving policemen inside the building had not seen the speeding bus until it was on top of them. The surprise had been complete. Several attempted to charge the bus, but were blinded by the gas or cut down by Mihalis' men. The others ran to escape the asphyxiating gas.

Inside police headquarters, the situation was desperate. Of the twenty men and women inside, four had been killed and five others had been wounded. All communications were out and the building was on fire and it was getting difficult to breathe from all the smoke. There would be no fire department responding. Most of the firemen were either too terrified to come out into the streets or had fled to their homes to protect their families from the insanity that was taking place in their city. Major Costopoulos was about to give the order to attempt a break out. At least they would die like men and not like trapped rats in a sinking ship.

"Major! I hear small caliber gunfire and see lots of smoke coming from, no wait! It's Manakos and his men! We've been rescued!" shouted one of the men posted at one of the windows overlooking the street.

Major Costopoulos hurried to the window to make sure for himself. "My god, it is Mihalis!"

A loud cheer erupted from the throats of the trapped policemen, who only a moment earlier, had written themselves off as dead.

"Okay everybody, let's move it, get off the bus and take up positions before the Muslims have a chance to regroup," commanded Mihalis.

While Mihalis and his handpicked team of five dashed inside the burning headquarters building, the rest of the team set up a 360-degree security cordon around the bus.

"Mr. Manakos, are we glad to see you. We had considered ourselves goners."

"Save the thanks for later, Major. We need to move right now before the gas clears and the Muslims recover."

"We're ready. Let's head for the bus!" said the Major. Assault rifles in hand taken from the armory and carrying their wounded comrades, they made their break for the bus and to safety. With the tear gas starting to clear, many of the Muslims quickly began recovering from its effects. Some of them who had taken positions in adjacent buildings, after having forcibly removed or murdered their occupants, began to shoot at the fleeing policemen. At first, their fire wasn't very accurate but it quickly improved, felling some of the running policemen.

"Hurry, pick them up and keep moving. If they get organized, we are all dead," yelled Mihalis. He himself had stopped to aid one of the fallen policemen, but kept on running when he saw that the man was beyond help, having had half his face blown off by a load of shot gun pellets. When all the survivors had boarded the bus, the driver, unable to turn around because the mob had blocked most of the side streets with overturned vehicles, put the bus into reverse. Mihalis' men, now armed with automatic rifles, were able to keep most of the Muslims at a safe distance as the bus continued its wild ride through the gauntlet. At the slow speed that they were going, it would take another couple of minutes before they would reach safety. Mihalis hoped nothing else would go wrong, it was taking too long to get away in reverse.

"Stop the bus! The road's blocked with overturned vehicles and rubble." yelled one of the rear look outs.

Coming to a stop less than twenty meters from the road block, the bus suddenly came under heavy fire from several directions. The Greeks began returning fire, keeping the Muslims at bay for the time being. "It's a trap. We can't stay here; we will all be killed, "screamed Major Costopoulos in terror.

"Damn it! Where is our rear guard?" shouted Mihalis in anguish. "We can't give up now, we're almost to safety. If we stay in here, we will all definitely die. Let's show them how Greeks fight."

"We are with you Mr. Manakos," said one of the lightly wounded policemen, as he picked up his assault rifle.

"Follow me, men!" Mihalis and the handful of survivors leaped out of the bus and charged the barricade. Mihalis and some of the men had even fixed bayonets to their Heckler and Koch G3 assault rifles. Not caring whether they lived or died, they continued their mad charge. With Mihalis in the lead, their pitiful number quickly dwindled from accurate shotgun blasts as they closed the short distance to the barricade. When Mihalis reached the barricade miraculously unscathed, he leaped between two overturned cars, his rifle spitting fire as he tried to clear a path for his comrades who were close behind.

"Look out, Mihalis, look out!" yelled one of the men running behind him. Mihalis glanced to his left and saw one of the Muslims running toward him carrying, what appeared to be an upraised axe. He brought his rifle up to fire and pulled the trigger only to hear the click as the firing pin went forward into an empty chamber. Reacting instantly, he plunged the bayonet into the other man's stomach, but it wasn't enough to totally ward off the blow. Fortunately, he was still wearing his riot helmet when the ax, with only the force of a dying man behind it, struck his head. The blade barely penetrated the helmet causing a slight cut to his head. Mihalis stunned by the blow, momentarily fell to the ground but recovered quickly and rejoined the fight.

Outnumbered almost three to one, the Greek policemen fought like lions. As the bodies began to pile up around the barricade, the rioters were beginning to lose heart. Sensing this, Mihalis rallied his men.

"Come on men, we have them beat!"

Screaming at the top of their lungs, the desperate policemen pressed the assault. Lacking discipline and effective leadership, the Muslim rioters broke and ran. As they fled up the street, they ran into Mihalis' rear guard which had been joined by a large contingent of the town's Christian residents. The rioters never had a chance as they were cut down in their tracks by heavy rifle and shot gun fire.

"Well, it's the cavalry to the rescue," said Major Costopoulos.

"It's over. We won! They're running!" someone yelled, as a loud victory cheer went up.

The battle had not lasted more than a few minutes. Victory did not come cheap as Mihalis looked around him. Flames could be seen coming from the vicinity of the telephone exchange and from other parts of the town. Scores of bodies littered the street. Over half of his force had either been killed or wounded. Mihalis knew in his heart that it was far from over. Too many on both sides had been killed.

"It looks like they are falling back to their part of the town.

We must establish communications with Athens and request immediate military assistance," said Major Costopoulos.

"I believe that they're probably already on their way, sir," said Mihalis looking skyward at the sound of an approaching helicopter. The helicopter momentarily circled the surrounding area and departed toward the west.

"It's probably a scout, sir. The lead columns should be here within the hour."

"Thank God for that," replied the Major.

"Mr. Manakos! We must get organized before the Muslims come back in force. Make sure all the wounded get proper medical attention. Then set up roving patrols composed of armed citizens and police to patrol the Greek sector of town. I am going to city hall if it's still standing to await the army's arrival and to set up a command center. You can almost rest assured, we will be hearing more from them. Too much blood was spilled here tonight."

"You're right on that one, sir."

"Oh, and Mr. Manakos, go and have your head looked at, you're bleeding all over the place."

"I will, as soon as I take care of the more pressing issue of attending to our seriously wounded," said Mihalis as he turned around and headed back to the bus where the wounded were being gathered.

Kommotini, the city Mosque
2355hrs, 17 May

After leaving Mohamid in charge at police headquarters, Osman went to the mosque and set up his command center. All their activities against the Greeks would be directed from there. Until the arrival of the Turkish army, they would be facing the Greeks alone. He had sent runners to all the nearby Muslim villages asking for their help and requesting they sabotage all power and communication lines in their area. When a messenger sent by Mohamid had advised him of the rescue of the trapped Greek policemen, he had initially become furious. But he knew that he shouldn't expect too much from a bunch of illiterate sheep herders. His main concern was to prepare for the arrival of Greek reinforcements that were sure to come. He had seen the army scout helicopter circling above the city. Osman was positive that the first Greek army units would be arriving very shortly and that didn't leave him much time to prepare his defenses.

One of the first things that he had done was to establish some type of command structure. He had taken several of the community's religious and political leaders who were present at the demonstration and gave them the title of Lieutenant. Then Osman had divided the men which now numbered more than one hundred and fifty, into seven teams and appointed an officer to lead each team. Osman knew that his rag tag forces whose weapons consisted of shot guns, some ancient rifles and a few pistols would be no match for the well-armed soldiers that would soon be arriving. So he tried to stack the odds in his favor as best as he could. His first order had been to barricade all the streets leading into the Muslim section of town with overturned cars. Lacking any type of explosives, he had instructed one of his teams to begin making gasoline fire bombs which could be used against armored vehicles. Another step that he had taken to better their odds was ordering the disruption of the town's power supply. Five of his men had gone to the town's transformer substation and set the structure ablaze. As of a few minutes ago, all of Kommotini had been bathed in total darkness. Their only light source was now coming from their flash lights, oil lanterns or from the glow of burning buildings.

Soon afterwards, he was joined by Mohamid who had returned with fifteen assault rifles and ammunition which they had collected from the abandoned police station.

"You have done well, my friend," said Osman.

"Those were all the weapons I could rescue from the burning building before the flames got too bad. I had momentarily left police headquarters to contact Istanbul. The fools, in my absence, let the trapped dogs get away. We could have gotten more weapons."

"It doesn't matter, we have done better than I ever expected. We must now prepare a welcome for the Greek army that will soon be arriving with the intention of restoring order. This is why I have ordered the barricading of all the streets leading into the Muslim district."

"Surely they will not move immediately against us?" Mohamid asked.

"I don't think they'll come rushing right in. First they must set up a battle plan. Then they will attempt to negotiate with us. We will stall them as much as possible, hopefully till morning. By then it'll be too late for them. When our army begins the attack, their troops will leave the city for the front and leave us alone."

"I hope you are right, Osman."

"You will see I' m right. Now go and supervise the making of the Molotovs, just in case we are attacked. Time is short."

Chapter 7

D-day, the Saronic Gulf
0140hrs, 18 May

It was a dark and moonless night over the Saronic Gulf, perfect cover for the Shatila's mission. Her voyage from Benghazi had so far been uneventful. Saleem, with a 9mm automatic pistol strapped to his side to deter any crew member from having a last minute change of heart, nervously paced the bridge. Their present position was nine miles southwest of Faliron bay and their intended objective. Saleem had instructed the crew to remove the fake superstructure housings from the missile launchers and the missiles be given a final inspection. However that had proved unnecessary, they were in perfect working order. In a few minutes, he would unleash his deadly cargo at the American Jew lovers and finally reap his revenge.

"Suilliman, what is our present position and are there any other ships nearby?" he asked his radar and weapons tech.

"We are eight miles southwest of Faliron bay. The closest ship is a large ferry, five miles due south of our present position. She is headed for the port of Piraeus."

"Yes, I saw her lights in the distance," said Saleem.

"Thank you, Suilliman. We will launch from six miles. Prepare for firing," said Saleem, electrified at the prospect of finally consummating his revenge.

"At this range, the Americans will have no time to react, before the fiery sword of Allah is upon them. Nothing will save them!"

It took the Shatila almost seven minutes, at her present speed of fourteen knots, to reach her firing position.

"Saleem, we are now six miles from the target," advised Suilliman.

"Commence the launch!"

"Switching tactical radar to search mode," said Suilliman who had already previously armed the missiles before he began his active radar sweep. The Shatila's radar and weapons specialist was in real life a trained Turkish naval NCO operating under the guise of the Islamic front. Since Suilliman knew the general position of his target, it took less than a full radar sweep before he established a "lock on," after which he immediately returned to passive mode. Only an alert ESM operator on the American warships might have detected the Shatila's brief radar emission, except this was not to be the case. With most of the crews ashore and anchored in a friendly port, no one saw the need for taking added precautions.

"We have radar lock," said Suilliman.

"Fire," commanded Saleem. The Shatila shuddered as the missiles leapt from their launchers, trailing a long plume of fire and smoke which lit up the morning sky.

"Turn us around and get us out of here."

Faliron Bay, USS Lincoln
0156hrs 18 May

Corporal Leroy Johnson USMC, a twenty-year-old African American marine from New York City, had just assumed the 0130-0300hrs starboard watch on the USS Lincoln. Armed with an M-4 assault rifle, he anxiously paced the starboard side flight deck. His one and only duty was to prevent any unauthorized individual or individuals from attempting to board the carrier. Holding a Styrofoam cup of coffee, he slowly sipped the hot brew to warm his body, chilled by the cool sea breeze that was blowing over the immense flight deck. Johnson looked out over the water at the neon lights which adorned the restaurants and clubs that dotted the beach front. He could hear loud disco music spilling out of one of the clubs on shore. This was his first time in Greece and he was stuck with guard duty. He could hardly wait to begin shore liberty in the morning. Most of his buddies who had gone ashore had come back hammered. Some of them had even gotten laid from the numerous hookers that worked the bars where the sailors tended to spend their shore leave and money. He could just taste the cold beer and fantasize what he would like to do with one of the hookers when his turn came to go on shore. He hadn't had a drop of booze or seen a woman since his last liberty in Naples and that had been almost three weeks ago.

As Johnson stared at the lights of an approaching ferry boat heading for the main harbor entrance, he saw what looked like lightning flashes out at sea. Almost immediately, the flashes became two very fast moving bright lights, one following the other. What was strange about it was that they were heading towards the carrier. Before he had assumed his post, he had been briefed by the Master at Arms to immediately report anything unusual to security control. He figured that this was something unusual. Taking his portable radio, he called security.

On board the Aegis cruiser Ticonderoga, anchored a half mile away, petty officer Anderson, the on duty radar operator, had suddenly picked up two high speed blips on his screen heading their way. The two blips had originated from the vicinity of a small ship which they had been tracking for the last hour. At the speed they were traveling, the blips could only be one thing, missiles.

"Sir," Anderson called excitedly to the duty officer who was only a few feet away pouring a cup of chicken soup from his thermos. "I think you need to see this. I've detected two small unidentified contacts, possibly missiles. Range four miles, speed three hundred knots and accelerating. They're heading this way!"

"Jesus! Sound general quarters, activate the air defense system and notify the Lincoln," screamed the duty officer to the bridge crew after seeing the incoming missiles on the radar. The last order though was not necessary. The Lincoln had also detected the incoming missiles. As general quarters sounded throughout the anchored American warships, the air defense systems on board the Lincoln and the Ticonderoga slowly began coming to life. Nonetheless, it would be too late for them. Saleem had been correct on his assumptions. With the missiles launched from such a close distance, there wasn't sufficient time for the air defense system to come on line.

On the Lincoln, the bridge crew could visibly see the bright exhaust trail of the incoming missiles which were now only seconds from impact.

"Lunching chaff canisters," yelled her ESM operator, "it's our only chance." The night erupted into a brilliant fireworks display from the exploding chaff canisters launched into the air by the anchored war ships. The chaff canisters let loose thousands of aluminum strips intended to confuse the missile's acquisition radar. When the first Exocet neared its target, its radar was only momentarily confused by the chaff, but its sophisticated circuitry quickly burned through the interference and reacquired its target. The last thought on Corporal Johnson's mind before the missile plowed into the carrier's side, ten feet from where he was standing, was that he wasn't going to have that cold beer after all.

The Exocet which had been cruising at more than 500 miles an hour struck the carrier amidships, just under her island superstructure. The missile tore through the main hanger deck and continued its path of destruction through several more compartments before its 165 kilo warhead and unused load of rocket propellant detonated in the ship's combat information center. The resulting explosion was tremendous, shaking the 91,000-ton behemoth from bow to stern. Super heated gases created by the missile's detonation, ripped through the confined spaces of the lower decks, killing and injuring over a hundred crewmen and setting off numerous large fires and secondary explosions.

When the second missile which had been following a half a mile behind encountered the aluminum chaff cloud, its radar momentarily lost the carrier, confused by the many ghost images caused by the chaff. A split second later, its radar burned through the interference, acquired and locked onto another close by target. Within a fraction of a second, the new target data was transmitted to the missile's flight computer and it instantly corrected the Exocet's flight path.

It had been a busy day for the Captain and crew of the inter-island ferry boat Poseidon. The 15,000-ton car ferry was returning to Piraeus with a full load of vehicles and passengers. Many of the ship's 900 passengers were out on deck enjoying the night scenery when their attention was suddenly drawn to a fireworks display emanating from several nearby anchored warships. In the next few minutes, most of these passengers would be dead. The second Exocet which had been confused by the chaff, slammed into the Poseidon's port side, slicing through the un-armored hull of the ferry like a knife through butter. The deadly missile detonated deep inside the ship's interior amongst its cargo of parked vehicles. The powerful blast set off a chain reaction of explosions immediately as the dozens of gas tanks of the vehicles she was carrying began to catch fire. In less than a minute, the car ferry had become a floating Viking funeral pyre. Scores of passengers, many of them on fire, jumped into the cold dark waters preferring to drown than be burned alive. With no one at her helm, the Poseidon veered sharply to starboard, out of control. Her new course was taking her toward the stricken American carrier, less than a mile away. Everyone on board the American warships watched in terror at the disaster unfolding before their very eyes.

On board the Aegis cruiser Ticonderoga, Captain Paulson, her commanding officer, entered the warships' bridge, still clothed in his pajamas. He had been asleep when general quarters had sounded.

"My God," he uttered out loud, as he took in the scene before him. The screams from the hundreds of passengers still trapped on board the doomed ship could be clearly heard across the waters.

"Jesus! She's on a collision course with the Lincoln, can't we stop her?"

"We're too close for a missile, sir, "replied the ship's weapons officer.

"What about our main guns?"

"We can give it a try, but our guns might not be able to

depress low enough to engage the target at this close a range."

"Hurry! She's closing on the carrier. Try a couple of shots, aim at her stern. Maybe we can knock out her steering."

"Aye, aye, skipper."

The cruiser's forward gun depressed as far as it would go and spat out two 127mm shells in rapid succession. The first shell barely missed and exploded harmlessly in the water. The second shell struck the ferry's fan tail where thirty or forty survivors had huddled together to escape the spreading flames. The shell failed to damage the steering and only added to the carnage, blowing many of the passengers into the sea.

"Cease fire, cease fire!" Captain Paulson yelled.

What the Ticonderoga could not accomplish with all of her latest state of the art weaponry, the flames which had been consuming the Poseidon's vitals did. The fire which had rapidly spread to the ferry's engine room had damaged the controls to the point where the engines shut down.

"By god, she's slowing!" Captain Paulson shouted.

"She sure is," said Lieutenant Commander Harris, the bridge duty officer.

Even with her engines dead, the blazing 15,000-ton ferry that had been cruising at nineteen knots continued toward the helpless carrier, now only with her momentum propelling her forwards.

"She won't stop in time, she's going to ram the Lincoln!" shouted Captain Paulson.

Seconds later, with a loud crash of tearing metal, the Poseidon plowed into the anchored carrier. The ferry's bow tore a fifty foot gash in the Lincoln's hull and ripped the carrier from her anchorage. The fire consuming the ferry's insides had finally reached the ship's fuel bunkers. It set off a searing explosion which blew out the ships bottom and engulfed the forward part of the Lincoln in flames which quickly spread to the F-18 fighters that were on the carrier's flight deck. As bits of debris and body parts rained down on the nearby Ticonderoga, what remained of the ferry quickly sank to the bottom of the shallow bay.

Captain Paulson and most of his crew were momentarily in a state of shock after witnessing the incredulous series of violent events that had just transpired before them. However, that didn't last long. The professionalism, instilled into the American sailors by years of training, quickly took over.

"Commander Harris, I want the ship's boats out with rescue and medical teams to look for survivors. Get us immediately under way and next to the carrier. Have damage control rig the fire hoses."

"Aye, aye, Captain."

"Captain, I have the Greek coast guard on the radio, they are requesting to know what exactly is going on," said radio man second class Kounts.

"Tell them that we were attacked by anti-ship missiles. Two were launched at us. One of the missiles struck the Lincoln and the other hit a car ferry causing it to veer out of control and crash into the carrier. The ferry has exploded and sunk with large loss of life. Tell them we need a couple of tugs, fire boats and all the medical assistance that they can send us." Captain Paulson turned to his radar man. "Smith, do you have a fix from where those two missiles came from?"

"Yes sir, but not for much longer. The terrorist ship will soon be behind the island of Aegina. I believe they're making a run for it."

"I want those bastards. Commander, send out our chopper to track the terrorist ship."

"Aye, aye, sir."

"Captain. I've lost radar contact with the terrorists."

"Damn it. I hope the chopper finds them before we lose them in the dozens of coves and small inlets that dot the coastline."

"Sir, message from the Lincoln, they're requesting our assistance. They are unable to move on their own power. They have fires burning out of control in one of the aircraft hangers and the lower decks. She's also taking on water. They aren't able to provide us with an accurate damage and casualty report at the moment, though casualties are feared to be in the hundreds. Her skipper, Captain Taylor, is among the missing."

"Holy mother of God! Commander, draft a classified top priority message for 6th Fleet Naples and Washington, briefing them on what has happened here tonight. Let me see it before you send it."

"Aye, aye, sir."

"Sir, the anchors are up and we are ready to move," said the Helmsman.

"Okay, put us alongside the Lincoln."

"Aye, aye, sir."

Saronic Gulf, five miles northwest of Aegina
0236hrs, 18 May

Immediately after the Shatila had unleashed her deadly cargo, Saleem had the helmsmen go to flank speed of 19 knots and alter course toward the Poros straits. They would attempt to make their escape by sailing behind the island of Aegina which would shield them from detection by American radars. In the event that they were discovered, they would be close enough inshore to the Peloponnesian mainland to beach the Shatila and attempt to escape overland.

"Look! Brother Saleem," one of his crewmen yelled, pointing to the sky. "There is a helicopter closing in on us." The feeling of elation that had originally swept over them after successfully carrying out their attack on the hated Americans, quickly evaporated. They had now become the hunted.

The small Sea Sprite helicopter that had been launched by the Ticonderoga had quickly found the terrorist ship. It had positioned itself almost a thousand meters behind the Shatila in order to track her until the arrival of an Albatross patrol plane which the Greeks said they would soon be dispatching to the area. Once on scene, the Albatross would assume the job of tracking the terrorists and coordinating any subsequent moves against them. In the mean time, the unarmed Sea Sprite continued to transmit the terrorists' current position and heading to the Ticonderoga, which in turn was relaying the information to the Greeks. The noose was quickly tightening around the Shatila. Immediately after the attack, the Greek coast guard had requested assistance from the Hellenic air force to help in locating and tracking the terrorists. An alert had been put out to Elefsis air force base and an HU-16B Albatross and its crew had been put on recall.

One of the units that had been dispatched to intercept the terrorist ship was the Hellenic navy gun boat Mykonios. She had been conducting night training exercises in the Saronic Gulf with units of the Greek army special forces near their base, twenty kilometers west of Corinth. When the Mykonios had received the message to intercept the terrorist ship, her Captain, Lieutenant Commander Markos, had immediately set sail at full speed to intercept the Shatila. The intercept orders had not come as a complete surprise to him. He had heard of the terrorist attack on the American carrier over the naval command net. If he managed to catch up with them, he would make sure that the terrorists did not escape. They would pay for the pain and embarrassment they had caused to his peaceful country.

With the Greek gun boat racing across the Saronic gulf at 25 Knots, her quarry had already rounded the west end of the island of Aegina. On the Shatila, Saleem was deciding on how to rid himself of his annoying pursuer. Before they had set sail from Benghazi, he had requested a number of Sam-7 Grail surface to air missiles from the Libyans. At first, the Libyans had refused, but eventually backed down and provided him with three of the missiles.

"Hadji" Saleem called to one of his crewmen. "Bring me one of the Russian anti aircraft missiles that are stored in my cabin."

"Yes Saleem!" A few minutes later, the crewman arrived with one of the deadly Grail missiles.

"Help me unpack it. I want to give our infidel friends a nice surprise."

Faliron Bay, USS Ticonderoga
0255hrs, 18 May

With the aid of the numerous rescue and fire boats that had arrived at the disaster scene, salvage and rescue operations had quickly gotten under way. From the nearby harbor, two tugs had arrived to help secure the drifting behemoth which had taken a 10 degree list from the hundreds of tons of water that had flooded several of the carrier's compartments. With the herculean efforts of both the Lincoln and tug boat crews, tow lines were passed to the carrier which still had large fires burning throughout several sections. Once she was secured, the battle to bring the fires under control began. Captain Paulson quickly maneuvered the Ticonderoga alongside the stricken ship enabling the cruiser's crew to use their high pressure fire hoses on the raging fires that had engulfed the Lincoln's forward section. With the significant efforts of the carrier's damage control parties and all the other fire fighting vessels, the fires were eventually contained.

"Sir, our boats are back from their search for survivors from the ferry."

"Well Commander, how many people did they rescue?"

Commander Harris hesitated for a moment before answering. "They found only thirty alive, sir. Many of them have been badly burned and not expected to make it."

"My God, there were hundreds of people on that ship. What about the Greeks?"

"They didn't do any better, sir. They're estimating 700-800 killed on the ferry alone."

"We can only hope that they get those bastards and they're made to pay for their horrible crimes. Oh, and Harris, here is the message you drafted. Just add those casualty figures and have Sparks send it Flash priority one."

"Aye, aye, skipper."

Captain Paulson, now fully dressed and wearing a flack vest and helmet like the rest of the bridge crew, turned around and walked out of the bridge to get some fresh air and gather his thoughts. This was a disaster of epic proportions. The US navy's only carrier battle group in the Mediterranean put out of action and God only knows for how long. Hundreds of innocent civilians and American sailors killed or injured. Looking at the smoking and listing carrier, he thought of the future of his military career. Someone would have to eventually pay for this. Washington would soon be looking for heads. He wanted the bastards that did this, and the ones that had put them up to it, to pay!

"Captain." Paulson was jolted from his thoughts by Commander Harris who had come out to brief him on the latest update on the terrorist ship.

"Yes, what is it Harris?"

"We have identified the terrorist ship by the information relayed to us from the Sea sprite. She is the motor ship "Shatila," of Lebanese registry."

What an appropriate name, thought Captain Paulson. Paulson turned and walked back into the bridge command center. He had been to Beirut in the early 1980s and remembered the massacre of the Palestinians by the Christian Lebanese militias at the refugee camps.

"What's the latest update on their location?"

"They are heading for the straits of Poros, sir."

"That's interesting. They are either trying to lose themselves in the heavily traveled narrow channel, but that would be a little difficult with the helicopter trailing them, or they will soon attempt to beach the ship and escape overland."

"Captain! The Sea Sprite reports that they are under missile attack," said radio man second class Kounts.

"Sir, I've lost all contact with the Sea sprite."

"God damn them. I want those bastards dead!"

"Sir, our only hope now is with the Greeks. One of their gun boats, the Mykonios is attempting to intercept them. They are twenty minutes out. It will be close. If they enter the straits, we might lose them."

"What about other aircraft?"

"I was just briefed that a Hellenic air force Albatross seaplane just took off from Elefsis air base, their ETA is fifteen minutes. With the Sea sprite presumed lost, it will be very difficult for the Greek aircrew to spot the ship, once they enter the Poros channel. It's still dark and the channel is very narrow, only 200 meters wide at its narrowest point."

The Pentagon, Washington, D.C.
0300hrs, (1900hrs EST) 18 May

Admiral Henderson, Chief of Naval operations, had just finished telling his wife over the phone that he was on his way home for dinner, when his intercom buzzed. The call was from the Pentagon communications center switch board, advising the Admiral that he had an urgent incoming call on his STU-3, from the commander of the US 6th fleet in Naples, Italy. When the STU-3 rang, Admiral Henderson opened his desk drawer, took out his phone key, inserted it in the phone and went on secure mode to talk to Admiral Kimmel.

After being briefed on the news of the disaster in Athens and reading the hard copy message sent by the Ticonderoga's skipper, Admiral Henderson's immediate reaction was one of shock and disbelief. What if this was a prelude to an all-out attack by a hostile power on US forces in the Mediterranean? With his only carrier battle group out of commission, there was very little he or the Navy could do to stop it. Quickly pulling himself together, he thought it best to immediately brief his boss, General Jason Coleman, chairman of the JCS. While picking up his phone to call the General, he immediately had second thoughts and put it down. First, he needed to get an update from the senior naval commander at the scene before calling General Coleman. This way he would be in a better position to answer the General's myriad questions.

"Captain Henry," the Admiral called to his aid, sitting at the adjacent desk and listening to the conversation. The Captain, who had turned pale from the shock of what he had just heard, could only stare at Admiral Henderson.

"Captain, snap out of it man!"

"Ah, excuse me, sir. This is just awful. The Lincoln's skipper is a good friend of mine. We were classmates together at the academy."

"I know. But we need to pull ourselves together and try to

salvage as much as we can out of this disaster. Now get me a voice link with the Ticonderoga's skipper. After that, locate General Coleman."

"Yes, sir."

It only took a couple of minutes for the satellite voice link to be established with the Ticonderoga. After receiving an update from Captain Paulson, Admiral Henderson had a true understanding of the scope of the disaster and what was being done to collar the perpetrators of this terrible deed.

"Sir, I have General Coleman on the line."

Henderson didn't even bother to acknowledge his aid, he just picked up the phone. He dreaded what he knew was coming from his boss. "Sir this is Admiral Henderson."

The six foot three, two hundred and thirty-pound chief of staff could be just as intimidating over the phone as in person to his subordinates.

"Cut the formalities, Admiral!" the General remarked.

"Tell me just what the fuck is going on in Greece with your aircraft carrier?"

"Sir, watch what you're saying, this line is unsecure."

"Screw the unsecure line! Turn on your god damn TV," said the General in a sarcastic tone. "I just got off the phone with the president and his national security advisor. It seems that CNN broke the news first on the disaster in Greece over national TV. Turn your TV on Admiral."

Admiral Henderson motioned to Captain Henry to do so.

"With all the billions that we have spent on state of the art communications, we were bested by a god damn civilian TV crew. CNN is calling it a new Pearl Harbor for the US Navy. As you can probably imagine, the "boss," wasn't very happy that he had to hear about this disaster from the TV."

When the TV came on in Admiral Henderson's office, they could see close up footage of the listing ship with fires still burning in the forward part of the carrier. They could hear the commentator stating in the background that the loss of life might exceed a thousand, taking into account the hundreds of passengers that were still missing and unaccounted for from the ferry boat.

"My God, General. It's worse than I thought. I see what you mean. Sometimes the wonders of modern telecommunications just work too well. The civilians don't have a military bureaucracy to contend with and they aren't worried about security."

"You're fuckin' right, Admiral! That's exactly what I told the President. The civilians don't care about security, nor do they have to encrypt and decode their messages. And they don't have a chain of command that wants to be briefed on every step of an operation! Heads are going to roll for this, Admiral. It's hard to believe that our only carrier group in the Med was taken out by a bunch of rag heads inside a friendly port. What the fuck were your guys doing? Out drunk, running the whores?"

"General, those missiles were launched from a distance of

less than six miles. That's point blank range for an anti-ship missile. It took just a little over a minute for those missiles to arrive on target. Our ships didn't have enough time to get their defense systems on line. They were in a friendly port in peace time. It was a miracle that they got any chaff or flares off at all. Lucky for us the second missile was deflected by the chaff."

"You're right, Admiral. If you want to call it luck," the General said sarcastically.

"Tragically at the cost of over 700 lives on that ferry boat. I am still trying to figure what would have caused less damage to the carrier, the ferry boat collision and subsequent explosion and fire or taking the other missile hit?"

"That couldn't be helped, sir. It was by pure chance the ferry was sailing by at the time of the attack."

"You can tell that to the victims' families, or to the Greek government, Admiral. Now what are you doing to get the bastards that are responsible for all of this?"

"We have a helicopter following a ship of Lebanese registry named the Shatila, which we believe is responsible for the attack," said Admiral Henderson, too terrified to tell the General that the helicopter no longer existed.

"We should have them within the hour, sir. The Greeks have dispatched forces to intercept them."

"How are rescue and salvage operations preceding, Admiral?"

"The carrier is secured and under tow to the Skaramagas

ship yards for emergency repairs Most of the fires are under control. The ship is listing slightly and can't proceed on her own power. We still don't have a clear picture on the number of casualties, but it's feared to be in the hundreds. The exact extent of her damages hasn't been determined. But she is effectively out of operation for weeks if not longer."

"Any word on her Captain?"

"He's been seriously injured, but he will pull through."

"Well Admiral, see what you can do to salvage your career. Before the day is through, we will all probably be looking for another job. Just keep me informed of any new developments. I'm on my way to a press briefing. As you can probably guess, the media is already having a field day over our new Pearl Harbor, as they're calling it."

"I will keep you informed, sir." Putting the phone back on the hook, Admiral Henderson thought of what the General had just said. He couldn't believe that almost thirty years of service had just gone down the toilet.

"Sir, we just received another message from the Ticonderoga, they have lost contact with the terrorists," said Captain Henry."

"Damn it! That's all I need. Coleman will really have my ass now. Get on the line to the Ticonderoga. They are to get those bastards at any cost. I don't want any more failures!"

"Easier said than done," the Admiral's aid quietly mumbled under his breath.

Sick Bay, USS Lincoln
0312hrs, 18 May

It had been a night of pure hell for Captain Taylor and the scores of injured crewmen who now lay in the Lincoln's sick bay. Taylor had been awake in his cabin when the general quarters alarm had sounded once the missiles had been detected. He had just returned after being the guest of honor for dinner at the U.S. ambassador's residence in downtown Athens. When the alarm had sounded, Taylor had immediately left his room and quickly headed for the bridge. He had not gone more than a few steps when he was knocked off his feet by a tremendous explosion. Stunned for several seconds, he lay in the dark passage.

It had been the smell of thick acrid smoke and the cries of the injured which quickly brought him back to reality and urged him into action. The smoke, coming from the several fires, started to fill the dark passageway making breathing difficult. He had suddenly realized that he had to get to the bridge and find help for the injured crewmen trapped below in the wreckage. Getting back up on his feet and using what little light was provided by the emergency battle lanterns, he had attempted to make his way back through the passageway toward one of the hatchways which led to the upper decks. Reaching the hatchway, he had climbed the ladder to the next level. Most of the crew had awakened and the passageways had filled with running sailors, heading for their duty stations. Spotting a group of crew men, Taylor had instructed them to go help the injured below. When he turned to leave, there had been a tremendous crash followed by a powerful explosion which slammed him into the bulkhead and knocked him unconscious.

When Captain Taylor regained consciousness, he found himself lying in a cot in the ship's sick bay. The strong odor of antiseptic burned his nose. His left arm was in a cast and his upper body was swathed in bandages. He looked around and saw that he was not alone. The whole of sick bay was filled with injured crew men.

"Someone help me. I need to get to the bridge!" he said out loud as he attempted to sit up.

One of the orderlies, tending a patient a couple of beds down, saw the Captain and rushed to his bed side.

"Sir, please don't move, you will only hurt yourself. I will go get the doctor."

A minute later, Commander Stevens, the ship's medical officer arrived at the Captain's bedside, his white smock was stained with blood making him look more like a butcher than a medical doctor.

"I am glad that you're awake, sir. You received a nasty bump on the head along with a broken arm and some superficial burns."

"I don't feel much pain, doc."

"That's because you were given a shot of morphine."

"How long was I out?"

"About an hour to the best of my estimates."

"I need to get to the bridge, my ship has been damaged. I've got to go." As the Captain tried to get up, he fell back down onto the cot.

"Take it easy, sir," the doctor said while having to physically hold the Captain down. "You received a nasty bump on your head and some other injuries. The ship's in competent hands."

"Okay doc," said Taylor, not having the physical energy to argue.

"Tell me what happened. All I remember was being knocked down by an explosion as I was trying to reach the bridge after "general quarters" had sounded. When I got up, it was dark in the passageway, only the emergency lights were on. I tried to get help for the injured and in about a minute or two later there was a big jarring crash and another explosion. That's when the lights went out for me."

"Someone launched two missiles at us, sir. One hit the carrier, that was the first explosion. The other one was decoyed away but struck a passing ferry, setting it ablaze and out of control. The ferry veered into our bow, then exploded and sank."

"That must have been the second explosion I heard."

"The collision put a large hole in our bow and tore us from our anchorage. The missile and the ferry explosion started several large fires, but they are all under control."

The Captain, visibly shaken from what he had just heard, once again attempted to get out of bed, but was held down by the doctor.

"I need to get to CIC and find out what our current status is."

"Sir, CIC is gone. The missile took it out, killing all those inside."

"Oh, God! What are our casualties?"

"Captain, I don't think I should . . ."

"Tell me Doc. That's an order. I am this ship's Captain."

The doctor thought about it for several seconds. It wouldn't really hurt to tell the man

. "If you insist. So far we have suffered 200 killed, 175 injured, many seriously and thirty missing, feared dead."

"And the ferry, are there many survivors?

"Very few, sir. She went down fast. It's feared that the death toll will be in the hundreds."

"Jesus! Have they got the bastards that are responsible for all this?"

"They are hunting them down as we speak, Captain."

"Have the senior officer in charge of this ship report to me as soon as he has time." The doctor made a motion to his orderly, who then handed him a hypodermic needle.

"What's that for?"

"It's a sedative."

"But I need to be awake. My ship...,"

"Sir, I am in command of this sick bay and what you need right now, is rest."

"Okay doc. But promise me that you will have the ship's senior officer report to me once I awake."

"I will, sir."

A few moments later, Captain Taylor was asleep as the sedative began to take effect.

"Poor bastard." Doctor Stevens muttered to himself, as he left the Captain's bedside to go tend to the other injured sailors that were awaiting his services.

The Poros straits

0323hrs 18 May

The Shatila's hull vibrated fiercely as she raced full speed toward the Poros straits and safety. Saleem prayed that the old rust bucket would hold together for a few more minutes. What he intended to do was beach the ship once in the straits and escape overland on motor bikes that they had brought with them. By now every Greek military and coast guard unit in the area would have been alerted and out searching for them.

"Brother Saleem. I have picked up a ship on the radar. It is six miles behind and closing on us fast. It will intercept us in about fifteen minutes."

"We will be entering the straits in about ten minutes. Have all the men break out the weapons. We still have teeth left."

"It will be done immediately!"

Weapons consisted of AK-47 assault rifles and RPG-7 rocket propelled grenades, were quickly handed out amongst the crew. One of the men shouted to his comrades and pointed skyward. While everyone looked up to see what Jamal was pointing at, the sky above the Shatila was suddenly illuminated by several flares which had been dropped by a Greek HU-16 Albatross seaplane. The Albatross had finally arrived and taken up station a thousand meters above the Shatila. A few miles behind the terrorists, the gun boat Mykonios had seen the flares dropped by the Albatross. Her target was clearly illuminated.

"Mykonios to Albatross, we see your flares and the target. We now have the terrorists on visual, ETA 8 minutes to intercept," acknowledged the Mykonios' communications officer.

Lieutenant Takis Mavridis cursed his bad luck. He had just gotten home with his new girlfriend Sophie, a hot blond whom he had met at one of the local clubs, when the phone call came. He had been originally scheduled for a mission later that morning, but he and the rest of the crew had been recalled to the base after the terrorist attack on the carrier. When Takis arrived at Elefsis airfield twenty minutes later, he met the rest of his crew. They were met by Wing Intel and briefed on the terrorist attack on the US warships in Faliron bay and ordered to take off immediately and find the terrorist ship. Takis had heard on the news earlier that evening of the riots in

Kommotini. Now he was really worried that something sinister was going to happen. Ten minutes later, they were airborne over the Saronic Gulf.

With the terrorists nearing the entrance to the straits, the local coast guard station on the island of Poros had been alerted to the Shatila's approach. The Station commander had immediately dispatched one of his patrol craft to attempt to intercept the ship. It had not been difficult for the small patrol boat to locate the Shatila, now clearly illuminated by the parachute flares that were being systematically dropped by the Albatross patrol plane which was orbiting overhead. Both Saleem and Hadji saw the approaching patrol boat at the same time.

"We are trapped," shouted Hadji, the panic clearly evident in his voice.

"Shut up you fool! We aren't finished yet. Prepare the men and don't fire until I say so!"

"But Saleem, they will kill us all!" Hadji yelled, who was now almost to the point of hysteria.

Saleem gave his Lieutenant a murderous look. "Do as I say, Hadji, or I will kill you this minute!"

"Yes Saleem," said Hadji, quickly recovering his composure.

"Keep everyone under cover and fire only when I give the signal which will be a blast on the ship's horn."

The Greek patrol boat which had finally caught up with the Shatila was keeping pace fifty meters behind the terrorist ship.

Saleem noticed that the patrol boat's .50 Caliber machine gun was manned and one of her crew was holding what appeared to be a bullhorn.

"This is Lieutenant Mandis of the Hellenic coast guard. You are ordered to immediately heave to or we will open fire." Just to clarify his point, the gunner fired a few rounds in the air. Hadji ran to Saleem.

"Everyone is ready and in position, Saleem."

Saleem stepped inside the bridge. "Mehmet, slow to one third," Saleem said to the helmsman. With the drop in engine revolutions, the ship began to slow. The small patrol boat was now within twenty meters of the Shatila's bow and closing on them. Saleem pressed the ship's horn. Almost in unison, several AK-47s and two light machine guns opened up. The patrol boat's gunner attempted to return fire but he was quickly cut down by a hail of lead. A second later there was a loud whoosh followed by a small explosion on the Greek patrol boat. The small boat, struck by an RPG-7 rocket propelled grenade, immediately started to burn. Those of her crew that had survived the initial attack jumped into the sea to escape the sinking boat but they were ruthlessly gunned down by Saleem's men as they tried to swim away. Saleem's crew cheered their easy victory as the burning boat fell behind them. Their cheering was interrupted only when the flames reached the patrol boat's fuel tanks causing it to explode in a bright ball of fire. The whole action had lasted less than a minute.

"The bastards!" yelled Lieutenant Mavridis in rage. He and the rest of the crew had witnessed the brief encounter from the Albatross orbiting overhead. Their only hope now was the Mykonios.

"Albatross to Mykonios, the attempted intercept by the coast guard was a total failure. The terrorists have sunk the patrol boat. I doubt there were any survivors," Takis said.

"Roger Albatross, we now have them in visual. ETA to intercept, four minutes. Let's see how they do against some real competition. Mykonios out."

From the Shatila's bridge, Saleem could now clearly make out the approaching gun boat which had turned on its spot light.

"Hadji, run and bring me our last two rockets. We must slow them down if we are to have any chance in escaping." Saleem looked back at the lights of the approaching warship. The Shatila would soon be in cannon range.

"Mehmet, make for that point and put the ship aground," commanded Saleem, pointing to the location where he wanted the helmsman to head for. Once aground, they would steal a car and escape overland through the Peloponnese.

"It will be very close, brother Saleem. The infidels are gaining on us."

"Don't worry, with the help of Allah we will make it, Mehmet."

With the gun boat rapidly closing in on the terrorist ship, her

Captain was taking no chances. As soon as the Mykonios was in cannon range, he would open fire and force the terrorists to surrender. If they refused to surrender, he would sink them.

"Gunner, what's our range?" Commander Markos asked via the intercom.

"Eight hundred and fifty meters, sir."

"Prepare to open fire. I also want a torpedo fix on them, just in case we have to use one," said Markos to his weapons officer.

"Yes, sir."

"Helmsmen, slow to one half."

"Yes, sir.

"Sir, they aren't answering any radio calls."

"To hell with them. Open fire!" The first few cannon rounds overshot the Shatila, but the gun boat's gunner quickly adjusted his aim and began pumping a steady stream of 30mm shells into her superstructure.

"Close on the shore, now!" screamed Saleem, as the world around him erupted in screams of pain and shattered glass. Saleem's man at the Shatilas's stern returned fire, but it was ineffective against the much heavier warship. The Shatila veered toward the shoreline which was only a half a mile away, but her speed was beginning to drop from the damage caused by the Mykonios' cannon shells.

"Cease fire, cease fire," ordered Commander Markos, fearing that a stray shell might strike the shore which was now lined with scores of onlookers who had heard the previous shooting and had rushed to the shoreline to see what was happening.

With the Shatila's bridge in shambles and several of his crew dead or injured, Saleem was now left to his own resources. The apparent lull in the firing gave Saleem the opportunity that he needed. Bleeding from a dozen cuts caused by flying glass, he grabbed the two remaining Grail missiles that Hadji had brought and headed for the ship's stern.

"Sir, it looks like the terrorists are going to ground the ship and attempt to escape overland," said the gunboat's weapons officer.

"No they won't, prepare to fire a torpedo."

When Saleem reached the stern, it looked like he had entered a slaughter house. Several of his men had been blown apart by the cannon shells and their bodies, or what was left of them, were scattered in bits and pieces all over the deck. The Shatila was making barely any headway and the shore was still several hundred meters away. Saleem needed to do something to buy them some time. He quickly prepared the missile for firing. Finished, Saleem looked up and saw that the Greek gunboat was less than a thousand meters behind the Shatila. At that distance it wouldn't be too difficult for him to hit her with the missile. Saleem braced himself against the handrail and aimed the SAM-7 at the gunboat's bridge. He knew that the missile's small warhead wouldn't do much damage to the gunboat, but it might buy them the few more minutes needed to beach the ship. Saleem remembered that ironically a U.S.

warship had accidentally launched an anti aircraft missile at a Turkish destroyer back in 1992 during NATO maneuvers. The missile had demolished the destroyer's bridge and killed her commanding officer along with several of the crew. Saleem was hoping for a repeat tonight.

"Fire the torpedo," ordered the Captain. Just as the Mykonios' torpedo entered the water, Saleem squeezed the trigger. The small anti aircraft missile streaked across the short distance separating the two ships. It struck the gunboat's Cannon, instantly killing the gun crew and setting off the nearby 30mm ammo. The exploding ammunition sent shrapnel ripping through the bridge wind screens, killing or wounding almost everyone inside. One of the dead was the gunboat's helmsman.

With nobody at the helm, the gunboat veered toward the nearby shore. It was only a moment before her keel struck the channel's sandy bottom, her still turning screws driving her hard aground. The guide wire on the Mykonios homing torpedo had been cut when Saleem's missile had struck the gun boat, causing it to momentarily lose its intended target. It wandered lost for a few seconds before her sonar went to active mode. Fortunately for the Mykonios, she had run aground and her screws had stopped turning. The only noise that the torpedo's sophisticated sonar was picking up was the beat of the Shatila's prop. The torpedo quickly reacquired its new target.

Saleem and his surviving crew had cheered and praised God

when they saw the gunboat hit and go aground. They had eliminated their last pursuer. Their escape road was now open. The Shatila's helmsman seeing the demise of the Greek patrol boat, immediately decided to ground her in a more favorable location, a couple of kilometers further down the coast.

Saleem was preparing to rid himself of the patrol plane with his last missile when his luck finally ran out. Looking toward the grounded gunboat which was now more than a mile distant, he caught the wake of an object in the water that was heading right for him. Saleem immediately knew what it was. He only had enough time to utter his dead brother's name before the torpedo hit. The force of the warhead's detonation ripped off most of the Shatila's stern and sent off a chain reaction of explosions that tore through the small ship. Her death was relatively quick as the Shatila settled under the dark waters. This had not been the case for some of her crew members that had been unlucky enough to have survived the attack and sinking. The explosions that had ripped through the Shatila had also shattered her fuel bunkers, covering the area where she had sunk in blazing fuel oil. Their screams could be heard on the Greek gun boat almost a mile away, as they roasted alive in a sea of burning oil.

High overhead the Albatross' crew had observed the battle and the terrorists' violent end. After briefing headquarters of the their demise, Lieutenant Mavridis requested that a tug be dispatched to assist the Mykonios which was still aground and a coast guard boat to search the water for any survivors. Takis doubted there were any. After repeated attempts to contact the gun boat, Lieutenant Mavridis finally was able to establish communications with the stricken ship.

"Albatross to Mykonios, do you read me?"

"This is commander Markos of the gunboat Mykonios. How do you read us?"

"Loud and clear Mykonios," replied Takis.

"Hey, you guys all right? We saw an explosion and your grounding."

"They probably hit us with a small shoulder launched antiaircraft missile. It killed three of my crew and wounded five others. A shrapnel splinter has damaged our radio, but fortunately not too seriously."

"That explains why we lost contact. Congratulations on getting those bastards."

"Thanks, I will pass that on to my crew, they deserve the credit."

"Salamis is sending out a tug to help you."

"We'll need it. I think we lost our screws and bent the shafts when we grounded."

"Do you guys need anything else?"

"No. We can see the lights of ambulances coming from Galatas. We will be all right."

"Good luck then. Albatross out." With the chase finally over and not needing to refuel, the Albatross was ordered by

Elefsis to proceed to its Aegean patrol zone.

Takis pressed the intercom button. "Hey, commander!"

"What is it Takis?"

"I have already plotted a course to our intended patrol zone."

"Let me have it then," replied the pilot.

"Turn to a heading of forty-two degrees. Our ETA to the patrol zone will be one hour and fifteen minutes. Now if you don't mind, I am going to try to catch thirty minutes of shut eye. Wake me if you need me."

"Okay Takis, sweet dreams," replied the pilot.

Chapter 8

The Attack, Ramstein AB

18 May, 0358hrs

After a hectic day of final preparations, Major Bankasi's commando team, dressed in unmarked camouflage uniforms, was finally ready to go into action. If all went according to plan, in a single stroke, they would eliminate a good part of USAF's fighter strength in Europe. For the past hour, they lay hidden in the bushes outside the Southwest sector of Ramstein Air Base, monitoring security operations.

"Lieutenant Olzum, it's time to begin the operation," Major Bankasi whispered to the commando team leader who was lying in the damp grass beside him.

"It is almost 0400hrs. Set the charges for 0440hrs. Most of the aircraft are parked in the western area of the sector. You and your men know the area well. Remember, if you are discovered, you are to set off the charges and then attempt to destroy as many aircraft as possible at all costs. The security team will buy you the time you need."

Both officers looked at each other without speaking. The younger man understood fully the meaning and ramifications of what his superior had just said.

"Lieutenant, it is vital to our nation that you and your men succeed tonight. I know that you have not been briefed on the full details of "Operation Medina" and I do feel that you have a right to know more."

"Sir, I am a soldier. I will do my duty regardless."

"Lieutenant, you and your men are the key players in all of this. You will be striking the first blow against our nation's enemies. In the next few days, our armed forces will destroy our historic enemies, the Greeks, and our nation will once again attain the glories and triumphs of its proud Ottoman heritage."

"Praised be the prophet. Sir, my men and I will not fail our people."

"I know you will not, Olzum. I wish I could go with you," said Major Bankasi with all sincerity.

Both men got up and Lieutenant Olzum prepared to leave. Major Bankasi, with tears in his eyes, embraced the younger officer. He knew it would probably be the last time he would be seeing him.

"Go now and may the prophet always watch over you." With these words the two men parted. Bankasi headed for the safe house to send the message that the operation had begun.

Observing that everything was clear, Lieutenant Olzum motioned to his squad leader, who was hiding behind a tree a few meters away, to cut the fence. Sergeant Bullant crawled the few meters to the perimeter fence, took a pair of wire cutters from his ruck sack and cut the wire. The first to enter were the security team who quickly fanned out into the area and took their positions. Soon after, the all clear came in over the radio for the rest of the team to commence their deadly work.

Ramstein AB, the Security Force barracks
18 May, 0412hrs

Smoking a cigarette, Layla pondered her next move as she lay naked in bed. The clock on the wall showed 0412hrs. In less than thirty minutes, all hell would be breaking loose when the explosive charges, planted by Bankasi's commando team went off. She glanced at Mike, who lay beside her passed out drunk and almost felt sorry for him. She thought of the night's events. Everything had gone according to plan. Thanks to this young fool, she had gotten her explosive laden vehicle on base without the slightest hassle.

After being escorted onto the base by Mike, she had driven both of them to the Security Force barracks and parked the car in the lot directly across the street. They then walked the couple of blocks to the enlisted club where they met some of Mike's friends. It was a typical Friday night. The disco club E was packed with patrons. Layla miserably spent most of the evening in the noisy and crowded smoked filled club, sipping cokes and fending off the numerous obnoxious drunks that kept asking her to dance. As the night progressed, Mike and his friends had lapsed into advanced stages of intoxication. Yet, it wasn't the conduct of the men that had surprised her the most. It was, in fact, the behavior of the American females who carried on just like their male counterparts which astonished her. She was glad that she was a Muslim woman and not one of these infidel sluts. Islam, she was sure, would eventually triumph over the corrupt ways of the West.

By 0300hrs, she had reached the point where she could no longer tolerate the annoying drunks and loud music which filled Club E. Besides, it was time to leave. In an hour, Bankasi's men would penetrate the base. Using her ample female talents, she had convinced Mike to leave the club and go back to his room to have some fun. She would let nothing jeopardize the mission, not even the thought of having sex with a disgusting drunk American pig. When they left the club, she had to practically carry Mike the couple blocks back to his barracks room. After she had gotten him back to the barracks which had not been an easy task, they both went to bed. Layla went through the motions of having sex but he quickly spent himself and passed out in a drunken stupor.

Layla heard a moan which jarred her back to the present. It had come from Mike who was still passed out beside her. She looked at the clock on the wall and saw that only twenty minutes remained before she would have to execute her part of the mission. She put out her cigarette, got out of the bed and quickly began to dress.

The 512th Squadron area, Ramstein AB
18 May 0420hrs

Lieutenant Olzum glanced at his watch, the luminous dials said it was 0420hrs; so far everything had gone very smoothly for his team. So smoothly, that he was beginning to think that they might even pull the whole thing off and escape with their lives. Except for some wild rabbits running loose, there was no one else in the area. Thanks to their previous surveillance and scouting missions of the sector, his men knew exactly which structures contained aircraft. Most of these structures were located in the eastern zone of the area which was spread out in a horse shoe pattern. The two security teams had set up at each end of the horse shoe and could monitor any traffic approaching the area. Their specific instructions were to fire only if spotted or instructed to do so. In the brief twenty minutes they had been in the area, they had planted explosives in twelve of the structures. The number of structures they had found open, so far, astonished Olzum. The Americans had become very complacent with security after the end of the cold war, he thought. Well, they would surely be in store for a surprise tonight.

"Hurry, Jemal."

"I am trying, sir. This particular lock is a little stubborn."

"Cut it off."

"I think I got it. Yes, it's open." The heavy security lock fell to the ground. Lieutenant Olzum pulled the hasp and opened the door. When they entered the structure, he turned on his flash light and shined it on the structure's sole occupant, a gleaming F-16C Falcon fighter. He stared at the plane, rejoicing at the thought that soon it would be just a pile of smoldering junk instead of a sophisticated weapon of war that the infidels could use against his people. Without any further hesitation, he reached into his pack, pulled out a small demolition charge, set the timer, flipped the switch activating it and placed it inside the plane's air intake.

"That's one more that we won't have to worry about, Jemal." The radio suddenly sprang to life.

"Security One to team leader. Vehicle is approaching my vicinity."

Lieutenant Olzum looked at his watch. "Shit, fifteen minutes till the charges blow," he said out loud. Security One was situated at the northern tip of the horse shoe.

"Let them pass," he said.

"Let's go do the next structure. I'll stay outside and provide cover this time," said the Lieutenant

It had been a run of the mill boring midnight shift for Alpha 5, the two man security response team assigned to patrol the sector known as Alpha land. Ever since the nuclear weapons had been removed from Ramstein due to the European denuclearization agreements a couple of years ago, there wasn't much for the Security forces to do except guard the aircraft. The most strenuous task for the patrols, besides making sure no one stole a plane, was staying awake. Tonight was no exception for Alpha 5 patrol, Sergeant Joe Kelly and Airman Tim Swift.

"Wake up, Swift!" Kelly hollered, shaking the young airman awake. "If the flight chief catches you snoozing, he will have both our asses."

"Chill out, Sarge. He won't see us. Pull over. I got to take a leak."

"Okay Swift, I'll pull over by that structure so you can take your piss."

When Olzum saw the approaching headlights, he quickly jumped behind one of the bushes growing next to the structure he was standing by. "Damn the rotten luck," he said to himself, praying that the Security patrol would just drive by. But this was not to be the case. The M1008 pick-up truck stopped ten meters from where he lay hidden. Fearing the worst, he flipped the safety off his MP5 submachine gun and laid it right beside him. He then unsheathed his commando knife and lay still hoping that the truck would leave. Olzum's worst fears were suddenly realized. The passenger opened the door, got out and began walking toward his hiding place. There was no way the American would miss seeing him. In a flash of speed, Olzum threw the commando knife, the weighted blade catching Airman Swift in the stomach. Swift let out a short gasp and collapsed in a heap, only ten feet from where Olzum lay hidden. The only thing that Sergeant Kelly saw from inside the truck was Swift grabbing his stomach and falling to the ground. Rolling down the window, he hollered out to Swift who was lying on the ground motionless. *What is this dumb shit up to, he wondered?*

"Hey Swift, you okay? Hey Swift, quit fucking around." Getting no answer, Kelly opened the door and dismounted the truck, leaving his M-4 rifle behind.

"Hey asshole, cut the bullshit. I said, are you okay?"

Kelly, who was now starting to get worried, began walking towards Swift. "Okay shithead, if you're fucking . . . ," before Kelly could finish what he was saying, Lieutenant Olzum got up from where he was laying and lunged toward him, taking him by complete surprise. The struggle was brief. The highly trained commando made short work of Kelly. Lieutenant Olzum felt a pair of hands on his arms. Sergeant Bullant and the rest of the team were helping him to his feet.

"Sir, we saw the American patrol too, but we would have been spotted if we exited the structure."

"Don't worry about it. I'm okay. Let's hurry Sergeant, we don't have much time left."

They all heard a voice and froze in their tracks. "Alpha 5, this is security control."

"It's the radio," said Lieutenant Olzum.

A few seconds later, they heard it again. "Alpha 5, this is CSC. What is your status?

"What should we do," asked Sergeant Bullant.

Before Lieutenant Olzum could answer, they heard another transmission, this time it was more ominous than the others. "Control to all post patrols, be advised this office could not come into contact with Alpha 5. This unit is under possible duress. If anyone comes in contact with this unit, treat it as such."

"Hurry Sergeant, hide the bodies and let's finish up. They will be coming to search for their lost patrol. I think that our luck has just run out."

Sergeant Wilks, the on duty Security Controller, had just finished drinking his fifth cup of coffee. Tonight for some unknown reason, he was really having a hard time staying awake. Wilks looked up at the clock and saw that they only had two more hours to go on shift. If he wanted to get off on time this morning, one of his units had to go to the Law Enforcement desk, on other side of base, to get him some toner ribbon for Central Security Control's laser printer. The printer had run out of toner and he was unable to finish the night's blotters. He had wanted Alpha 5 to make the run, but they were not answering their radio. Wilks was starting to really get pissed off at his SRT unit.

"Hey Sarge, I can't raise those two assholes in Alpha 5."

Master Sergeant Watson, a tall and slim African American in his early thirties, put down the book of operating instructions that he had been reviewing and turned to his security controller, "send Alpha 6 and Alpha 7 to check on their status. If they are asleep, their ass is mine."

"Will do Sarge," replied Wilks with a grin on his face.

The Security Force Barracks, Ramstein AB
0428hrs, 18 May

Layla looked at her watch for the fifth time in as many minutes. It was 0428hrs. She had seven minutes to go, before she would make her move. The plan that she and Major Bankasi had come up with, to take out the Security Police back up response force, was very simple. She would take her car which was packed with one hundred and fifty kilos of C-4 plastic explosives and drive it right up to the barracks. She would set the timer for ten minutes and then make her escape on the bicycle that she had chained to the bike rack on the back of her car. In five minutes, she would be out the back gate with time to spare. Her car bomb would detonate at 0445hrs, five minutes after Lieutenant Olzum's charges had gone off. Layla had calculated that the blast would take out most of the face of the building, along with the Security Force armory that would be used to arm the back-up response forces.

Alpha land, Ramstein AB
0430hrs, 18 May

After having stashed the vehicle and bodies in the trees, Lt. Olzum and his men continued their mission of planting explosives, knowing that their time was quickly running out.

"Security Two to team leader."

"Go with your message, Security Two," answered Olzum.

"There is another vehicle approaching my location."

"Let them pass."

"We have to take them out, sir. There is no more time left. The charges will blow in ten minutes."

"I know Sergeant. Deploy the men."

"Security One to team leader. I have a vehicle approaching my location, also."

Olzum now knew that the game was definitely up for him and his men. "Take them out and hold out as long as you can. May Allah watch over you."

The first of the two American security patrols had been allowed to enter the area unharmed. They approached the vicinity where Alpha 5's vehicle had been abandoned. Sergeant Hannon, Alpha 6 leader, spotted the abandoned vehicle off the road between two trees. He picked up the mobile radio mike to transmit.

"Alpha 6 CSC, I have located Alpha 5 parked near structure 105. We are . . . ," before he could finish his transmission, the vehicle windshield was shattered by a burst of automatic weapons fire. The driver instinctively floored the accelerator and the vehicle rolled forward a few meters before it careened off the road embankment and rolled onto its side.

The second patrol, Alpha 7, heard the shots, but before they could respond, the truck was struck by a 60mm anti tank rocket and disintegrated in a blinding flash. The rocket had been fired by one of Lieutenant Olzum's security teams perched atop an aircraft structure.

"Good work Corporal Hamaz, the infidels never knew what hit them," said Lieutenant Olzum, congratulating his men after eliminating the security teams.

"Roger sir, I hope they are now burning in hell."

"Let's hurry men; we now must destroy as many planes as we can before the Americans arrive in force."

Ramstein AB, South
0434hrs, 18 May

Just as Layla was leaving Mike's room, she heard an explosion originating from the other side of the base. Going back inside, she closed the door behind her. Her experience and training told her something wasn't right. There should have been a lot more explosions. She looked at the time, it was still too early for the charges to have detonated.

"Oh my God, they've been discovered!" She said out loud, barely able to control the panic that was beginning to come over her. She would now have to act immediately. In a couple of minutes everyone inside the barracks would be awake. Her nerves quickly began to settle as her training began to take over. Layla knew what had to be done, opening the door, she ran out of the room as the barracks was beginning to come alive.

It had been a relatively quiet night for the Ramstein Law Enforcement desk, considering it was a pay day weekend. The desk hadn't even received a single noise complaint, which was rather unusual for a Friday night. Unfortunately, all this had suddenly come to an end, when the quiet was shattered by the sound of explosions and gunfire from across the base. Picking up the direct line with Security Control, the desk sergeant spoke to his security counterpart on the other end.

"I've got Master Sergeant Watson on the line," the desk sergeant rose from his chair and yelled. "He says that the explosion was caused by armed intruders who have taken over Alpha land. They have already wiped out three of his units. He wants us to initiate a 30/30 recall."

Master Sergeant George Pappas, the on duty Law Enforcement flight Sergeant and eighteen year Security Police veteran, did not hesitate in issuing the alert order. He had practiced the 30 men in 30 minutes recall procedure on numerous occasions. "Do it, but make sure you brief everyone, especially the command post on what's going on."

"I will, Sergeant Pappas."

"Initiation time is 0438 hrs. Don't forget to also send a patrol to building 2112 to wake everyone up over there. Dispatch police 4 to help with weapons issue. I am going to the armory."

"Hustle Thompson, this is for real," said George as he ran from his desk.

"Don't worry Sarge, I can handle it," replied a rather excited Staff Sergeant Thompson, but George was already out the door.

When Layla had exited the barracks, she quickly ran across the street to where her car was parked. With her hand shaking uncontrollably, she put the key into the lock, opened the door and sat in the driver's seat. She looked across the street and saw that the barracks was beginning to hum with activity. Some of its occupants were already beginning to file out and head for the armory, which had not been opened yet.

When she saw the patrol car drive up to the building, she nearly panicked. Nervously, Layla glanced at her watch and saw that it was 0440hrs. The charges should have exploded by now, she thought. She wondered if the mission had been a total failure, but that speculation was quickly changed as a deafening series of explosions originated from the southwest sector of the base. When the cacophony of the explosions subsided, the sound of automatic weapons fire could now be clearly heard.

Senior Airman Pete Saddler had been dispatched by the desk to the alternate armory to help with the 30/30 weapons issue. He was trembling with excitement. The explosions he had just heard confirmed that all hell was breaking loose in Alpha land. The twenty-two-year-old red head from Montana had never heard a shot fired in anger. All that had now changed; he was finally going to see some action. A good cop despite his lack of experience, Saddler had noticed a woman sitting alone in a parked car across the street in the barracks parking lot. Thinking that this was rather suspicious, especially with what was going down on the other side of the base, he decided to check her out. Walking up to the car, he noticed that the woman had already rolled down her window.

"Excuse me ma'am, are you waiting for someone? he asked her.

"Ah yes, I am waiting for my boyfriend, Mike Jones, he is a cop," Layla nervously replied.

"Saddler knew Jones, but to be on the safe side he would check her base pass and identification papers. Besides this girl was too good looking for a dork like Mike Jones. She was probably a hooker, he thought. Master Sergeant Pappas, his flight chief, would be arriving any second, so he had better hurry up and check her papers.

"Ma'am, may I see your base pass?"

"Oh, I didn't get one; Mike Jones just drove me through the gate. You know him. He's a cop. I just left his room," said Layla trying to bluff her way out of a rapidly worsening situation.

Saddler would not buy her story and by now beginning to get really suspicious. "Let me see your German ID card and car papers now!" he said rather curtly, no longer polite.

Layla realized that her mission was now blown. She might still be able to bluff her way out, especially if they located Mike Jones who would verify her story, but she had failed Lieutenant Olzum and his men. The 30/30 response force had not been neutralized; the Lieutenant and his men would soon be wiped out. She would never be able to live with herself, knowing that her failure had cost the mission. As all this raced through her mind, the American cop had become more persistent as it quickly became evident to him that she was stalling.

"Okay lady; get out of the car now!" ordered Saddler, at the same time unsnapping his holster, and reaching for his 9mm Berretta."

"Oh, here they are, I found my papers," said Layla as she reached into her hand bag and pulled out a small .32 caliber automatic pistol. Saddler, who had partially withdrawn his weapon from its holster, momentarily let down his guard when he heard her say that she had found her papers. His carelessness cost him his life.

"Here's my ID, you pig," said Layla. The small automatic pistol barked twice, the rounds hitting Saddler full in the chest. Layla looked at the clock in the dash. It was 0443hrs. A couple of individuals across the street had seen Saddler fall to the ground and were beginning to run toward her. She knew what had to be done if the mission was to succeed. Layla started the car and gunned the engine. The last thing the few who survived that night remembered, was a woman screaming at the top of her lungs, Allah Akbar, as she crashed her bomb laden vehicle through the front doors of the Security Force barracks.

Master Sergeant Pappas was only a block away when the car bomb detonated. He had been stuck in the parking lot behind the Law enforcement building for last few minutes attempting to get his patrol car started. The delay saved his life. The force of the explosion was so great, that it caused him to lose control of his vehicle and crash into a parked car. Not wasting any time, the five foot ten, one hundred and ninety-pound, nineteen year Security police veteran exited the vehicle and ran with the speed of an Olympic athlete toward a parked truck twenty meters away. George dove under the vehicle just as pieces of rubble began raining down all around him.

Once the debris stopped falling, George crawled out from underneath the truck and ran the last few hundred meters to where the barracks once stood, all that remained of the three story building was a choking cloud of dust and a pile of smoldering ruins. Where the main entrance stood, there was now a three meter deep crater filled with debris and twisted metal everywhere. The area around the building looked like a scene from a war zone. All of the vehicles around the building were now a twisted pile of smoking ruins. The scene reminded him of the pictures he had seen of the Beirut Marine barracks bombing. He gazed at the floors of the three story structure that had collapsed on one another. Bodies and limbs were strewn across the debris.

My God, another minute and I would have been in there, he thought to himself, thanking his stars for the crappy mechanical condition their vehicles were in. "Jesus! That's one of our blue and whites!" Running up to what remained of the patrol car,

George looked inside for a body. Not finding one, he wondered if Saddler had been inside the building at the time of the explosion. He was answered when one of the responding firemen who had just arrived from across the flight line, found Saddler's body in the parking lot.

"Hey, Sarge, over here." George sprinted across the street to the prone form. "He's dead," said the fireman who had found the body. "Shot in the chest. How about you? Are you okay?"

"Yeah, I'm alright." Still shaking from the effects of the explosion, George took his portable radio which was attached to his side. "Police One to Ramstein control." Getting no answer, he gave the radio a quick check. "I guess it helps if I turn it on." This time he got an immediate answer.

"Jesus, Sergeant Pappas. Are you okay? We have been trying to reach you ever since we heard the explosion. The Wing Command post is on the line and they want to know what is going on!"

"Listen, I don't have time to explain, the barracks and the armory are gone. Whoever did this knew what they were doing. They have effectively taken out our 30/30 response force. I need you to send every available patrol to building 2112 and shuttle every available body that they can find to our primary armory and have them arm up and respond to Alpha land. Brief U.S. Forces downtown and have them send us as many personnel as they can scrounge up. Tell the command post what we know so far. They will in turn brief the Wing

Commander. We need all the help that we can get."

"Roger, Sarge. What about the barracks? We can't locate Police 4, he had responded over there."

"I've found Police 4. He's dead. He was not killed in the explosion. He was shot. Don't worry about the barracks, there are enough emergency units and people responding to help," he said having to yell into the mike to be heard over the din of the sirens of the arriving emergency vehicles. "Just do as I told you. We must neutralize the threat at Alpha land. Police 1 out."

Putting the radio back into its case, George spotted the Wing Commander's vehicle pulling up. He walked up to where the vehicle had parked and was surprised to see that Colonel Rider, the Security Forces Commander, was with the General. Both men exited the vehicle and for a few seconds remained silent as they took in the devastation that was spread out before them.

"Mother of God!" was all that Brigadier General Pope could initially say. Quickly recovering from the shock of the devastation around him, he noticed Master Sergeant Pappas.

"What happened, Sergeant? We were both on our way to Alpha land when we heard the explosion."

"It was a car bomb, sir" said George pointing to the crater and the few pieces of what remained of the terrorist's car. "I believe it was meant to take out the 30/30 response force. Whoever did it shot one of my men," he said, pointing to the now covered body of Senior Airman Saddler. He must have caught them in the middle of activating the bomb."

"How many casualties so far, George?" said Colonel Rider.

"Just those so far, sir," said George as he gestured to the growing number of bodies that the fire and rescue crews were beginning to drag out of the rubble."I don't think there will be many survivors."

"God! There were over one hundred of my cops living in that barracks."

"Sir, I'm positive this was a coordinated plan to take out the 30/30 force to buy time for whoever hit Alpha land," reiterated George. As if to clarify George's a point, the sound of automatic weapons fire could be clearly heard coming across the flight line. "Colonel, I sent all my available units to gather personnel from 2112 and transport them to the armory to gear up. The 569th has also been contacted and they should be responding with assets.'

"Good work Sergeant, I believe that all your assumptions are right. This was a well-planned attack, not the work of amateurs. My initial reports tell me that a well-armed commando team now controls Alpha land and they've already destroyed a dozen of my aircraft if not more."

"General, I'm going to CSC to assume command of the recapture forces," said Colonel Rider.

"Very good idea Colonel, I want those bastards taken out as quickly as possible before they do any more damage," replied the Wing Commander, knowing good and well that his chance for a second star had just gone down the crapper.

Landstuhl, Germany
0450hrs, 18 May

Logan sat up in the bed. He was jarred from his drunken sleep by a loud boom that rattled the house's windows. At first he thought it was a thunder storm, but the noise did not repeat itself. I wonder what that was, he thought as he could feel the first symptoms of a hangover coming on. He had drunk too much, having several beers at the club and a bottle of wine at Helga's. Helga stirred next to him.

"What is it Jack? Why are you up?" she said.

"Didn't you hear it?"

"Hear what, Jack?" she said as she also sat up, the down cover falling off her breasts, the sight of her ample bosoms causing Logan to get excited again.

"That was thunder or an explosion?"

"I didn't hear it. But I usually sleep very heavily after drinking. It might have been a plane breaking the sound barrier. You've told me that you guys do it all the time even though it's forbidden over Germany."

"I don't think so, we aren't night flying."

"Oh, go back to bed Jack, it probably wasn't anything", said Helga as she slumped back down into the bed.

"You're probably right," said Logan, as he did the same, putting his hand on Helga's left breast.

"Mmmm . . . , are all you pilots early risers?" she asked as she touched Logan.

"Only the best, baby," said Logan as he entered her.

Alpha Land, Ramstein AB
0458hrs, 18 May

It had taken Sergeant Harrison several seconds to orient himself and remember what had happened. The last thing that he recollected was the truck's windshield shattering and the lights going out. When he had come to, he had found himself lying on his side and his partner's body on top of him.

"Damn, my head feels like it's going to explode. What the hell happened? Did we have an accident?" he mumbled. He reached for Airman Torres who was lying beside him.

"Hey Joe, wake up. Are you all right? Oh shit, blood!" He glanced at Torres's face which had been shattered by a bullet. "What the hell is going on here?" A long burst of automatic weapons fire coming from somewhere in the area, answered his question. Slowly unbuckling his seat belt, he pushed his partner's body out of the way and slowly began crawling out of the vehicle cab from where the windshield used to be. Halfway out of the truck, he spotted Torres's M-4 rifle with its attached M-203 grenade launcher lying in front of him. Thinking that he might need it, he grabbed the weapon, popped the seals on the 203 ammo box, loaded the grenade launcher and stuffed several extra 40mm grenade shells into his BDU pockets. Making his way clear of the vehicle, he crawled into the underbrush. Hearing the sound of weapons fire coming from nearby Tab Vee structure, he slowly began to make his way toward that direction.

Once they had been discovered, things for Lieutenant Olzum and his team had rapidly gone downhill. Knowing that he had only a few minutes left before the Americans responded in force, he had instructed his men to begin randomly destroying aircraft. His men began blowing the locks off of the remaining aircraft structures and tossing grenades inside. They were only able to destroy three more aircraft this way before they were pinned down by heavy machine gun fire from one of the responding security units. Just when they thought that all was lost, the night was split by a tremendous explosion coming from the other side of the base. Olzum immediately knew what that explosion signified and thanked Allah that Major Bankasi had come through on his promise to buy them some extra time.

With their spirits boosted, Olzum's men quickly rallied and took out most of the security units that had responded to the area, but at the cost of one dead and another slightly wounded. The surviving Americans hastily withdrew to a more secure location. Now was the time for them to act before the Americans regroup.

"Sergeant Bullant, take two men and our remaining LAW rockets and use them against the structures. We will hold them as long as possible. When your mission is completed, attempt to escape and save yourselves."

"But sir, we can't leave without you."

"Go. That is an order! Our nation will need well trained and experienced soldiers in the next few days. I will try to join you if possible."

Sergeant Bullant knew that the Lieutenant and Corporal Mehmut would be sacrificing their lives for them.

"Okay sir, I will obey your order this time," he said with sadness. "Good luck sir, may the prophet always watch over you." With tears in their eyes, Sergeant Bullant and his men grabbed the remaining LAWS and headed into the area.

While the fire fight had been going on all around him, Sergeant Harrison had slipped unnoticed toward one of the still undamaged aircraft structures. There he rested and quickly contemplated his next move. Looking at the luminous face on his watch, he saw that the time was 0455hrs. "Damn! It's soon going to be light out here and I really don't know what the hell is going on," he whispered to himself. As if that wasn't enough, he heard voices and movement coming through the bushes directly behind him. "Fuck!" he said as he ran and dove for cover behind a tree. After waiting several seconds, Harrison poked his head out and saw three individuals carrying what appeared to be LAW rockets. The three men stopped about thirty meters in front of the aircraft shelter he had been resting behind. One of the terrorists began arming one of the LAW rockets they were carrying.

"Oh Shit! They're going to blow the structure door! Not if I can help it."   Harrison checked his M-203, it was loaded. Remembering that the 40mm grenade needed at least twenty meters to arm, he mentally calculated the distance between himself and the three terrorists and concluded that it was just barely enough. Bringing his M203 to firing position, he took aim and fired a 40mm high explosive grenade at the three terrorists at virtually point blank range. Sergeant Bullant heard the distinctive thump of a M203 grenade launcher firing, the 40mm shell landed just a few meters in front of them and detonated.   The exploding shell sent hundreds of bits of shrapnel tearing through the three commandos. Drifting off into a deep sleep of which he would never awaken, Sergeant Bullant's last earthly thoughts were of Lieutenant Olzum. At least they would be sharing the joys and pleasures of heaven together.

Chapter 9

Northern Aegean
0500hrs, 18 May

The formation of Hind E attack helicopters flew southward over the dark waters of the Aegean. Flying at night at low altitude over the sea, even at the best of conditions is a very demanding task, but tonight though it was especially difficult. Flying with radio silence, their navigation lights off and at an altitude of ten meters over the wave tops to avoid radar detection, the aircrews strained to keep their helicopters from crashing into the sea. The Hinds, which had been purchased from the Russians during the early 1990s to help combat the Kurdish PPK, had been modified to carry and dispense a special cargo. The tanks that had been attached to their pylons were filled to the brim with a deadly Hydrogen Cyanide chemical blood agent. The Hinds would be spearheading the surprise attack on Limnos and its defenders.

Major Echever in the leading Hind glanced at his instrument panel. He prayed the executing order to begin the attack would arrive soon. If they delayed much longer, his helicopters wouldn't have sufficient fuel to carry out their mission. Fortunately, he did not have to worry long, as the anticipated code word "Medina" was broadcast over their command net frequency. Throughout the Aegean and Eastern Thrace, in the air, on the ground or on the sea, Turkish military units went into action.

"Praised be Allah! The time has finally come to even the score with the Greeks, Abdul," Major Echever said to his weapons systems officer, who was sitting a few feet in front of him in the WSO's cockpit.

"Yes sir, I heard the message too."

Breaking radio silence, Major Echever switched to the prearranged frequency that every ship in the formation was monitoring and broadcast the execution order.

"Cobra leader to all units, Medina! I repeat, Medina! Proceed with plan."

With their attack confirmation orders received, the six ship formation slowly swung westward while increasing their speed to 160 knots. Their objective, the island of Limnos, was only fifteen miles away.

Plaka, Limnos
0506hrs, 18 May

Nineteen year old Private Nikos Yiannakos let out a long yawn as he walked the narrow dirt path leading up to the defense emplacements. It was almost daybreak. The first predawn rays of light were just beginning to be visible in the east. In another hour, he would be back in the barracks having breakfast with the rest of his squad who would be just waking up. Pulling the last guard shift was a pain in the ass. It was always the hardest one to stay awake and tonight had been no exception. He had been stationed as a draftee at this god forsaken garrison post for the last ten months. The weather really sucked. It was very hot in the summer and cold and damp in the winter. The only thing that Nikos could think about this morning was his warm bed in the garrison post a couple of kilometers away. The post also housed the two infantry companies which would man the defense emplacements he guarded if they were ever invaded by the Turks. Most of the defense emplacements had been carved out of the rocky cliffs with explosives. All of them had weapons and ammunition and were ready for use at a moment's notice. He remembered many occasions of back breaking work, having to help rotate the ready ammunition by manually lugging out the old cans and carrying back new ones.

Private Yiannakos glanced at his watch and saw that he had less than an hour to go on his shift. *I'll go see how Stathis is doing and bullshit with him for a while,* he thought to himself. Both of them had been posted together on the island after being drafted into the army. Walking toward the area where his friend was posted, Nikos heard the sound of approaching helicopters which were coming in low out of the East. He looked eastward but could not yet see the helicopters in the early morning twilight. Those guys must be crazy flying so low and with no lights on, he thought.

The noise from the approaching aircraft was now beginning to get very loud as they neared his position. He saw some lights coming on at the nearby garrison post. Nikos looked up and only caught a glimpse of the aircraft as it passed overhead. For a moment, he thought he felt a cool mist touch his face. "I'll bet that those pilots will get in some hot shit for waking up the Colonel. He's probably already on the phone to headquarters," he mumbled to himself.

Nikos' chest suddenly began to feel very heavy. *That's odd. I haven't been running. Why I am out of breath?* His breathing had become very labored as though for some reason he was getting no air. He looked at the lights of the garrison post and his head began to spin as he fought to take in a breath. Unable to take another step, Nikos collapsed in his tracks, gasping for air. Saturated with the deadly gas, his lungs were unable to process the oxygen they took in. Within another minute, he was dead.

The nearby garrison never had a chance. When the helicopters buzzed the post, many of the soldiers who were awakened by the noise opened the barracks doors and windows to catch a glimpse of the low flying aircraft. When the deadly chemical dispensed by the Hinds drifted to the ground, it quickly entered through the open doors and windows and did its lethal work. In less than two minutes, the whole garrison had been incapacitated. Most of the soldiers died quietly in their sleep. For those unlucky enough to have been awake, they had to only briefly suffer the effects of dry land drowning caused by the quick acting blood agent, before they too lapsed into unconsciousness and death. In the next ten minutes, this was to be the fate for many of Limnos's military garrisons and defense emplacements that dotted her Eastern coast line.

The cat and mouse game that had been played by Turkish aircraft all throughout the week's war games had paid more dividends than anyone could ever have imagined. The round the clock exercises and continual harmless violations of Greek airspace by Turkish aircraft had lulled the island's air defense radar controllers into a false sense of security. When the helicopters carrying the deadly load made their dash for the island, none of the air defense controllers wanted to be the first to cry wolf. So no one alerted headquarters, in fear of being chewed out by some pissed off Colonel for awakening him at five in the morning. The same flight patterns had been flown by the Turks for the last week and they had always turned around. When the radar operators finally realized that the Turkish aircraft weren't turning around, it was too late. The gas carrying gunships had begun their deadly work. The radar operators did not have much longer to live either. Volleys of HARM missiles fired by Turkish fighters which homed in on their radar emissions quickly knocked them off the air. With the island's radar network silenced, the Turks had complete air superiority over the island.

Limnos Airport, Air Defense Batteries
0518hrs, 18 May

The Turks were soon to find out that not everything had gone as planned. After the air raid sirens at the island's only airport finally stood silent, the men manning the field's anti aircraft batteries stood ready at their posts. When the first of several missiles landed on the airport, most of the air defense gunners had immediately put on their gas masks. Luckily for them, they had been one of the few fortunate units that had been issued with gas masks over the weekend. Those that had not, had paid with their lives. When the blood agent finally dissipated several minutes later, the airfield's air defense network had remained virtually intact. Unfortunately, this had not been the case for the rest of the airfield's personnel. The pilots who flew the four Mirage 2000 alert birds which were part of the island's air defense, sat strapped to their planes. They had died while attempting to start their aircraft engines, joined in death by their ground crews who died where they stood, trying to launch their aircraft against the enemy.

Limnos, at the airfield
0531hrs, 18 May

The surprise attack on Limnos had left most of the island's defenders in total disarray. The blood agent had effectively decimated much of the island's combat units, especially those that were tasked with the coastal defense role. Most of the island's coastal defense positions were now either unmanned or were severely undermanned. Immediately following the devastating chemical attack, two squadrons of Turkish F4E Phantom fighter bombers having taken off from Cigli air base, just outside of Izmir, began striking targets on the island. With a good part of the Hellenic air force grounded by chemical attacks or committed in northern Greece, the Turkish air force enjoyed complete air superiority over Limnos and much of the northern Aegean. Because no Greek fighters had sortied from the island, the Turks had initially believed that the chemical attack on the airfield had been a total success. This belief had been reinforced after two Turkish F4Es had buzzed the airfield without drawing any triple A fire. The F4E pilots spotted the island's alert birds still in their pens which meant that the gas had neutralized the airport's air defenses. Needing the airfield intact for future use, the Turkish air force left it alone.

Ten miles to the north, after having dispensed their deadly cargo, Major Echever's flight of six MI-24 Hinds waited for the arrival of ten Chinook helicopters at their prearranged rendezvous point. The huge helicopters were carrying three reinforced companies of marines, whose objective was to secure the island's only airfield. Once the rendezvous was made, Major Echever's flight of gunships would escort them to their objective. Neutralizing and then taking the air field was a crucial step in the overall campaign of securing the island. Once the airfield was captured, the MI-24s would land and be refueled from the airfield's own stocks and rearmed with ammo carried by the Chinooks. Soon afterwards, heavy transport aircraft would begin landing with supplies and reinforcements.

"Sir, I see the Chinooks, twelve o clock," said Captain Abdul.

Major Echever looked out and spotted the giant helicopters crossing the coast line, three miles to the north.

"Cobra leader to shuttle one, we have you in sight."

"Roger, Cobra leader. Proceeding to objective, reconnaissance states all is clear. ETA to objective is six minutes."

"Roger Shuttle one, you will stand by two miles from the field and await my signal to proceed."

"Roger Cobra leader, that's a good copy."

Ten miles to the south, the Hellenic air force anti-aircraft gunners had stood by their guns waiting for the air raid that never did appear. They had heard the sound of jet fighters and explosions in the distance, but so far, the air field had not been attacked. Except for a high speed pass over by a Turkish F4 soon after the Scud attack, everything had remained quiet. The gas had done its work extremely well, not even the chirp of birds or an insect could be heard anywhere around the airfield. This had led Captain Papademas, the battery commander, to correctly speculate that the enemy apparently believed that everyone had been killed by the chemical attack and that they were more than likely saving the airfield for their use. Presumably, this was the reason they had not been bombed. Well, he would have a hot surprise for the Turks when they did come.

Immediately after the initial missile attack, Papademas took the initiative and instructed two of his Stinger missile teams to deploy atop the control tower and remain out of sight until he gave the order to open fire. The remaining Stinger teams had deployed to various strategic locations throughout the airfield. They too had been ordered to remain under cover. To ensure that the surprise would be complete and not be sprung too early and lose its maximum effect, he had given orders to his gunners to shut down their radar and withhold fire until he gave the order to go operational.

While he waited for the enemy to appear, Captain Papademas thought back to the events of the past hour. The air raid sirens had sounded immediately after the first missiles hit the field. His men had gotten out of bed and put on their gas masks and chemical gear without delay. This, and the fact that their barracks had been upwind of the first Scud landings had probably saved all their lives. Very few others had survived the deadly chemical agent. Only those that had been up wind of the attack or had gas masks now remained alive. Captain Papademas thanked God for giving him the inspiration to have issued his men the gas masks, immediately after the message ordering their distribution had arrived on Friday. It had initially resulted in several hours of overtime, tons of paper work and heckling from his other peers for not wanting to wait till Monday. But some unknown inner hunch had made him order the issuing of the masks that evening. Had he not done so, he and his men would now be laying dead besides their comrades.

Papademas looked to the east from his camouflaged position and could hear the load thump made by the rotors of approaching helicopters. A grin appeared on his sun tanned face. He had been right. Glancing eastward once again, he could now make out a formation of enemy troop carrying helicopters under escort from several large gunships, which he correctly guessed to be MI-24s. The enemy would now have hell to pay for the unprovoked act of aggression against his country. Picking up the field phone, Papademas rapidly turned the crank, rang his gun batteries and ordered the gun crews to remain out of sight or lie down and play dead. Meanwhile, the enemy helicopter formation had by now reached their objective. The lead gunship, piloted by Major Echever, made a low reconnaissance pass over the airfield while the rest of the flight stood by waiting a couple of kilometers away, ready to come to his assistance if fired on. All Echever could see were the scores of bodies that lay where they had fallen after succumbing to the deadly gas which the missiles had earlier delivered. Even the three Mirage 2000 alert birds were still in their protective revetments. He was certain that no one had survived the deadly attack.

"Our surprise attack went better than I had expected, Abdul. Look over there. Their planes are still in their revetments."

"Yes, I see. They never had a chance," said the weapons officer.

"Cobra leader to Shuttle one. You may proceed and secure the airfield. The enemy has been eliminated."

"Roger, Cobra leader. We will proceed with landings. Shuttle one out."

When the large enemy helicopter formation crossed over the airfield's perimeter, Captain Papademas ordered his Artemis AA gunners to prepare to open fire.

"Battery commander to all units, stand by to go active on my order." The gunners immediately sprang into action and began ripping the camouflage netting off their guns.

The ten Chinook troop carrier helicopters were now well inside the airfield perimeter. The Chinooks were flying in three groups, each escorted by a Mi-24 gunship. Major Echever, who was in the rear of the formation, was considering them fortunate that they wouldn't be facing any opposition. Because of the previous heavy load of gas that they had carried, his flight of gunships was only armed with their 12.7mm nose gun. Hopefully, this would soon be remedied after the airfield had been secured and the transports began landing. Once they were armed up, they would be able to use the massive fire power of the Hind against any remaining enemy units on the island.

When the first group of helicopters approached the vicinity of the airfield field control tower which was also intended to be their landing zone, Captain Papademas gave the order to open fire. Several of his troops, carrying Stingers, came out of their hiding places and they along with the Artemis gunners quickly and methodically went to work. With the Artemis fire control radars going active, the threat indicators on the forward two escort gunships lit up and began to buzz.

"It's a trap! There is enemy Triple A emplacements and missile gunners everywhere! Oh God they've locked onto us!" screamed the weapons systems officer of the Hind closest to the tower. But before the Hind could take any evasive action or begin dispensing flares, it was hit by a Stinger missile, launched by one of the teams posted on the tower. The Stinger struck just above the engine exhaust port, peppering the transmission housing with metal fragments that tore through several hydraulic lines. The pilot of the Hind, who had been flying at very low altitude, did not have sufficient time to switch to auto rotate before the ten ton helicopter slammed into the ground and exploded. The same fate awaited most of the helicopters of the first wave. The huge Chinook troop helicopters, unable to take evasive action because of their large bulk, were cut down like sheep in a slaughter house by the Stingers. When they hit the ground, they broke apart, rupturing their fuel tanks, dousing their human cargo with burning JP 4. The Parking ramp facing the control tower had rapidly become an inferno filled with burning machines, exploding ammunition and dying men.

After most of the first wave of helicopters had been eliminated by the Stingers, the Artemis anti aircraft batteries came on line and quickly added to the carnage. Captain Papademas had ordered the crews of two of his mobile AA guns mounted on Leonidas armored personnel carriers, to hide inside one of the aircraft hangers. When the word was given to open fire, the mobile guns charged out of the hangers which happened to be right in the flight path of the second wave of helicopters. Within nine seconds, the guns had locked on and opened fire, decimating the entire group of five helicopters that had been caught in the cross fire of another gun battery while attempting to escape. Major Echever who had been flying in the rear of the formation had just crossed over the airfield's northern boundary when the ambush was sprung. Instead of a secure landing zone, it had turned out to be a death trap.

"Cobra leader to all units, abort! It's a trap!" Echever screamed over the radio net.

For most of the helicopters, the warning was already too late. The majority of the two lead elements had already been blown out of the sky either by missiles or anti aircraft fire. Now, his surviving element was coming under fire. Looking to his left, he saw a giant Chinook troop carrier disintegrate in mid air, spilling men and equipment after being hit by a stream of 30mm anti aircraft shells. He knew that the whole operation was now a complete failure. Their only hope for survival was to make a break for it by charging toward their ambushers. Hopefully, he would get them before they got him. Pushing his throttles to their back stops, the two 2200 shaft horse power 120-TOV turbo shaft engines roared to full power.

The MI-24 Hind E gunship leaped forward, hugging the deck and seeking out its hidden enemies. Seeing all his threat indicators going off, Major Echever knew it would only be seconds before his helicopter would be riddled by 30mm shells or blown out of the sky by a heat seeker.

"Release the counter measures!" he screamed into the intercom while putting the Hind into a series of violent maneuvers, trying to escape the shells, which he knew would soon be coming. Fighting for his life, he put the gunship into a steep bank to the right as a string of 30mm shells passed over them, missing only by a few feet.

"There's the gun, five hundred meters away, at the two o'clock position," his WSO pointed out. Major Echever looked to his right and spotted the gun that had just attempted to shoot them down, hidden in a clump of bushes. Knowing that it would take the gun's fire solution radar several more seconds to compute its new fire coordinates, he flew toward it.

"Our gun is armed, sir."

"Roger I copy...,. Oh shit, we have been required Abdul. Take him out now!" screamed Major Echever, his threat indicators lighting up like a Christmas tree. Before he could say another word, the gunship's quad 12.7mm gatling gun fired, spitting out hundreds of rounds a minute. They were quickly rewarded by the sight of the enemy anti aircraft gun being blown off its mount.

"We got the bastard, Abdul! Now let's get the hell out of here."

Unfortunately, Major Echever was unaware that the Greeks had taken additional defensive measures and deployed jeep mounted Stinger teams as a back-up for each anti aircraft gun. One of these vehicles, hidden under camouflage netting was directly between the gun they had just destroyed and their escape route from the airfield. The jeep which had driven out from its place during their brief engagement with the anti aircraft battery was now in front of their flight path.

"Enemy vehicle 12 O'clock, 900 meters," screamed Echever in panic.

"I have them. But just as Captain Abdul pressed the firing button, the enemy fired off two missiles.

"Got them!" said Captain Abdul joyfully, after seeing the Mercedes jeep fire ball. But his joy was short lived.

"Oh, no, God! Missiles! Missiles," screamed Abdul in terror. Major Echever immediately put the helicopter into a steep climbing turn and hit the flare dispensers and pushed counter measure jammer. The first Stinger, decoyed by the flares and jammer, missed the gunship but the second did not, hitting the helicopter's left engine. With its left engine on fire, the ten ton gunship skewed violently toward the right, trailing thick smoke.

"I got a fire warning light on number one engine. I am shutting it down. I can't hold her in the air for long, Abdul," said Echever, quickly sensing their contribution to the war effort was about to come to a quick end."

"Just keep her flying a little bit longer, sir. Once we make the coast, we should be safe."

With more warning lights coming on and the helicopter bucking like a wild horse, Major Echever knew that they would never make the coast.

"She's not responding to the controls. I am losing her!" With black smoke pouring out of its engine compartment, the stricken Hind flew on for another minute before it suddenly lost total power. Echever threw the transmission into auto rotate. "Brace yourself Abdul, we're going to crash!"

Unable to control the copter's descent, the gunship plunged nose first into a freshly plowed field. Major Echever badly shaken but unhurt, hit his canopy's quick release button and jumped to the ground. The first thing he thought of was to help his WSO, but after looking inside his canopy, he saw that Abdul was beyond help. The nose first impact had pushed the gun turret into the front cockpit, killing his WSO instantly. With flames beginning to spread from the helicopter's engine compartment and the smell of JP4 permeating the air, it would be only a matter of seconds before the gunship exploded.

Echever began running from the now burning craft. He had covered only thirty meters before the helicopter blew. The last thing he remembered before being knocked unconscious by the blast wave was flying through the air and landing head first. When he came to several minutes later, he was rewarded by the sight of a Greek soldier pointing a rifle at his head. He also had the additional distinction of becoming the first Turkish POW of the war.

The battle had lasted less than ten minutes, but it would prove to be decisive. With the airfield still under Greek control, the Turks were unable to establish a base of operations for their attack copters which could have been used to provide fire support to their forces. Neither could they now airlift supplies to their troops by air if need be. Captain Papademas and his men were later joined by other Greek army units who dug in around the airport, which soon became the main rallying point of the island's defenders.

The Northern Aegean
0601hrs, 18 May

The Greco-Turkish war was only an hour old but it had seemed like an eternity for Lieutenant Yiannis Vassiliou. His ship had been out on night patrol, keeping tabs on Turkish naval movements. When on the return leg, all hell had broken loose. At 0511 hours, they had intercepted a radio call for assistance from their sister ship, the Batsis, which had been en route to relieve them. The message said that they were under air attack, eight miles northeast of Mirina, before all contact was lost. Yiannis had tried to re-establish contact with their sister ship but the Batsis had gone off the air. Fearing the worst, he immediately ordered radio silence and his ECM implemented. His suspicions of a Turkish attack were quickly confirmed when Naval Headquarters Limnos had gone off the air a couple of minutes after broadcasting that the port was under heavy air attack by Turkish fighter bombers.

The realization of Yiannis greatest fears had come to pass. Greece and Turkey were at war. He momentarily thought of his fiancée Eleni, who was now trapped on the island, but quickly put her out of his mind. His first concern now was for the safety of his ship and forty man crew. Yiannis' first order had been to put them on a southwestern course away from the island. The Hydra was no match against a well-coordinated air attack. He would not foolishly, in an act of bravado, squander away his ship and the lives of his crew.

As the Hydra cruised deeper into the Aegean, they received a long coded message from Naval Headquarters Athens, confirming that they were at war. The Prime Minister had ordered all Hellenic military units to begin hostilities against the forces of the Islamic Republic of Turkey. The message went on to say that Turkish military forces had launched a surprise attack, both in Western Thrace and in the Aegean, using in many instances missiles containing a chemical weapons payload. Military targets in Athens and Thessaloniki had been hit with conventional ballistic missiles and by enemy aircraft, which had been repulsed with heavy losses. General mobilization had been ordered throughout all of Greece. The message ended by reminding everyone that the fate of the nation was at stake and that every Greek was expected to fight till the bitter end.

After reading the contents of the message to his crew, Yiannis had attempted to tune the ship's radio to a civilian station for further news updates. Almost every station had gone off the air, except one of the government stations, which was only broadcasting patriotic and martial music and giving coded instructions to reservists where to report to their mobilization stations.

"It must be bad, sir, if they stopped commercial broadcasting,"

"I'm afraid that you are right Mr. Georgiou. It's probably worse than we can imagine, especially if those bastards used poison gas. We are probably the only Greek warship that's left in this area." Looking at the charts spread out in front of him, he spotted the small island of Agios Efstratios, which was located approximately fifteen miles south of Limnos. Their position was just a few miles southwest of the island.

"I got an idea Mr. Georgiou.".

"Helmsmen, set a course for Agios Efstratios to bring us up

the island's eastern coast line. We should be shielded from enemy radar there by the island's bulk. When we come up around the island's Northwestern tip, we might catch some targets of opportunity and pay the bastards back."

Washington, the White House Situation Room (2242hrs, EST), 18 May

On the other side of the world, President Bill Davis sat at the head of the table in the White House's underground command bunker briefing room, listening with interest to the briefing given by his chairman of the JCS on the rapidly deteriorating situation in the Balkans. He had called this latest emergency meeting with the heads of the JCS, CIA and the NSC as soon as he had been notified of the Turkish invasion of Greece. He was never a big fan or supporter of the military, but he was now facing the greatest political and military crisis in his presidency. At this moment, the military were probably the only ones capable of pulling his nuts out of the fire. The last twenty-four hours had to have been the worst in his political career. The President, a tall, handsome, charismatic African American man in his late 40s and a liberal democrat, had been elected to his first term on a platform of economic and social change. Before he had assumed office, the country had been in its worse economic slump since the great depression. Millions were unemployed, the nation's deficit was sky rocketing and government spending had to be brought under control. During his first term, he had reduced the deficit by almost fifty percent, the economy had rebounded and millions of jobs had been created. But many of the economic stimulus programs had required large sums of money. The only way he could have afforded these programs and cut the deficit at the same time was to make drastic cuts in other federal programs and departments. One of the departments that he had turned to had been the department of defense.

With the collapse of Soviet Communism and an emerging era of trust and cooperation between the former cold war adversaries, many in the new democratic administration didn't see a need for maintaining a large military any longer. NATO was now only a hollow shell of what it had once been, as almost every member nation had made huge defense cuts. Davis believed that the billions spent on defense could now be better spent in the domestic sector which had suffered from neglect in the previous Republican administrations. So the axe fell. Scores of military bases in the U.S. and around the world were closed or realigned. Dozens of ships were either sold to our allies or decommissioned. Many air force wings were restructured or eliminated and hundreds of thousands of military personnel had been retired or discharged. Some of his advisors had warned him against such drastic cuts, but they were only a small minority, scorned by the others as prophets of doom. Billions of dollars had been saved. Now, these decisions were coming back to haunt him. He wished that he had listened to some of these prophets of doom.

The President had faced other minor international crises during his first administration. One of these had been the Islamic revolution in Turkey. At the time, he had been accused by his political opponents of abandoning one of America's most loyal allies in the region to its fate. It was irrelevant to them that most of Turkey's armed forces and people had sided with the Islamic revolutionaries. Hundreds, perhaps thousands of Americans lives would have been lost in putting down the revolt. His opponents wouldn't have been the ones facing the grieving parents or spouses mourning the loss of their loved ones. Furthermore, he could find no allies willing to get involved in another nation's domestic affairs. To make matters worse, US's Arab traditional allies were being pressured by their own Islamic fundamentalists and risked open revolution if they supported the US against a fellow Muslim state. Many of the Islamic states had even threatened America with an oil embargo if it actively intervened. As a token gesture, he had only sent a couple of fighter squadrons to help the secular government, but these were quickly withdrawn when it became apparent that other Islamic states were throwing in their support to the Islamic revolutionaries and were getting ready to send thousands of "volunteers" to join the jihad against the infidel. Unfortunately, his political opponents now would be having the last laugh. He could just hear them in the halls of congress with cries of, "we told you so."

To add insult to injury, his so-called experts had convinced him that two fighter wings and an aircraft carrier group in the Mediterranean would be sufficient military muscle to handle any contingency in post cold war Europe. From what he had been advised earlier concerning events in Ramstein, the U.S. was now left with only one operational fighter wing in Europe. America's only other tangible military assets in the region, the aircraft carrier USS Lincoln, was now under tow to a Greek ship yard. It too having been seriously damaged by a terrorist attack, most probably carried out with the help of Turkey. Well, his experts were dead wrong. In the span of a few hours, the United States had been reduced to an impotent giant in the region. Greece, America's only ally and friend left in the Balkans, was being attacked from all sides. This time he would act quickly and decisively.

"Excuse me General Coleman, but how long before we can muster enough forces in the area to stop this aggression?"

The General looked up from the thick stack of messages he was reviewing, genuinely surprised that the President was contemplating military action. His respect for the man had just gone up a notch. He had considered him a spineless bureaucrat. "Mr. President, it will be at least a week, if not longer, before we have enough military units in the area to effectively intervene. From what our latest satellite photos tell us, the Turks have thrown an entire army Corp against the

Greeks in Thrace. The Greeks are in full retreat in the north. But we only have sketchy reports on the fighting on Limnos. Some of my sources said the island is in danger of falling."

"General, I just got off the phone with Mr. Samarakis, the Greek Prime Minister. His forces have suffered heavy losses from the surprise WMD attack. He fears the northern front might totally collapse. In a week, the Turks will have captured all of northern Greece if we don't do something."

"Mr. President, I am well aware of the Greece's situation. Unfortunately, our closest carrier, the Roosevelt, is in the Indian Ocean and the Egyptians have refused her transit through the Suez. The Egyptian Military fears renewed riots and violence instigated by the Muslim Brotherhood if they openly backs us. They barely survived the fundamentalist uprising a year ago."

"I remember it very well. What about our other carriers, Admiral Harrison?"

The chief of naval operation was also prepared for the President's question.

"Sir, the Reagan is in the Pacific, it would take her at least two weeks to redeploy to the Mediterranean. The Midway is in dry dock and the Nimitz is in South America on a goodwill tour. It would take her ten days to reach the Mediterranean. As for our other surface ships, they would be sitting ducks without air support."

"General Coleman, can we send any planes from Germany?"

"Mr. President, we lost over half of the 86th fighter wing at

Ramstein from the commando attack. All that's left there is a squadron of F-16s from the 526th fighter squadron and we can't spare any F-15s from Lakenheath. That's all that we have left in fighter assists in Europe."

"Then send the 526th to Greece. And have the planes in Lakenheath put on alert."

General Mc Dugan, the Air Force Chief of Staff, rose from his seat. "Mr. President, it's suicide. They'll be out gunned and outnumbered."

"General, the Greeks need our support. Their backs are against the wall and they're fighting for national survival. I will not stand by and see a historical friend and ally of the United States destroyed! Even this token gesture will help bolster their morale."

"Yes, sir."

"Admiral Henderson, issue immediate orders to the Nimitz. Have her steam at full speed to the Med. . . . "Before the President could finish issuing the order, the pentagon hotline rang. General Coleman picked up the phone, his face registering shock upon hearing the latest news. Everyone in the room suddenly turned to him after he had hung up the phone.

"Mr. President, I have just received some more bad news. While the Lincoln was being towed to the ship yards in Skaramagas for emergency repairs, Athens and the port of Piraeus came under heavy Turkish air attack. During the raid, the Lincoln was hit by a large bomb which destroyed her port elevator and started several large fires in the already damaged aircraft hanger bay. The Ticonderoga was hit by an air to surface missile, which knocked out her Aegis system, but not before she herself had shot down six of the attackers. Her commander and twenty of her crew are dead and fifteen others have been injured. The raiders struck the main Greek naval base on Salamina Island, but achieved only moderate results. Targets in the city were also hit, causing heavy civilian casualties. Fourteen of the attackers were reported shot down. I don't have any figures of casualties on the Lincoln, but there has been considerable additional loss of life. The ship will be out of commission for months."

"Dear God! Two American ships attacked, hundreds of American sailors and airmen killed and injured in the span of a few hours. Has Kemal gone totally off the edge?"

"Mr. President, if I had to take an educated guess, I would say that Kemal is going for broke," said Dan Otis, the head of the National Security council. "He's gambled that if our only carrier in the Mediterranean is put out of action, he would have a free reign in the area for about a week. And in a single stroke, he has accomplished just that. We are powerless at this moment to take any serious military action against him. In a week, he would have most likely accomplished most of his military objectives. If I were then in his shoes, I would force a negotiated surrender or imposed settlement on the Greeks."

"And don't forget Ramstein, gentlemen," interrupted the

head of the CIA, a short, skinny, middle age man wearing thick glasses. "We are almost positive that the attackers in Ramstein were Kemal's boys. It's been only 2 years since we realigned Ramstein from a transport base back to a fighter base and now he has masterfully taken out most of our air power in Europe."

"But he surely must know that no American president would let such acts of aggression go unpunished," said President Davis.

"True sir, but he is also gambling on the fact that an American president might not want to sacrifice the lives of thousands of American service men and women on an already lost cause. General Kemal would be in a position of strength if his army and his allies controlled most of northern Greece," said the head of the NSC.

"Well Dan, we must not let this bastard achieve such a position," said the President. "Hundreds of American lives, were lost tonight. The American people will demand that someone pay for this!"

"Tom, is it possible to bring any diplomatic pressure on this mad man? What about the European Community? Greece is a member state."

Tom Gaston, the U.S. Secretary of State, an older man and respected diplomat, answered the question. "Mr. President, we don't have much, if any, diplomatic leverage in the area. We broke off diplomatic relations with Turkey when the fundamentalists overthrew the elected government. Their leader, General Mohamid Kemal, is vehemently anti-Western. He believes in the rebirth of a new Turkish Ottoman Empire, an Islam under one banner, his banner. As for NATO and the E.U, it's still too early to tell. If the old Yugoslavian crisis was any indication of how the E.U. reacts diplomatically or militarily in a crisis, Greece will be overrun before they consider any type of action to be taken. As for NATO, we know that most of our allies have undertaken massive military cuts. It would be weeks before a sizable force could be put together. By then, the war would be over."

"What about any of our Arab friends? Can any one of them talk some sense into him, before things totally escalate out of control?"

"No, Mr. President. He considers them puppets of the west and traitors to Islam. I am afraid we are on our own," said the Secretary of State.

"Well, it was a thought. After this meeting is over, I want you to request an emergency meeting of the UN Security Council Tom," said President Davis.

"I know it will probably be useless, but we need to give that body a try."

"I also want to call an emergency meeting of the North Atlantic council.

"It seems gentlemen that General Kemal has us over the proverbial barrel."

"Yes, Mr. President, it does," replied the Secretary of State.

"In the mean time Admiral Henderson, you will alert the First marine Division. I want them sailing for the Mediterranean within the next twenty-four hours. Also, I want to see a plan as to what other naval forces and options we have to use against this son of a bitch!"

"Yes, sir."

"And Admiral, do we have any subs in the area?"

"The Reagan sir, she's an improved Los Angeles class and can be on station in thirty-six hours."

"Does she carry any missiles?"

"Yes, she does Mr. President. Besides her normal load of torpedoes, she carries a complement of twelve Tomahawk cruise missiles. Both conventional and nuclear tipped."

"As soon as she is in range, I want her to launch her Tomahawk missiles, conventional of course, at military targets in the Turkish capital. As I mentioned before, the American public will be expecting some sort of response in retaliation for the attack on our ships."

A smile appeared on the Admiral's face. "With pleasure, sir."

"Now, General Coleman, what can the army do in the next twenty-four to forty-eight hours to help the situation?"

"The only quick reaction units that we have in Europe are elements of the 81st airborne in Vicenza, Italy. They can be alerted and ready to go in twenty-four hours. We can probably have two to three Apache gunship squadrons in Greece within forty-eight hours and I can alert the 10th Mountain division in Fort Drum, New York. They can be ready and in the air for Europe in the next twenty-four hours. That's all we can do in such a short notice. The troops will be lacking heavy weaponry."

"What about air lifting their heavy weapons?"

"We will do that, sir. But our transports can only carry very limited amounts of tracked vehicles per flight."

"General Mc Dugan!"

The Air Force Chief of Staff hearing his name, looked up from the stack papers which he was reviewing. "Yes, Mr. President?"

"How many squadrons can we have in Europe in the next twenty-four to forty-eight hours?"

"Mr. President with all our base closures in Europe . . ." Before the General could finish, the President angrily cut him off.

"Damn it, General! I am aware of all our base closures. I ordered most of them! My question was how much air power we can have in Europe in the next couple of days!"

"We will have to coordinate with our remaining European allies on using their facilities."

"Well you just do that, General."

"Yes, Mr. President."

"I am not finished, General. Can we mount long distance bombing raids with our B1s and B2s? We spent so much money on all that expensive hardware, we might as well use it and get our money's worth."

"Yes, sir. It can be done with tanker refueling. But sending them in unescorted might cause losses."

"General, those planes were supposed to penetrate Soviet defenses, once thought to be the best in the world. I want a plan and a full report by morning."

"Yes, Mr. President. I'll get right on it. And I'll also alert some of our remaining B-52 units. They can fly a long distance and carry a considerable pay load."

"Do whatever you see fit. Now gentlemen, the situation is very grave. The survival of a long time democratic friend and ally is at stake, along with the reputation of the United States as a world power and the backer of freedom and democracy. If this mad man succeeds, there will be no stopping him. I have the utmost faith in each and every one of you. We must make sure that freedom and democracy prevail. General Coleman, please keep me briefed on any new developments."

"Yes, Mr. President."

"Then, gentlemen, this meeting is adjourned."

Agios Efstratios
0712hrs, 18 May

While on course to the small isle of Agios Efstratios, Lieutenant Yiannis Vassiliou and his crew had received another communiqué. This time the news was even grimmer. The message had reported that Albanian aircraft had attacked and bombed targets in Epirus and Macedonia; they too were throwing in with the Turks. Greece was fighting for her very survival as a nation.

Yiannis scanned the horizon with a pair of binoculars looking for the enemy, just as generations of sailors did before the invention of radar. He didn't dare turn on his air and sea search radar for long, out of fear of being detected. They were now slowly cruising less than a hundred meters from the rocky shores of Agios Efstratios. The Hydra was using the dozens of coves and inlets that dotted the southeastern coastline for cover. Yiannis made note of some of these coves which could later be useful to hide in. For now they were all safe, it would be very difficult for enemy radar to detect them because the boat blended in with the islands' bulk.

"Mr. Georgiou, what's it looking like on the radar?"

"I have been running random sweeps on our navigational radar. I don't want to stay active for too long. If by any chance we are detected, they might just think it's some merchant ship or a ferry's navigation radar. If not, then we are . . . "

"I understand, Mr. Georgiou."

"Let me show you something, sir." Yiannis stepped over to the radar and looked at the screen. "Watch very carefully. I won't leave it on for more than a sweep."

"Okay."

As the radar made its 360 degree sweep, several blips appeared on the screen.

"There is a lot of traffic out there Captain, but what looks most interesting is this six ship slow moving convoy about twenty-five miles northeast of us. They're on a westerly heading towards Limnos, estimated speed twelve knots."

Yiannis looked at the screen and saw the ships that Ensign Georgiou was referring to. "It looks like they may be sending reinforcements and supplies to the island."

"That's exactly what I think, too," said Georgiou turning the radar off.

"Probably a few escorts and LSTs, transporting tanks, artillery and other heavy equipment."

"Turn on the radar for another sweep."

"Ensign Georgiou gave his Captain a worried look. "I will Captain, but we are really pushing our luck." As the radar made its 360 degree sweep, Yiannis could clearly see the convoy sailing unhindered toward Limnos. Hopefully, not for much longer if he had anything to do with it.

"What's it looking like above us Mr. Georgiou?"

"It's fairly quiet now, sir. There was a lot of rotary and heavy fix wing traffic going back and forth earlier."

"Probably helicopter assault troops and Paratrooper transports," said Yiannis.

"There hasn't been any high speed fixed wing traffic for the last twenty minutes."

"Anything being transmitted over the air waves from the island, Mr. Faniou?"

"I have picked up several calls for help from Army units on the island. It seems that they were attacked by chemical weapons and suffered heavy casualties. Now they're under attack from Turkish airborne units. Some of these units are very desperate and can't hold out much longer."

"Anything from Mirina?"

"No, sir. They've been off the air since their last message stating that they were under air attack."

"Thank you, Mr. Faniou."

"Mr. Georgiou, that convoy we've picked up will be arriving at their destination probably within an hour or so," said Yiannis, his thoughts momentarily shifting to Eleni. "Let's give our soldiers a hand and make sure that convoy never reaches its destination."

"Mr. Panou, plot an intercept course that will take us within twenty miles of that enemy convoy. If we have any chance of succeeding, we must hug Agios Efstratios's coastline as long as possible. Once we are in open seas, their radars will most likely detect us. Just pray they have no planes in the air in this area."

"Yes, sir!" said Mr. Panou as he and the rest of the bridge crew became elated at the prospect of going into action.

While the Hydra cruised toward her intended quarry, both Lieutenant Vassiliou and Ensign Georgiou completed their battle plans in the ship's combat information center. Yiannis ordered the boat's galley to make coffee and sandwiches and give them out to the crew at their battle stations. His men had been up all night and needed some food and something warm in their stomachs. In the next few minutes their lives would depend on every man doing exactly what he had been trained to do and Yiannis wanted his men to be comfortable and wide awake. Their chances of success depended on staying undetected as long as possible. If they were not detected by enemy radar immediately after they cleared the island's shores and entered open sea, they would be, once they activated their tactical combat radar. If by a miracle they weren't sunk after their attack on the convoy, Yiannis planned to hide the boat in one of the myriad of inlets or coves that dotted Agios Efstratios and wait it out till nightfall. If they were fortunate enough to survive that long, they would make their escape across the Northern Aegean to the Halkidiki peninsula. The Hydra didn't have enough fuel to go much farther. Her four 4500hp MTU diesels had eaten up fuel at an alarming rate during their high speed dashes. Yiannis counted on finding fuel in one of the dozens of fishing villages along the coast. Once refueled, they would sail for Thessaloniki, where they would resupply and rearm their missile launchers. But first they had to survive their engagement.

The Hydra drifted a hundred meters off the island's northeastern tip, with her engines idling to conserve fuel while they waited for the enemy convoy to close the range. Yiannis had gone inside to the combat information center (CIC), picked up the bridge intercom phone and called his weapons officer. "Mr. Georgiou what's our range now?"

"Sir, the targets are now at twenty-two miles."

"Thank you Mr. Georgiou. Stand by for further orders." Switching channels to the ship's public address system, Yiannis spoke to the crew.

"Men, in the next few minutes, you will be asked to risk your lives for our country. The odds will be heavily against us. We will be attacking a numerically superior force, which enjoys complete air and naval superiority in the area at this time. Our brothers, who are fighting on Limnos, depend on us to stop these reinforcements from arriving. Like our forefathers before us, who themselves, outnumbered and outgunned challenged the might of the Ottoman Navy to win their freedom, we will do the same and use our superior seamanship and training to overcome the odds. We will launch our fire ships against this modern Ottoman enemy, which now threatens our freedom. We may not come out of this alive, but we will die like Greeks, as King Leonidas and his men did at Thermopile, with sword in hand. I am proud to have served with all of you. Long live the Hellenic nation!"

After Yiannis had finished his short speech, the crew had broken out in cheers of "long live the Captain." He knew that his crew would follow him through the very gates of hell if he asked them to. "Mr. Panou, let's give those bastards a taste of their own medicine."

"With pleasure, sir!"

Within a few seconds, the ship's four powerful engines were roaring at full throttle, propelling the Hydra away from her shelter and into harm's way. Yiannis pressed the intercom button, "What's the enemy's range?"

"Twenty miles, sir."

"Lock onto the two transports and give them two missiles apiece."

The Hydra's tactical radar immediately went active and locked onto the two transports. Her emissions were immediately picked up by the enemy escorts. "Sir, we have been detected by enemy radar," said Ensign Georgiou."

"All we can do now is pray, Mr. Georgiou."

"I have a positive lock."

"Fire."

The Hydra shook as the four Exocets left their launchers. "Missiles off and running."

"Give her all she's got and get us out of here, Mr. Panou. Head for that small cove right behind that point," said Lieutenant Vassiliou pointing to the location which was a couple of miles away.

"Sir! I've picked up an enemy missile launch. There are two missiles headed our way! Mr. Georgiou yelled. The look of elation in going into battle quickly faded from the faces of the bridge crew, as they realized that death was only a few minutes away.

While the Hydra had been homing in on the two heavily laden LSTS, one of the convoy escorts, a Kartal class fast attack boat, had picked up the Hydra's radar emissions. It immediately launched its two Penguin missiles against her. The Hydra was now running for her life. If she made the shelter of the rocky cove, the missiles might just lose her.

"Sir, three minutes before our missiles impact. Three and a half till theirs arrive."

"At least we will know if we hit them," said Yiannis.

With the four Exocets closing in on the Turkish convoy, a feeling of panic gripped the Escort commander. According to naval headquarters in Izmir, all enemy units had been eliminated in the vicinity of Limnos. Now there were four enemy cruise missiles bearing down on his precious charges, which contained the tanks and artillery needed to secure the island. He did the only thing that he could do in such a situation. He ordered the escorts to close on the two LSTs and form a protective shield around them. It was better, he figured, to lose a frigate or destroyer than one of the valuable LSTs. Unfortunately, most of his escorts were spread out, conducting ASW sweeps. Only a couple of them were in the immediate position to comply with his orders.

When the Hydra's Exocets had neared their targets, their internal guidance systems went active. The first missile attempted to lock on the lead LST, but its acquisition radar was momentarily fooled by chaff fired by an escort that had positioned itself between the target and the missile. The Exocet's radar locked onto the next closest target, the frigate itself. The ship's point defense gun went active and attempted to shoot down the missile, but failed. The missile struck the ship's bow and penetrated into the forward magazines which contained Harpoon missiles before exploding. The resulting detonation of the ship's magazines was of such great magnitude that it ripped the entire bow section off the frigate. With her engines still pushing her forward at more than twenty knots, what was left of the ship's bulkheads rapidly gave way, causing her to quickly fill with water and nose dive to the bottom, leaving few survivors.

The second Exocet, only seconds behind, now unhindered, locked onto its programmed target and struck the LST amidships. The missile penetrated all the way into the ship's huge cargo bay before the 165-kilo warhead and missile fuel detonated amongst the parked military vehicles with catastrophic results. The cargo bay quickly became a flaming inferno as ammunition stored inside the vehicles began to catch fire and explode. Many of the hundreds of soldiers inside the ship, some with their clothes on fire, jumped over the side to escape the roaring flames. With fires burning out of control, her Captain gave the order to abandon ship. Still burning and listing, she was sunk several hours later by a torpedo launched by one of the surviving escorts. The crew of the remaining LST watched in horror and prayed for salvation, while the rest of the missiles streaked toward them. They were given only a temporary reprieve. The destroyer Kalil-Ali-Pasha which had positioned itself in front of the LST, fired off chaff and flares to decoy the incoming missiles. Unfortunately for the soon to be ill-fated ship, only one of the missiles was decoyed away. With the missile homing in on the escort destroyer, her point defense Phalanx gun opened fire and destroyed the missile just fifty feet from the ship. The blast from the incoming missile killed three of the Kalil-Ali-Pasha's crew, dismounted the port side Harpoon missile launcher and wrecked the communications and radar dishes mounted on the ship's mast.

The last Exocet continued on course and struck the LST's stern section, ripping through several decks before detonating in the ship's engineering compartment. The blast buckled the ship's propeller shafts, sprung several hull plates and started a large fire. Lying dead in the water, her crew fought valiantly to save the ship and her precious cargo. Later that morning, after her fires had been partially extinguished and power restored, a tow line was passed from one of the escorts. Unfortunately for the Turks, her cargo never made it ashore. While under tow to Moudros bay, Limnos, she was torpedoed and sunk by the Greek submarine Katsounis. It would be a couple of days before anyone fully realized the impact of what Lieutenant Vassiliou and his crew had accomplished in their daring attack.

Chapter 10

Macedonian Border

0751hrs, 18 May

Lieutenant Colonel Mihalovic had stayed by the radio most of the night, awaiting the green light from headquarters to cross the border. Much to his relief, the coded message giving the go ahead had finally come at 0535hrs. Twenty-five minutes later, the first units of the 3rd Macedonian Mountain regiment had crossed the Greek border. Like in most military operations, everything had not gone according to plan. The fifteen man advance commando team, which had infiltrated the Greek border town of Doiranis an hour prior to the commencement of hostilities, had unexpectedly run into difficulties. They had expected to completely surprise the Greeks and quietly neutralize the police station. Instead, the police had been alerted and had posted guards at 0530hrs. The team could only speculate that the Greeks had been alerted by their higher headquarters after the Turkish attack.

Having no other choice but to proceed with their original plan, the commandos cut the phone lines to Doiranis at 0555hrs and neutralized the police station at the cost of one man killed and two others wounded. This short but violent gun battle had awakened most of the town's inhabitants prompting several of them to grab their hunting rifles and head toward the direction of the shooting. When they spotted the Macedonians, the lightly armed civilians opened fire. The Macedonians returned fire, killing two and wounding four others. Luckily, the only thing that averted a bloody show down between the Macedonians and the town folks was the arrival of the lead elements of the Macedonian 3rd Mountain Regiment. By 0635hrs, Doiranis had been secured, but not without the loss of two more Macedonian soldiers and several civilians.

While Doiranis was being pacified, the second battalion of the 3rd Mountain regiment made a dash to Drossato, a larger town a few kilometers to the south. Drossato had been a harder nut to crack. Like Doiranis, an advance commando team had infiltrated the town with instructions to neutralize the police station. Like Doiranis, the Macedonian commandos hiding in an adjacent field watched helplessly as the police were alerted at 0530hrs and posted additional sentries. At 0555hrs, the commandos cut the telephone wires leading to a small microwave antenna above the telephone exchange. A few minutes later, much to the commandos' dismay, the sounds of gunfire could be heard coming from the direction of Doiranis. Hearing the shooting, the Macedonian team leader decided to scrub the mission, fearing heavy casualties. Pulling just out of the town, they awaited the arrival of reinforcements.

Fifteen minutes later, the first contingents of the second battalion, 3rd Mountain Regiment entered the town. After a fierce twenty minute battle, the town of Drossato had been secured. The police station lay in ruins, its defenders killed by a hail of bullets and high explosive anti tank rockets. In a repeat of Doiranis, several of the town's citizens lay dead, killed in the cross fire or resisting the Macedonians. Lieutenant Colonel Mihalovic stared disappointingly at the rubble of what had been Drossato's police station. He admired the courage shown by its defenders who had refused to surrender, even under insurmountable odds.

"Colonel, we have secured the town," said Major Ziad who had just returned from the town square.

"How many casualties did we suffer, Major?"

"Two killed, five wounded. One soldier was shot and killed by a civilian with a hunting rifle."

"Is the civilian in custody?"

"Well . . . , no sir" said Major Ziad hesitantly.

"Where is he, Major?"

"Sir, Lieutenant Amir had the man and his family shot, as an example to the Greeks."

"Did you know about this beforehand?" Colonel Mihalovic, visibly irritated at the turn of events.

"I found out afterwards. You know I would never condone such behavior."

"The stupid, fool! I want Lieutenant Amir relieved of all command responsibilities. I will deal with him later. I will not have my soldiers shooting civilians except in self defense. If word of this gets out, the Greeks will brand us as war criminals and resist us even harder."

"Yes, sir. He was only thinking of his men."

"I realize that Major and I will take it into account. Now, are we ready to move into the mountains? I will feel more comfortable if the men were in an environment they better understand."

"The regiment will be ready to move as soon as the Infantry Brigade arrives to take over occupation duties from us. They are due within the hour. Our advance scouts are already in the Mavrovouni foothills. They've reported everything is quiet."

"Excellent. I want us ready to move once the 4th Infantry Brigade is on station. We must be dug in by nightfall."

Kesan Command Bunker, Turkey
0832hrs, 18 May

General Kemal stood in the command bunker's gallery looking down on a large map of Greece and the Aegean Sea. The command center hummed with activity. The General watched as Staff Officers moved back and forth, removing and attaching small colored flags to the maps surface. The flags, colored red for Turkish and blue for the Greek forces, were marked, each identifying a specific unit. Each flag attached to the map indicated where each unit was supposedly located. There were now more red than blue flags on some areas of the map which was a good sign. So far the operation had gone better than expected. The chemical attack had caught the Greeks completely by surprise. It had succeeded in grounding much of the Greek air force and devastating their front line defenses. In fact, the attack had been so successful, that within twenty minutes of its initiation, the first tanks of the Suilliman armored division had crossed the Evros River and breached the Greek front line positions virtually unopposed.

With the General looking on, one of the Staff officers moved the flag that represented the Suilliman division moving deeper into Thrace. It was now less than fifteen kilometers from its main objective, the city of Alexandroupolis. He expected the city to fall by nightfall, if all went well. In northern Thrace, his tanks had easily captured the border towns of Soufli and Didimotiko, but heavy fighting was still raging in the small border city of Orestiada. The only major setback that the whole operation had so far suffered had been on Limnos. For some reason, the defenders of the island's only airstrip had not succumbed to the gas attack. When his airborne forces had attempted to seize it, they had been repulsed with very heavy losses. This failure had cost him one of his best Marine battalions and a squadron of irreplaceable transport helicopters. Hearing footsteps, the General turned around and saw a naval officer carrying a stack of papers.

"Sir, we have just received an immediate message from Naval Headquarters Izmir," Captain Turket, the Naval Staff Duty Officer, stood at attention in front of the General.

"Well, what is it man?"

"Sir, there has been a serious setback. The convoy carrying the heavy weapons and reinforcements to Limnos was attacked. The frigate Yavuz was lost with all hands . . ."

Kemal banged the desk with balled fists. "I don't give a dam about one measly frigate! What about the LSTs carrying the army's equipment?" screamed Kemal in a fit of fury.

All activity in the bunker had momentarily ceased, as everyone stood spellbound by the exchange that was taking place between the General and the now visibly terrified naval officer.

"Sir, both the LSTs were hit by anti-ship missiles. One of the ships is burning out of control and has been abandoned. The other has received serious damage to its engine compartment and is taking on water. The fires started by the missile have been put out or are under control. They are attempting to put a tow line on her as we speak."

The General flew into frenzy. "You stupid incompetent fools! How did this happen? This will set us back days!"

"Sir, the report relates that the attack on the convoy was probably executed by a lone missile boat. One of our Kartal attack boats fired two missiles at her. It's believed that the enemy boat was destroyed. It disappeared from the radar screens," Captain Turket said, visibly shaking with fear.

"Believed sunk! I want the infidel dogs that did this, dead! Do you understand, Captain?"

"Yes, sir."

"I also want the Escort Commander relieved of command and shot for incompetence!"

"Sir, the Escort Commander went down with the Yavuz."

"Good! Then justice has been done. Now get out of my sight!"

"Ye . . .yes, sir," said Captain Turket, as he quickly scurried away, fearing that the General might have him shot for bringing the bad news.

General Hasan, who had heard the shouting, had gone up to the gallery to calm his commander and chief. His rage now dissipated, General Kemal saw his subordinate enter the gallery.

"Kismet has not been kind to us with Limnos."

"I heard the news, sir."

"The loss of those ships is a serious blow to our plans Imbrahim. Our soldiers fighting on the island need that equipment to quickly secure it. Pray that those incompetent fools manage to save the stricken LST. Otherwise, this will be a critical setback to our plans. We lost much of our heavy helicopter transport during the initial attack. It will take us a couple of days to muster up another resupply convoy, if we're lucky. Most of our reserves are committed to Thrace."

"Sir, General Guven's latest report from Limnos suggested that many of his initial objectives have been met. Except for some isolated pockets of resistance in the island's interior, the airport and around the port city of Mirina which should be captured by late afternoon, we now control most of the island's eastern coastal areas."

"We must press the enemy harder, even without the heavy equipment. They must not be given the time, or the opportunity to regroup and reorganize their defenses, Imbrahim."

"Sir, may I take the liberty to say that except for our setback on Limnos, your plan has succeeded beyond all our expectations. Our army crossed the Evros River and penetrated the infidel's main defense line virtually unopposed. Forgive me for ever doubting your wisdom."

General Kemal temporarily forgot the bad news and smiled. "You are forgiven Imbrahim. It's human nature to have doubts, especially for an endeavor as grand and daring as this. As for our successes, we have been very fortunate. But it's still very early in the game. The Greeks resolve will stiffen. That is why your men must quickly capture Alexandroupolis. We need the port."

"It will be done, sir. The Suilliman division is now less than fifteen kilometers from the city. If anyone can accomplish this task, it's Brigadier Karakoglou."

"You are correct in that assumption, Imbrahim. He is an excellent soldier and above all a superb tanker."

"Sir, has there been any official response from the Americans?"

"Not officially. They are still licking their wounds, from the damage they suffered at Ramstein and to their carrier in Athens."

"I just read an unconfirmed report that the carrier suffered additional damage from a bomb hit during our air force's raid on the city."

"It is true, Imbrahim. A CNN news broadcast confirmed it for us. It even showed pictures of the stricken ship."

"Your plan to cripple American air power in the region by striking both their carrier and Ramstein air base and making the attacks look like the work of terrorists was ingenious."

"Don't think that the Americans are total idiots, Imbrahim. They know that we were ultimately behind those attacks, but so what. They are now virtually powerless in this area of the world for at least a week, if not more. They can't possibly muster enough forces to effectively intervene against us in time to save their allies. Oh, they still have some men and equipment that they can send down here from northern Europe, but we can effectively deal with that threat when it comes."

"Sir, you should get a couple of hours of rest. You have been up all night. I will wake you immediately if anything occurs that requires your attention."

"Yes, I think I will, Imbrahim. I feel exhausted. My thinking is starting to be clouded by fatigue. Wake me in a couple of hours."

Limnos

0906hrs, 18 May

For the past couple of hours, while the sounds of battle grew nearer, Eleni and Anna stayed inside the pension, too terrified to go outside. Everyone had been awakened a little past five A.M. by the loud noise of low flying jet aircraft and explosions. Terrified, Eleni had quickly gotten dressed and proceeded down to the lobby where Petros, Anna and several of the other guests had also gathered. Trying to find out what was going on, Petros had attempted to call the Mirina police station without any luck. The phone line was dead and so was the cell phone. When he tried the radio, all he got from the local station was silence. It was only when he tuned to Athens, did they hear the news of the Turkish attack on Greece. When they heard the news, most of the foreign guests staying at the Pension had immediately panicked and requested transport to Mirina to leave the island. Petros had attempted to dissuade them from leaving by trying to convince them that it was safer at the hotel. But no one would listen. So Petros had everyone who wanted to leave board the pension's van and he drove them to Mirina. That had been at 0630 and he still had not returned.

Throughout the rest of the morning, the two women could hear the rumble of heavy gunfire coming from the sea. Anna speculated that it was naval gunfire striking targets inland. Only an hour ago, they had heard helicopters flying overhead toward Mirina. Both women were terrified at the thought that those helicopters might be carrying Turkish soldiers. Stories of the atrocities that had been committed by the Turks on Cyprus in 1974 flashed through Eleni's mind.

"Anna, I'm really scared. The shooting seems to be getting closer. Maybe it would be better if we packed some food and left for a safer location."

"I'm not going anywhere until Petros returns."

"I am sure he's okay, Anna. He's probably gotten cut off by the fighting," said Eleni trying to reassure her friend.

"What's that?" The two women heard a loud high pitched shriek. Several loud explosions rocked the building as a string of 127mm shells bracketed the pension, shattering the front plate glass windows. "Anna, get down!" screamed a terrified Eleni.

A tremendous explosion ripped through the building as another string of shells landed, one of them hitting the structure. All that Eleni remembered was being picked up by the force of the explosion and slammed into the ground with such strength that it temporarily rendered her unconscious. When Eleni awoke, a few minutes later, she found herself covered in dust and broken plaster. Getting slowly back up on her feet, she checked herself for injuries. Except for a headache and a couple of minor scratches, she had escaped relatively unscathed. She looked around her. The lobby was in a complete shambles, broken glass and masonry were strewn everywhere. "Help me!"

"Oh my God," Eleni suddenly remembered her friend.

"Anna, where are you?"

"Over here, help me." She rushed to Anna's aid and found her on the other side of the lobby covered by boards and broken masonry. Lifting the debris off the woman, she helped her to her feet, noticing a large bruise on Anna's forehead.

"Are you okay?"

"My head hurts."

"You received a good size bump on it. But you should be okay."

Anna looked around at what was left of the lobby and burst into tears. "All our life's work, gone."

Eleni hugged her friend. "Don't worry about it. You're alive. We could have been killed. Everything can be rebuilt."

"Hilfe!"

Both women quickly made their way to the area where the cry came from. When they got there, they found a young woman covered in blood holding a man in her arms.

"It's the German couple who had decided to stay," said Anna.

"Please, help my husband. He is badly injured and needs a doctor."

Eleni bent down to see what assistance she could offer the injured man, but saw that he was beyond help. He had taken a piece of shrapnel through the head. Eleni looked at the women with tears in her eyes. "He's dead; there is nothing we can do."

"No, he isn't. You are lying!" shouted the woman as she began sobbing uncontrollably. Eleni pulled the woman away from her husband's body and comforted her, while Anna who had gone to the kitchen, returned with a tablecloth and covered the dead man.

"She will be okay, Anna. She's not injured."

"I think that we had better get out of here. The Turks will most likely be here soon."

"I think you're right, Eleni. Go into the kitchen and fill a couple of plastic bags with food, while I go find us some clothes to take along."

Ten minutes later, Eleni emerged from the kitchen, with a couple of bags full of food. The German woman had calmed down and had even made an attempt to clean the blood off her.

"Eleni! I hear a vehicle. Maybe it's Petros." Both women rushed to the window.

"Oh my God, it's Turkish soldiers!" Eleni said, who was now almost to the point of panic.

"What are we going to do?"

"Take the German woman with you and hide in the food storage locker in the kitchen."

"No Anna, I am not leaving you alone."

"Go! Hurry, there isn't much time."

Eleni grabbed the German woman and went into the kitchen. She opened the storage locker door, but before going inside she grabbed a large butcher knife that was lying on the counter.

Anna who was standing in the lobby awaiting the arrival of the Turks, could now hear the three soldiers approaching the door way. The three soldiers burst inside with their rifles at ready position and spotted Anna. Seeing that the woman posed no threat, one of the soldiers shoved her to the ground and stood over her as the other two checked the immediate area. Finding no one else except the body of the dead German tourist, the other two returned to the lobby.

"Well, well, what do we have here?" asked the NCO who accompanied the two soldiers.

"An infidel slut, Sergeant," replied the soldier.

"Yes, I can see. A nice one at that," said the Sergeant, pinching Anna's check.

Anna swung her arm slapping the Sergeant. "Don't touch me, you pig!"

The Sergeant turned and back handed her across the face, knocking her to the ground.

"You infidel whore must be taught some humility. Anna could barely stand up, her head still spinning from the Sergeant's blow. Unable to understand their conversation, she understood from their actions what was about to come. She was grabbed by the two other soldiers and held up. The Sergeant reached to his belt and unsheathed a sharp knife. In one quick move he grabbed her shirt by the collar and ripped it from her body. Anna began to scream in terror.

"Hold her well."

"No! No! Please don't! Using his knife, he cut away the rest of her cloths. When he had finished, he pushed her to the ground. To stop her screaming, he slapped her several times. As the three soldiers took turns raping Anna, Eleni who was hiding inside the kitchen could hear her screams, which soon turned to whimpers. After what seemed like hours, the whimpering stopped.

Hearing the sound of approaching footsteps, both women held their breath. Holding the butcher knife, Eleni was determined to defend herself and the German woman no matter what the cost. Eleni began to tremble uncontrollably as she heard the footsteps come closer. She heard the footsteps suddenly stop and the new sounds of opening and closing of drawers. "Oh, God! They're going to find us," she whispered.

Suddenly the storage locker door swung open. Facing her was a soldier, probably not much older than her own brother. Surprised by his find, the soldier momentarily hesitated. Eleni, who had been holding the butcher knife at the ready, lunged at the soldier and plunged the knife deep into his chest. The soldier who had been holding his rifle in one hand, collapsed to his knees holding the protruding knife handle with his other hand. Bringing his rifle up, he was able to fire off a quick shot before collapsing, face forward into the storage locker.

"Jesus! I just killed a man," said Eleni as she looked at her hand which was covered with the soldier's blood.

Hearing the shot, the other two soldiers rushed into the room with their weapons drawn. When they saw Eleni, they determined that she was no longer hostile and did not shoot her. The young private rushed to his fallen comrade's aid. "He's dead, Sergeant. The bitch killed him."

The Turkish NCO walked over to Eleni and with a gun in one hand pointed it at her head. "Why you murderous infidel whore," he said smacking her sharply across the face with his free hand, knocking her off her feet. Pulling out his knife he bent over Eleni.

"Hold her Ali. She will provide us with better entertainment than the other slut did."

"Yes, Sergeant."

Grabbing Eleni's shirt, he began to cut it from her body. "No, please!" she screamed in terror.

Two shots rang out in rapid succession. The sergeant who had been standing over Eleni, dropped the knife and fell over backwards. The soldier, who had been holding Eleni, let go of her and made a grab for his weapon, but he was shot down before he had taken a step.

"Oh, Petros! Thank God you're here," Eleni got up and hugged him.

Quickly recovering from the shock of almost being raped, Eleni noticed that it was conspicuously quiet and remembered the German girl in the closet. Letting go of Petros, she rushed back to the storage locker and saw that the German woman was dead. The bullet fired by the soldier Eleni knifed, had struck the woman in the chest, killing her instantly. "Oh God she's dead!" She turned and looked at Petros with tears streaming down her cheeks.

"Where is Anna?" She saw that Petros was also crying. She suddenly realized that something had happened to Anna.

"I got caught up in the fighting. That's why it took me so long to get back. Maybe if I were here . . ."

"Oh, no! Anna!"

Eleni tried to run to the lobby where she had last seen Anna, but was grabbed by Petros. "No Eleni, it's better that you not see her. She's dead."

Eleni began to sob. "Anna made us both hide in the storage closet while she stayed in the lobby to meet the soldiers. She sacrificed herself for me. We can't just leave her."

"Eleni we must go. The Turks are close by. They will soon be here in force. Mirina can't hold out much longer. I'll take you to a safer place, and then I'll return to bury my wife."

Grabbing the bags of food that she had collected for the trip, they made their way out of the building.

"Where are we going, Petros?"

"We must head for the island's interior. That's where our troops are retreating. You'll be safer there."

The Northern Aegean
1016hrs, 18 May

Lieutenant Mavridis munched hungrily on a candy bar that he found in his survival pack. He had been drifting westward for almost five hours and to the best of his reckoning, he figured he was about eighteen miles northwest of Limnos. The Albatross' last position had been ten miles north of the island, when they had gotten jumped by a Turkish fighter. Everything had happened so fast. Takis tried to think back to this morning's events. One minute they had been tracking a large contingent of Turkish surface units on their radar, the next they were being riddled by cannon fire and going down in flames.

The fighter had struck without warning. Not wanting to waste a missile, the enemy pilot had decided to use his guns on the lumbering sea plane. On its first pass the Turkish fighter jet had raked the forward part of the plane with its cannon, shattering the cockpit, killing the pilot, flight engineer and seriously wounding the copilot. Luckily, he had been inside the plane's cabin checking on some malfunctioning equipment and had escaped unscathed. Trying to shake the fighter, the wounded copilot had put the stricken plane into a nose dive and headed for the wave tops. But the ungainly sea plane didn't have a chance to get away from its nimble pursuer. On the next pass, the fighter's cannon shells ripped into the starboard nacelle, knocking chunks out of the engine and starting a fire. Takis knew the plane couldn't stay airborne much longer; he grabbed one of the emergency flotation devices hanging in the cabin and braced himself for the crash. He didn't have long to wait.

When the plane hit the water, he had been thrown hard against the plane's fuselage; fortunately his flight helmet had absorbed most of the impact. Momentarily stunned, the rushing sea water that had begun to fill the plane jolted him into action. Unable to reach the damaged cockpit to help the co-pilot because of the advancing sea, he had only enough time to find and deploy a life raft before the plane sank from under him. He was the only survivor.

During the course of the morning, while drifting in the open life raft, he had seen scores of fighter aircraft, heavily loaded with ordnance, pass overhead, heading toward Limnos. Takis hadn't fired off a flare nor had he activated his emergency locator beacon to get the planes' attention, figuring they were Turkish. He didn't relish the thought of becoming a guest of the Turks, who weren't particularly known for their hospitality toward their enemies. He would wait a few more hours and let the currents carry him further west and hopefully toward safety. Unfortunately, Takis knew that his luck wouldn't hold out. Before they had taken off from Elefsis to look for the terrorist ship, he had checked the weather forecast. It called for gale force winds and rain during the next twenty-four hours throughout the northern Aegean. Looking toward the northeast, he could see in the clouds of the expected front beginning to move in. Well he thought, much to his rotten luck, for once the weatherman happened to be right.

Army Headquarters, Argyrokastron, Albania
1130hrs, 18 May

General Hoxa put down the stack of reports and messages he had been reading. He was beginning to feel the immense strain and fatigue put on him during last twenty-four hours. Needing a break, he got up from his desk and went over to the window where he lit a cigarette. Looking outside, he could see a convoy of motorized infantry heading for the front, less than thirty kilometers away. So far, he thought, the Albanian contribution to "Operation Medina" had gone off very well. Hostilities had commenced at 0600hrs, with air strikes on Corfu, Igoumenitsa, the NATO AWACs airfield at Preveza and several other targets of military importance. According to some of the after action reports of the air strikes which he had read, the enemy had suffered substantial damage. The reports claimed Corfu's airport, communication, military and harbor facilities had been heavily damaged. And as an added bonus, one of the SU 27's had attacked and severely damaged an enemy Frigate that was anchored in the bay. As for the raid on Igoumenitsa, the planes had destroyed fuel storage facilities and sunk or damaged several merchant ships in the harbor. The only disappointment was the raid on Preveza. The bombers had not found the NATO E3A AWACS plane on the field. Still, significant damage had been done to the airfield's runway and support facilities. But the cost to Albania's small and relatively obsolete air force was heavy. Five of the older J-4 fighters had gone down during the long over water flight, an SU 27 had been shot down by antiaircraft fire over Preveza and a SU 27 as well as three J 2s were lost to F-4 interceptors scrambling out of Andravida air base in the Peloponnese.

The SU 27s had managed to shoot down one of the interceptors; still the Albanian air force couldn't sustain losses like this and remain a viable fighting force. From now on, he would have to use his remaining aircraft when absolutely necessary. The other bright spot, the army's ground offensive had gone better than he had initially expected. Albanian forces had advanced twenty kilometers inside Thesprotia province and captured the provincial town of Filiate. Further to the Northeast in Ioanninon province, his infantry had captured the town of Delsinakion and were battling for control of the small provincial town of Konitsa. He looked at a map of Northern Greece that was hanging on the wall. If his forces could only keep up their present rate of momentum, they would be at the outskirts of Igoumenitsa by tomorrow morning.

General Hoxa was amazed that the Greek response to the Albanian incursion had been only lukewarm. He speculated the Greek high command in Athens must have been totally caught off guard and overwhelmed by the scope and magnitude of the attack by Turkey and her Allies. If he were the Greeks, he would do one of two things to stabilize the worsening situation. Deal with the Albanian threat immediately or fight a holding action and concentrate the main effort and resources on the greater Turkish threat. He prayed that the Greeks would choose to deal with the greater threat. This would buy him the time needed to consolidate their gains and dig in. He picked up the phone to call his driver to take him back to his command bunker. He would get some rest there. It was safer than headquarters if the Greeks launched an air strike.

Kommotini
1210hrs, 18may

In the confines of their command post located in the city Mosque, Osman and Mohamid were recalling the past night's events and discussing their future plans over a meal of bread, cold lamb and goats' cheese. The Muslim quarter of the city was now relatively quiet, after the withdrawal of the Greek armored units. The two Turkish agents and their small command had just barely survived the assault the night before to crush the insurrection and to regain control of the Muslim quarter by the Greeks.

Osman, who had coordinated all operations from his makeshift command center in the city Mosque, had in the relatively short time available to him, effectively organized the Muslims' defenses. Under his and Mohamid's guidance, all streets leading into the Muslim quarter had been blocked off and several fighting positions had been quickly constructed throughout the district. Dozens of Molotov cocktails had been manufactured to be used against any armored vehicles that attacked them.

When the Greek assault did finally come, it had been spearheaded by two M113 APC's, both armed with fifty caliber machine guns and an AMX-10, armed with a 20mm cannon. Following behind the three APC's was a company of dismounted infantry. When the lead APC had approached the first street barrier, not a single Muslim could be seen. Thinking that the Muslims had fled in fear, the driver of the first APC had crashed his vehicle through the first barricade with the other APCs and infantry following closely behind. Having gotten safely through the first barricade, the driver of the APC was confident that the whole operation would be a walk over. He put the APC into gear and drove toward the next barrier of overturned cars and uprooted telephone poles, seventy meters down the road. Upon reaching the barricade, the driver had gunned his engine and began to drive his eleven ton vehicle over the obstruction. The Muslim fighters, who had remained hidden on the roof tops of the adjacent buildings, on Mohamid's orders, struck with a fusillade of gunfire and Molotovs.

Surprised by the sudden turn of events, the gunner of the

first APC didn't even have a chance to return fire, before being hit by a barrage of bullets. The gunner of the second M-113 had been set ablaze by a fire bomb that had landed on the vehicle's hatch. When the commander of the third APC saw the other two vehicles set alight, he put the vehicle into reverse and ordered the dispersal of smoke canisters.   With its 20mm cannon raking the roof tops, the APC began to slowly back out of the ambush and for a while it had looked like it would escape.

However, two Muslim fighters, each carrying several sticks of dynamite and screaming Allah Akbar at the top of their lungs, rushed out from one of the buildings and charged the APC. The APC's gunner had only been able to hit one of them with his 7.62 coaxial machine gun before the other dived under the vehicle. The resulting explosion ripped the treads off the vehicle and set it ablaze. The infantry company which had been following closely behind the three APCs had taken cover once the shooting had broken out and hastily retreated toward the Greek positions, leaving several dead behind them. Osman, who had seen the battle, had been elated at their initial success. But he knew that the Greeks would be back, this time in force.

The first heavy tanks did not arrive in the city until an hour and a half after the failure of the first assault. During the interlude, Osman had used the time to strengthen his defenses. Dozens of additional trees and telephone poles had been cut down and used to construct crude antitank barriers.

Construction equipment had been used to haul dirt and rocks to block building entrances and construct fighting positions. When the army launched its assault at 0335hrs, Osman's fighters were ready for them. The Muslims had fought like mad men and had to be blasted out of their fortified positions by direct tank fire or flushed out by infantry assault. Rather than surrender, many of them had rigged the buildings they were fighting in with dynamite and blew themselves up, taking many of their attackers with them.

Even though army casualties had been heavy, the outcome of the battle had never been in question. The Muslims knew that they could never defeat the heavily armed soldiers. Much to the Muslim fighters' surprise, the army assault had suddenly stopped a little past 0500hrs. The units had begun a hasty withdrawal from the Muslim quarter. The fighters came out of their strongholds and gave thanks to Allah for their miraculous salvation. This miracle had come as no surprise to the two Turkish military intelligence agents. They knew what had really saved their ass and just at the brink of time, the commencement of "Operation Medina."

It wasn't until a little past six in the morning when the rest of Kommotini's Muslims found out who their real saviors had been. At 0610hrs, a flight of Turkish F-16 fighter bombers swept in low from the east and began pounding targets in and around the city. When Osman's men saw the red crescent moon and star markings on the planes, they fired their guns in the air and cheered in delight. They had cheered even harder when they heard the sound of explosions coming from the east. The planes had found and severely mauled the armored brigade that had participated in the attack against them earlier that night.

Finishing their lunch, the two agents entered the central part of the Mosque and prayed to Allah, thanking him for their success. Over a hundred of the faithful had perished that night; but their plan had succeeded beyond their wildest expectations. After finishing their prayers, Osman and Mohamid met with their Lieutenants and instructed them on their next moves. Osman, not wanting to risk further confrontation with the Greeks, had instructed his fighters to "stand to," until the arrival of the Turkish army. When they were finally alone, Osman turned to Mohamid.

"Allah is great, my brother,"

"Yes indeed! We have dealt the infidel a heavy blow. They lost a whole armored brigade to our planes this morning. The General will be proud of us!"

"Don't ever mention the General, you fool! Those idiots must never find out who we really are!"

"I am sorry, Osman. I will be more careful."

"It's okay, Mohamid, We are all very tired. I suggest that you lay down and get some rest."

"You're right, my friend. I will rest after I check on the status of our wounded. I must be going now. May Allah watch over you."

Several blocks to the east, a temporary police station had been set up in the town hall building by Major Costopoulos and the surviving policemen. Once hostilities with Turkey had begun, the government had declared immediate martial law. The police station now served as a liaison between the police and the army. In one of the building's now empty offices, Mihalis lay in an army sleeping bag, exhausted from the previous night's ordeal. As he began to doze off, he had a premonition that last night's events were only a prelude of worse things to come.

Chapter 11

Ramstein, Germany

1424hrs, 18 MAY

After spending most of the morning in Helga's bed, Logan took a quick shower, jumped into his car and drove back to his apartment. On the way, he observed that the German Police had established road blocks on the autobahn entrances and were checking vehicles. He wondered what the hell was going on for the Germans to be tying up traffic for kilometers. After entering his apartment, Logan grabbed a cold beer from the fridge and checked his answering machine. He was instantly greeted by the voice of the acting Squadron executive officer telling him to report to base immediately. Well, there probably goes the rest of the weekend, he thought rather disappointedly.

The usual ten minute ride to the base had taken almost half an hour because of the huge traffic tie up at the gate. The Security Force personnel were searching every car entering the installation. While waiting in traffic, Logan had turned on the car's radio and heard the news of the terrorist attack and the Turkish invasion of Greece over AFN (The American Armed Forces Network). After being thoroughly checked by the guards at the gate, he entered the base and drove toward Wing Headquarters. When he reached the building, on account of all the debris that still clogged the streets, he was unable to park near the structure. Leaving the car a few blocks away, Logan walked the rest of the way.

Passing by what was left of the Security Force barracks, Logan observed that base fire and rescue personnel were still searching the twisted rubble for the dead and injured. He had heard on the news report that there had been over seventy-five killed in the bombing. Crossing the small parking lot that separated Wing headquarters from the Security barracks, Logan saw the devastation the bomb had done to the headquarters building. Shattered glass lay everywhere. From what he could see, not a single window had remained intact in the whole structure. Civil engineering crews were still working hard, trying to repair the blast damage and replace the shattered windows.

At the entrance to the building, Logan displayed his ID card to the Security sentry, which had been posted there once Threat con Delta (the highest state of alert during terrorist threat conditions) had been implemented and proceeded through. He continued downstairs to the Command Post where he was met by the duty Officer.

"Sir, the General's waiting for you in the conference room."

"Thank you, Major."

Logan went straight to the conference room and found General Pope sitting at the head of large mahogany table, glossing over a message. "Ah Jack, we've been trying to find you all morning."

"Well, I was preoccupied last night and I didn't get home till this morning," said Logan with a smug on his face.

"I bet you were, Logan," the General said, having heard of Logan's exploits with the ladies.

"Sit down, Colonel. I guess you want to know why I've called you here."

"I do have some idea, sir and I suspect it has something to do with last night's events and the subsequent war that's broken out down South."

"You hit it right on the head, Jack. If you haven't already heard, the 512th has been devastated. The bastards knocked out sixteen planes and killed over eighty of my cops."

"I saw the barracks, sir."

"It was a suicide bomber just like in Beirut, Colonel. OSI (Office of Special Investigations) agents, as we speak, are shifting through the wreckage to see if they can find any clues as to who is responsible for all this. The bastards that hit the flight line were killed to a man. We have no body alive to interrogate"

"I bet it was the same assholes that launched a missile against the Lincoln in Athens," said Logan.

"Those assholes, Colonel, are responsible for rendering the carrier inoperable and for the deaths of over two hundred sailors and eight hundred civilians. And if that wasn't enough, the ship took a direct bomb hit when the Turkish air force raided Athens. She'll be out of commission for months. The situation in Greece is critical. The Greeks have their backs against the wall. They are reeling from a surprise WMD attack and have been invaded on all fronts. To top it all off, the bastards who probably planned and carried out all this here, have us over the barrel. We really can't do much to help".

"So who did it? The Turks?" Logan asked.

"Washington believes that the Turks are directly behind both terrorist attacks."

"That's probably a correct assumption, General. Crippling most of our European fighter assets gives them a virtual free hand to do as they like in the Aegean."

"Well that's exactly what they are doing, Colonel. The Greeks are in full retreat and getting more desperate by the minute. They are requesting military assistance from us. In lieu of the critical situation there, Washington has decided to strip central Europe of our remaining fighter assets. They've decided to send the 526th to Greece. For the time being, you're it, Logan."

"But General, we're only seventeen airplanes. We'll be heavily outnumbered and outgunned."

"I know that, Jack. I used the same logic with Washington, but nobody's listening. Besides, after last night's fiasco, who would listen to me anyway? I'll probably be looking for a new job before the weekend is out," said General Pope.

"Oh before I forget, Captain Barnes will be going along with you, so that gives you eighteen aircraft."

"But sir, she's not really ready."

"Nonsense, Logan.   You yourself told me that she might have been given the shaft during her Stan Eval."

"Well maybe she was but...,"

"There is no but, Colonel! You will need every aircraft and pilot we have available for down there. Besides, this is a very touchy political issue."

"Excuse me, sir. I will not endanger the lives of my pilots for politics!"

"So what do you suggest, Colonel?"

"I will personally take Captain Barnes up and give her another Stan Eval and if she passes, I will gladly take her along."

"Okay, Jack. I know that you're a fair guy and I will respect your opinion."

"Thanks, sir."

"Now may I continue with the briefing?"

"Sorry, go ahead, sir."

"Well Jack, here's the scoop," said the General as he went to the front of the briefing room. Taking the Top Secret classified marking cover off the chart that was hanging on the board, he revealed a map of northern Greece.

"Before I call in the official briefing team, Jack, I would like to give you the courtesy of personally briefing you on your upcoming deployment."

Logan didn't say a word; he just stared at the map and shook his head. Taking this as his cue, the General continued. "You will be flying out of here, hopefully some time tomorrow afternoon and deploying to this airfield," said the General as he pointed to its location on the chart.

"The airfield is roughly eighteen miles east of the city of Kavala near a town called Piges. The field serves as the city's airport and it's used by Olympic Airways and Aegean air, the country's air carriers.

"Excuse me, sir," said Logan, interrupting the General.

"Is the runway large enough to accommodate fully loaded and fueled fighters? What type of facilities do they have in servicing our aircraft?"

General Pope, physically and mentally exhausted by the last twenty-four hours' events, was visibly perturbed at being interrupted. "Let me finish and then you can ask the questions, Colonel."

"Sorry, sir.

"I do share the same concerns as you do, Jack. To answer your question, the Greeks have assured Washington that the runway can handle combat loaded F-16s. Olympic operates medium size passenger jets out of there. So the runway is long enough to handle our combat loaded fighters. The Greek air force is working nonstop to bring the facilities up to par. Nonetheless, we must face the facts. You will be working out of a bare base with limited facilities. Okay, any other questions?"

"What about ammunition and air field security?"

"The Greeks, who always feared something like this would

someday come to pass, had planned for this airfield to serve as an auxiliary air strip in time of war. They had pre-positioned ammunition stocks at this site, mainly MK 83 thousand pound free fall iron bombs for their planes to use in time of war. Your squadron will depart Ramstein fully loaded for air to air combat. We at USAFE will re-supply you with AMRAAMS and smart weapons. The Greeks will be primarily responsible for air defense and security, but we will send a Security Force Air Base Ground Defense team along for support. If you have any other questions, please ask the briefing team, they will be more than happy to answer them for you. Much of the details have already been gone over with your staff this morning."

General Pope moved to the door and was about to leave the room and let the briefing team in, when he stopped in mid stride and turned to Logan.

"Jack, if you notice on that map, the Turkish army is less than 80 miles from that base. I know that the odds are going to be stacked against you, but you are the best! Your pilots are some of the best trained aviators in the world. You will have to go it alone, until we can send you reinforcements. Give um hell and pay the bastards back for what they did here. Good luck!" With that, the General turned around and left the briefing room.

A few blocks to the West, Master Sergeant George Pappas was waiting, half asleep, outside the 568th Security Police flight commander's office. Running his hand through his thinning brown hair, he peeked at his watch, and saw that it was 1541hrs.

He had urgently been recalled back to the base and told that the commander wanted to see him. There was a buzz and the commander's secretary picked up the phone.

"Sergeant, the Major will see you now."

George opened the door and entered the commander's office. Major Murry was sitting at his desk flanked by the rest of his operations staff.

"Have a seat George. I am sorry to have called you back, especially since you had just gotten to bed, but this is very urgent. It's been a trying day for all of us."

George plopped his stocky frame into the soft couch and rubbed his tired eyes. "I realize that, sir. How can I be of assistance?"

"I am sure, George, you have heard of what is going on in Greece?"

George knew good and well what was going on. He had been trying for hours to phone his parents who had retired in Athens several years ago, but was unable to get through.

"Yes sir, I am aware of the outbreak of war between Greece and Turkey."

"Things are going rather badly for the Greeks at this moment," said Major Murry. "They need our help and Ramstein has been tasked to deploy the 526th fighters to Greece."

George gave the Major a look of surprise. "We the 568th will be sending a forty-four man team to Greece for air base ground defense and security. Because of your fluency in Greek, the Colonel wants you to head the team on the enlisted side of the house. You will also act as Security Force liaison to the Greeks."

"Sir, where are we going to find the forty-four men to deploy after last night's fiasco?"

"Don't worry about the details Sergeant. USAFE will bring in TDY troops from Mildenhall air base, England and the States to cover the base. You will take a team consisting of personnel from the 568th and possibly even the 569th.

"When will we be leaving?"

"Some time tomorrow."

"That's rather short notice, sir."

"I realize that George, but the Greeks are desperate. I have been told by intelligence that the Turks have broken through their main border defense line and that the Greek army is in full retreat."

George cringed at the news while he thought of his parents and of the untold suffering and devastation that the war was causing on the Greek people. "Go home George, get some rest, pack your bags and be back here at 0600hrs."

"What about my family here, sir."

"Don't worry; we'll take care of any problems that arise. You're not the only one going; there will be over forty others with you. Any other questions?"

"Where are we deploying to Major, if I may ask?"

"I don't know George. The location is still classified.

However, I know it's somewhere in Northern Greece. You will be operating under bare base conditions in a hostile combat and possible chemical environment. So be prepared for the worst," the Major added.

"Thanks for the information, sir. Now I am going home to pack my bags and hopefully get some rest."

Ramstein Air base
1830hrs, 18 May

Logan quickly scanned the check list as he went through engine shut down procedures for his F-16 fighter. As the engine's turbines began winding down, he unsnapped his pilot's helmet and popped the canopy. It had been a grueling ninety minute flight, but he had definitely assured himself that Captain Barnes was a capable fighter pilot. Despite his years of experience, she had been a serious challenge for him when they had engaged in a mock dog fight. At one point, it appeared that she was going to get the best of him. Only his experience and the few tricks that he had learned over the years had helped him prevail. Releasing his seat harnesses, Logan climbed down the stairs and was met by his crew chief that had a worried look on her face. Logan read her thoughts. "Don't worry Cindy; I didn't abuse her this time."

He could see her instant relief. "Thanks, sir. I could use the time to finish packing and attend the chapel services for those killed in last night's attack."

"I'm sorry about your boyfriend, Cindy." He had been one of those killed in the barracks bombing.

"Thank you, sir. I hope we get a chance to repay the bastards in Greece."

"I am sure we will. Well, here comes the crew van. I'll see you tomorrow."

Climbing into the crew van, he sat next to Wendy Barnes. "Well, how did I do, sir?"

"Captain that was some fancy flying that you did up there. For a moment I thought that you'd even get my six."

Logan saw the look of relief on her face. She looked into his eyes and accidentally touched his lap but quickly withdrew her hand. "Gee, thank you, sir. This is what I've waited for all my life, to be a fighter pilot!"

Logan felt like putting his arms around her and giving her a kiss. Control yourself Jack, remember she's one of your officers and you're going into combat, he thought to himself.

"How about a drink to celebrate?"

"Sure."

Twenty minutes later, both of them were sitting in the casual bar of the officer's club sipping on Champagne. "Not too many people in here, today."

"After last night's fiasco, there isn't much to celebrate about," said Logan.

"I guess you're right, sir. Logan hated it when she called

him, sir.

"Wendy, call me Jack when we are alone and off duty."

"Okay, sir, I mean Jack."

"Jack, you've been to war before. What's it like for a fighter pilot?"

"It's not as glorious as the movies. It's fast and violent. Death comes quick and usually out of nowhere. The best man usually wins."

"Or best person," she said with a smile.

"An air to air missile or a cannon shell doesn't discriminate, Wendy. If you aren't well trained, you die. It's that simple."

"Well, am I good enough?"

It was a loaded question but he would answer her truthfully. "You fly well but I personally don't think you're ready for combat. You need more experience. Most of these guys have hundreds of hours of simulated mock air combat experience under their belts. If it was up to me, you wouldn't be coming along."

"Why, sir, because I'm a woman? I thought you were different. But you're just like the rest of your male chauvinist counterparts," she said and then stormed out of the club.

"Well, I blew that one," he said to himself while draining the remaining champagne in his glass.

The Northern Aegean
1950hrs, 18 May

After the attack on the enemy convoy and with only seconds to spare, the Hydra had made it to the rocky isle of Agios Efstratios. The enemy missiles that were fired at her locked onto the isle instead and exploded in the rocky cliffs. Yiannis quickly found the large cavern he was looking for, eased the boat in, dropped anchor and waited until dusk. During the course of the day, they could hear helicopters and other aircraft passing overhead. Finally with the sun beginning to set over the Aegean Sea, the missile boat Hydra pulled out of her hiding spot and headed into the Northern Aegean. With her radar turned off to avoid detection, Yiannis had posted extra lookouts to provide early warning.

"Sir, we have to slow to eighteen knots, the seas are becoming too rough to sustain this speed. The wind is already over force five and worsening," advised Warrant Officer Panou.

"Okay, Pavlos, you can lower our speed. Hopefully this weather will ground all Turkish aircraft, at least till morning."

"That's what we're all gambling on, sir. We still have about forty minutes of light left."

"Captain!" yelled one of the lookouts as he rushed into the bridge. "I've spotted a yellow object in the water, possibly a life raft, approximately a thousand meters off our port bow."

Lieutenant Vassiliou rushed outside, taking his binoculars

with him. Putting them up to his eyes, Yiannis could distinctly see a yellow object, possibly a raft, bobbing on the waves. "I think it's an overturned life raft, and there is someone in the water holding on to it," hollered Yiannis, loud enough to be heard over the wind and waves.

Rushing back inside, he ordered the helmsman to alter course toward the life raft. While the Hydra rapidly closed in on the over turned raft, several sailors stood by the ship's railing to help the man out of the water. The Hydra was maneuvered next to the raft and one of her sailors threw out a rope to the struggling man in the water. But the person was too exhausted to grab the rope that was tossed to him. Immediately, one of the sailors jumped into the rough water to give him a helping hand. Grabbing hold of the man, the sailor put a life vest around him and both of them were quickly hauled aboard.

"Captain, we've hoisted the survivor on board. He's a little worn out from exposure, but once he gets some dry clothes on and something hot to drink, he'll be okay," said Mr. Panou.

"Who is he?"

"He's a survivor from one of our scout planes which was shot down this morning. I think you will be in for a surprise."

Before Yiannis could reply, Lieutenant Mavridis walked into the bridge, covered with a blanket and dripping water. "Takis! What the hell..."

"Sorry to drop in like this, unannounced, Yiannis. But my plane was shot down this morning. I was the only survivor."

"Thank God for that, my friend."

"I've been drifting in that raft since 0600hrs. I was okay until the weather started worsening. The raft was capsized by a large wave about thirty minutes ago. I thought I was a goner until you guys came along and rescued me."

"It was lucky for you that we did. Now go down to my cabin and change into one of my uniforms before you get pneumonia."

"You don't have to tell me twice, Yiannis. I'll be right back."

"Sir, the wind is still picking up. It's at force six."

"I can feel it," Yiannis said to Mr. Panou, the on duty helmsman."It'll get worse before the night is over. Lower our speed to fourteen knots."

"Yes, sir."

"Two unidentified helicopters at three o'clock," yelled the starboard look out."

"Sound General Quarters!" commanded Yiannis.

The worst had happened, they had been spotted. While the crew rushed to their battle stations, Yiannis picked up his binoculars and saw the two helicopters coming in low over the water. The two AH-1 Cobra gunships had been returning to their base from a fire support mission and had been diverted westward to avoid a number of rain squalls. Spotting the Hydra in the dim evening light, they quickly moved in for the kill.

"Here they come," yelled Mr. Georgiou. At the same

moment, the Hydra's two 35mm anti-aircraft guns began filling the air above the boat with exploding shells. Luckily for all of them, the helicopters had expanded most of their heavy weapons on Limnos. Fighting a forty knot head wind, the two gunships fired off their remaining 2,75inch rockets at the weaving and bobbing missile boat. Most of the salvo passed harmlessly over the Hydra, except for a rocket that struck the ship and exploded in the engine room. The boat immediately lost power and thick smoke poured out of the engine room. The damage control parties, with hoses in hand, rushed to put out the fires and restore power to the ship. Lieutenant Mavridis, dressed in one of Yiannis' uniforms, raced into the bridge, just in time to shout a warning.

"Here they come again!"

The pilots of the two gunships, seeing the missile boat dead in the water, rushed in for the kill. However, in their haste to finish her off, they disregarded the Hydra's two 35mm cannons and made a head on pass. When the two helicopters were within eight hundred meters of the boat, the Hydra's guns opened fire. Now committed, the Cobras pressed their attack. As they were about to open fire, the lead ship disintegrated into a ball of flame after running into a stream of 35mm shells.

"We got the bastard," yelled Lieutenant Vassiliou.

But their success was short lived. The other gunship made its pass raking the Hydra with 20mm cannon fire as it flew by. The pilot of the surviving gunship, after seeing his partner blown out of the sky and not wanting to press his luck any further, broke off the attack and headed for home, trailing smoke.

With her engines out and the bridge in shambles, the Hydra was now at the mercy of the wind and seas.

"Get a medic," screamed Lieutenant Mavridis, as he attempted to apply a tourniquet to Ensign Georgiou, the weapons officer who had been wounded in both legs.

"Takis, take over Mr. Georgiou's post, I'll tend to his wounds. See if you can get power restored. Get us moving before we broach in these high seas," yelled Yiannis, loud enough to be heard above the noise of the roaring wind and seas coming through the smashed bridge windshield.

"I'll see what I can do in the engine room, Yiannis."

A couple of minutes later, several crewmen arrived with stretchers removing the dead sailor's body and the wounded so the job of clean up and repair could begin. After the dead and wounded had been removed, Yiannis picked up the bridge's phone and called the engine room. It was answered by Lieutenant Mavridis.

"Yiannis, the Chief says that he can restore power to at least two of the engines in a few minutes. The other two have serious damage. He's shorthanded on help, one of his men was killed and another wounded."

"I understand, Takis. Tell him to give it his best. We can't take much more of this beating. Besides, we're sitting ducks."

"I doubt the Turks will dispatch any aircraft to look for us in this weather,"

"You're probably right, Takis, but if they have any destroyers patrolling this area, we've had it."

The Chief, true to his word, had power restored to two of the engines fifteen minutes later. Once again, the Hydra turned her bow into the storm and continued on her journey to safety. Nightfall found the small missile boat plowing northward through heavy, rain swept seas. The weather had worsened to the point where the boat's crew had to tie life lines to provide some protection from being tossed overboard by the heavy seas. Inside the Hydras CIC, Lieutenant Vassiliou and his staff were debating their next move.

"Would any of you gentlemen like some coffee before we start?" asked Yiannis.

"No, I've had enough for now," said Takis.

"Chief?"

"No thanks, sir."

"I'll take some," said Mr. Fanopoulos, the boat's communication and electronics specialist.

"Ah! A man of my tastes," said Yiannis, getting a laugh from everybody around the table. *At least morale was still good*, he thought.

"Well gentlemen, I am open to any and all suggestions as to our next course of action."

Lieutenant Mavridis spoke first. "As you all can see

gentlemen, the weather has worsened. The boat, with only two engines running, is barely making headway in these heavy seas and we are extremely low on fuel. My suggestion is we head for Skyros. The weather is too severe for the Turks to mount any air patrols; I believe we'll make it through.

"Chief, what do you think?"

Chief Chronis didn't hesitate to answer. "I'm with the Lieutenant. We're very low on fuel, sir and the weather isn't helping any. Besides, I might be able to get the other engine going if I'm able to find the part on Skyros."

"Mr. Fanopoulos?"

"I agree with the Chief. We should head for Skyros. Our wounded need medical attention. Ensign Georgiou lost a lot of blood, he needs a hospital."

"Warrant officer Panou is on the bridge. I haven't asked his opinion, but I'm sure he would go along with all of you," said Yiannis.

Yiannis picked up the phone and rang the bridge. The phone was answered by Ensign Tasakis. Fresh out of Electronic Warfare School, the Hydra was his first assignment. He had joined the boat on Limnos.

"Bridge, Ensign Tasakis."

"This is the Captain. How is it out there? Are you picking up any emissions on the ESM?

"No, sir," screamed Ensign Tasakis into the mike, loud enough to be heard over the howling wind caused by the bridge's broken windshield which still hadn't been repaired. "Everything is quiet and we are not picking up anything on the radar."

"Thank you, Mr. Tasakis, that will be all."

"The lad has picked up his trade pretty fast."

"He had a good teacher, sir," said Mr. Fanopoulos.

Yiannis rang the bridge again. "Mr. Panou, set a course for Skyros immediately."

"Yes, sir." A few minutes later, the Hydra slowly came about and pointed her bow toward Skyros, seventy miles away.

Sea of Crete

0458hrs, 19 May

A couple of hundred miles to the south, the United States Navy hunter killer submarine U.S.S. Clinton, cruised silently three hundred feet beneath the dark waters of the Sea of Crete. Her crew was going through the procedures for launching her Tomahawk cruise missiles. The crew had practiced this procedure countless times, but had never actually launched a live missile. This time would be different. Her Captain walked through the hatch into the control room.

"Captain's in the control room," cried the officer of the watch. The Captain checked their position on the plotting board. They had been at flank speed for the last ten hours.

"I have the comm.,"

"Sir, the missiles have been programmed with the target coordinates and have been loaded into the launch tubes." said the sub's weapons officer.

"Excellent, bring us up to sixty feet."

The helmsman applied slight pressure to the aircraft type control wheel that controlled the dive planes and the giant behemoth began her rise out of the depths.

"How does it look up top, Chief?"

"Except for a small fishing boat three miles to the west of us, it's all clear, Captain."

"Thanks, Chief."

"Leveling off at sixty feet, sir," advised the helmsman.

"Make your speed five knots."

"Up periscope." The head of the periscope broke the surface and rose several feet into the air. The Captain swept the area. Except for the small fishing boat that was clear of the launch area, there was nothing else in sight. "Down scope."

"Make the missiles ready for firing."

"All ready, sir," said the weapons officer having previously fed all the target data through his command and control system to the twelve Tomahawks in the vertical launch system.

"Send the babies on their way, Mike," the Captain said to the weapons officer.

"Aye, aye, skipper."

Having been given the launch command, the metal hatch protecting the first missile clanged open, followed by the explosive charge which propelled the seven meter long missile toward the surface. The sound of the launch reverberated through the boat. It was immediately followed by the sound of the sea rushing in to fill the void left by the missile in the empty tube and the hatch clanging shut. This sequence went on for eleven more times as the Clinton sent her entire complement of Tomahawks eastward.

A few miles to the West, the crew of the fishing boat Agios Minas had just finished raising their nets as had dozens of generations of fishermen before them. Elated on their good haul, they had all taken a break for a shot of ouzo before heading home. As the ouzo began to take the night chill from their bones, they heard a rumbling coming from the sea a few miles east of their location. A couple of seconds later, twelve pillars of fire burst forth from the sea and quickly disappeared toward the northwest. Terrified, the three fishermen dropped to their knees and prayed to Saint Nicholas, the patron saint of seafarers, invoking his protection from the evil that had just erupted from the sea.

"All the missiles are off and running, sir," said the weapons officer.

"Johnson, send off a message and let headquarters know."

"Aye, aye, sir."

Salamina Naval Base

0751hrs, 19 May

It had been a pure night of hell for the Hydra and her crew. Their small boat was tossed about the waves and battered by the heavy seas, but the storm had also served as their salvation. It had grounded the enemy's air patrols and kept most of their ships in port, giving the Hydra the opportunity to escape. When she finally reached Skyros, her fuel tanks were practically dry. During their brief refueling stop on the island, all the wounded were dropped off so they could receive the proper medical attention which they needed.

Soon after the Hydra departed Skyros, the storm's intensity began to abate, enabling Lieutenant Vassiliou to order an increase of speed to twenty knots. This had become possible, thanks to Chief Chronis's uncanny scrounging abilities that enabled him to find the necessary parts to repair another engine. By daybreak, the missile boat had cleared Cape Sounion and entered the Saronic Gulf where the seas were much calmer. With her three working engines at full power, she was soon surging ahead at twenty-five knots.

Two hours later, the Hydra tied up to her moorings at Salamina naval base to the cheers of dozens of sailors and TV crews.

"Takis, what the hell is going on?" Yiannis said, surprised at the throng of people awaiting their arrival.

"I don't know Yiannis, but it seems that for some unknown reason we're suddenly quite popular..."

Once the boat was secured and the gang plank dropped, an entourage of senior officers, headed by Admiral Diyiannis, fleet commander, boarded the Hydra.

"Welcome aboard, sir," said Yiannis, as he rendered a salute to the senior officer.

"Thank you, Lieutenant,"

"May I ask sir, why the official welcoming committee?"

The Admiral gave Captain Tassiou, Yiannis's squadron commander and Commodore Ballas, the base commander, a puzzled look. "Gentlemen, I don't believe they know," said the Admiral.

"You're probably correct on that assumption, sir. They were maintaining radio silence the whole time," said Captain Tassiou.

"Know what?" asked a very bewildered Lieutenant Vassiliou.

"You're heroes," said Commodore Ballas.

"We're what! Heroes?"

"That's correct, Lieutenant," said Admiral Diyiannis."

"Your daring attack on the Turkish convoy that was steaming for Limnos saved the island from immediate capture. The two transports your missiles hit were, according to intelligence sources, carrying artillery and tanks to reinforce the enemy beach head," added Captain Tassiou.

"How did you ascertain this information?"

"The submarine Katsounis finished the job several hours later, torpedoing a damaged LST that was under tow. The other transport had been abandoned and was still burning when the Katsounis left the area," added Admiral Diyiannis.

"Sir, we were just doing our duty" said Yiannis, humbled at the thought he was now a national hero. He looked around the damaged bridge that still bore the scars of the encounter with the Turkish helicopters.

"The real heroes are the three sailors that didn't make it back," said Yiannis, as he pointed to the three body bags that were being carried off the boat and into a waiting ambulance.

"Lieutenant, before this war is over, many brave men won't make it back. Many good men are dying just as we speak. Nevertheless," added the Admiral, "the destruction of that convoy saved us from an immediate military disaster. Your actions and that of your crew, helped buy the time our forces needed to regroup and somewhat stabilize the situation on the island. Otherwise, the island would have surely fallen to the enemy."

"What is the present situation on Limnos, sir?"

"Not too good, Lieutenant. The enemy controls Mirina and much of the coastal areas. We control most of the interior and the island's only air strip. The situation is critical but our forces are tenaciously holding on." Yiannis prayed that Eleni had somehow made it into the island's interior and at least for now, temporary safety. "As for the rest of the front," the Admiral took a deep breath and went on to say, "our army in Thrace is strategically withdrawing to new defensive positions. The same goes for the situation in Epirus and Macedonia, which is more of a holding action as we concentrate on the main threat in Thrace."

In other words, the army has suffered a disaster and is in retreat thought Yiannis, seeing through the Admiral's bullshit.

"Oh, I almost forgot Lieutenant, excuse me, Commander. Your promotion to Lieutenant Commander is effective immediately," said Admiral Diyiannis.

"My what?" Said Yiannis, flabbergasted.

"Congratulations, Commander and well done!" Captain Tassiou held out his hand to congratulate Yiannis.

"Well Commander Vassiliou, I don't want to keep you any longer," said Admiral Diyiannis. Intelligence is waiting to debrief you and your crew. Remember Commander, you're heroes. The Greek people are in need of heroes at this point in the war. Good luck, Commander."

"Thank you, sir."

The Admiral shook Yiannis's hand and departed the bridge, Captain Tassiou had remained behind.

"You know he's right, Yiannis. The Greek people are in need of a few heroes right now to build their morale up after the military disasters that this country has just suffered. Right now, the war is going very badly for us. We are in danger of losing not only Limnos, but all of Northern Greece," said Tassiou with a very somber face.

"I wasn't aware that it was that bad, sir."

"It is, Yiannis. Fortunately, the navy only lost a few units in the opening attack and subsequent raids. I am sure you know that the Batsis was lost with all hands."

"I know, sir. We heard them over the radio calling for help." Yiannis looked across the dockyard at the destroyer Navirino, which had been sunk at its moorings.

Reading Yiannis's thoughts, Captain Tassiou replied at the unspoken question. "The Navarino was hit during the first bombing raid on the city."

"What else did we lose?"

"The Frigate Aetos was badly damaged by the opening Albanian raid on Corfu and we lost a couple of gunboats in the Aegean. Otherwise, the fleet is pretty much intact."

"Thank God for that, Sir."

"We need every ship we have if we're going to stand any chance in stopping the Turk, Yiannis"

"There are repair crews working round the clock. After the Hydra is repaired, she'll be back in action and you'll be in charge of a three boat flotilla."

"I am ready to go fight right now and I'm sure my crew feels the same way."

"No rush, Commander. There will be lots of opportunities to strike back at the enemy. What you need now is some rest. Now, let me give you a ride to fleet Intel."

"What about the boat, sir?"

"Don't worry about the Hydra. She'll be in good hands. The yard master will have her repaired in no time."

"Oh sir, I almost forgot. This is Lieutenant Mavridis," he said, introducing his friend who had been standing by the whole time. "We plucked him out of the sea yesterday evening. His Albatross reconnaissance plane had been shot down by Turkish fighters earlier in the morning."

Captain Tassiou offered his handshake to Lieutenant Mavridis. "Ah, yes Lieutenant, we were informed of your rescue this morning by naval headquarters Skyros."

"I'm very lucky that they came by, sir, or else I would be fish food by now. Too bad the rest of my crew wasn't as lucky."

"Those are the fortunes of war, Lieutenant. And by the way, Commander, since we are speaking of fortunes, that was a very wise decision that you made when you pulled into Skyros. It probably saved the life of Ensign Georgiou. The doctors say that he will recover."

"I'm glad to hear that, sir".

"Now, on the subject of Lieutenant Mavridis. As of this morning Lieutenant, you are being reassigned to the navy as the Hydra's new weapons and executive officer. I believe you served as a weapons officer on the missile boat Xenos before your assignment to the air force,"

"That's correct, sir, under commander Grapsas," said a rather surprised, but not disappointed Lieutenant Mavridis.

"I'll work for Yiannis any day of the week, sir."

"That's Commander Vassiliou to you, Lieutenant," said Yiannis, winking his eye to Captain Tassiou.

"Do you understand that, Lieutenant?" said Yiannis in a serious tone.

"But I thought, we . . . " both men burst out laughing, as Lieutenant Mavridis turned beet red. "Well the joke's on me."

"Let's go gentlemen, intelligence is waiting. But before we go, you will give a short interview to the cameras.

"Okay, sir, if you insist."

Ramstein AB. flight line
19 May, 1455hrs

Master Sergeant Pappas along with the rest of his forty four man air base ground defense flight, sat strapped in their seats while the C-130 transport waited its turn to take off for Greece. The six C-130s Hercules and two C-141 Starlifters that were departing Ramstein carried most of the basic items necessary to set up fighter operations at Piges air field. As the turbo prop engines revved to full power and the plane began its take off roll, George remembered his last few hectic hours at Ramstein. To begin with, this whole deployment had been the classic example of your usual cluster fuck from the start. Putting together the forty four man team had not been easy and finding the necessary gear and supplies, in such short order, had been almost next to impossible. George hoped the rest of their needed gear would be forthcoming, but he wasn't holding his breath. What had been worse was trying to sort and put one's personal affairs together in twenty-four hours.

While the plane climbed to cruise altitude, it was suddenly rocked by turbulence. George looked at their two Humvees which were secured by chains to the floor of the aircraft. "I hope those chains hold in this turbulence," he mumbled to himself. Each of the vehicles was equipped with an MK-19, 40MM grenade launcher, able to pump out a stream of grenades to distances of a thousand meters. *At least we'll have some fire power which may come in handy, he thought to himself.* The Greeks were supposed to provide most of the security forces and the heavy weapons needed to guard the air field. George, as well as anyone else in a position of responsibility knew that if the Turks attacked the air field in force, they were all goners.

The sleek F-16 Falcon fighter stood outside its shelter, refueled and uploaded with the latest air to air missiles in the USAF's inventory, ready to begin its two thousand kilometer flight south to harm's way. Logan had just finished his pre-flight check walk around and found everything to be in order. The fighters would be flying with a full air to air ordnance load out and a long distance fuel tank. Additional fuel would be provided by a KC-10 Extender tanker over the Adriatic Sea for the final run into Greece.

"She's all ready to go, sir. I've given her a thorough going over," advised Sergeant Tanner who was filling in for Logan's regular crew chief, now on one of the C-130 transports on her way to Greece.

"Thanks, Sergeant."

"Kick ass and take names, Colonel. Pay the bastards back for what they did here. Some of those cops were my friends."

"Rest assured we intend to."

Climbing into the plane, he secured his safety harness and closed the canopy. Pulling out his checklist, Logan began his engine start up procedures for the short but potentially dangerous flight to their new airfield.

Chapter 12

Northeastern Adriatic

1728hrs, 19 May

After taking off from Ramstein AB, the F-16s of the 526th, quickly formed up with Logan in the lead plane and turned southeast toward Italy. Two hours into the flight, the fighters rendezvoused with a USAF KC-10 Extender tanker over the Adriatic to top off their tanks for the run into Greece. Logan was first to gas up and after he was done, he came off the refueling boom and took his station on the tanker's right wing. His wingman next, stayed connected with the boom until his tanks were filled and was immediately followed by the next fighter. Having accomplished refueling, the flight of F-16s turned for Greece. Twenty minutes later, they entered Greek airspace over the island of Corfu, where they were met by their escorts, two vintage F-4E Phantoms armed with air to air missiles.

"Blue leader to Falcon leader."

"Go ahead Blue leader," replied Logan.

"Welcome to Greece. We're very grateful for your assistance."

"We hope that we'll be of some useful service to you.

"Rest assured. We're glad to see you. We will be your escort till Thessaloniki. There, you will pick up another escort for your final leg."

"Roger, Blue leader. Any sign of enemy air activity?"

"That's a negative in this sector. The Albanians haven't shown themselves since yesterday."

"Roger, Blue leader."

The flight continued westward, the endless blue sky sparkled with brilliance. Logan enjoyed the scenery below which was a panorama of greens, browns and rugged mountains which thrust skyward. Thirty miles west of Thessaloniki, Greece's northern capital, they picked up their new escorts. This time, they were met by two Hellenic Air Force F-16Cs, painted light gray. Both of the fighters were armed for air to air. Logan surmised that the Greeks were using their best equipment for the more dangerous Turkish threat. Thirty kilometers from the city, the country's second largest, they observed large plumes of black smoke rising high above it, the aftermath of a recent air raid.

"Falcon leader, this is Hermes control over."

"This is Falcon leader, go ahead with your message."

During his intelligence briefing at Ramstein, Logan had been told that Hermes control would be the call sign for the Greek air defense command of northern Greece.

"Roger, Falcon leader, we are picking up twenty-one Bandits inbound, altitude five thousand feet, heading 260 degrees, fifty miles east of the city. We are urgently requesting that you intercept inbound enemy aircraft," said the voice over the radio in heavily accented English.

"That's what we're here for, vector us in".

"Roger, Falcon leader, turn to a heading of one zero niner, descend to ten thousand feet. Bandits now at forty miles and closing."

"Roger, Hermes, Falcon leader out."

"Falcon leader to all pilots, we'll engage incoming bandits at maximum range with AMRAAMS. Prepare to salvo missiles at my command."

Logan pushed his throttle forward and toggled his weapon selector switch to air to air, selecting an AIM-120 medium range missile. Switching his radar from standby to attack mode, the missile's seeker head came alive as the plane's radar painted the enemy planes, twenty-five miles to the east, well within the missile's range.

"Falcon one to all birds, fire your missiles!" Almost simultaneously, eighteen AMRAAMS, one of the most sophisticated air to air weapons in the USAF's inventory, left their rails streaking toward the enemy formation.

All hell broke loose in the Turkish bomber formation when the air crews of the fifteen F4E fighter bombers and six F-16c escorts detected the incoming missiles. The once orderly formation quickly disintegrated as the fighter bomber pilots jettisoned their bomb loads and tried to run. With the missiles rapidly closing in, the enemy bombers and their escorts dumped flares and maneuvered frantically trying to escape almost certain death. The sophisticated missiles weren't easily fooled by the counter measures. The Turkish planes had been well within the AMRAAM's envelope. Ten of the missiles found their targets, filling the sky with disintegrating aircraft and parachutes. The few surviving enemy fighter bombers immediately hit afterburners, turned tail and headed for home. The five remaining escorts bravely turned toward the American fighters to buy time for their charges to escape.

"Falcon leader, bandit on your six!" called Logan's wingman over the radio. Logan heard his threat indicator warning go off indicating a missile lock. He punched in afterburner, pulled up and hit the chaff and flare button. Maybe they would save him. The G counter reached 6.9 as his suit inflated to keep him from losing consciousness. The enemy Aim-7 missile seeker head, confused by Logan's violent maneuver, momentarily lost the heat signature of the American fighter and acquired the decoys. It exploded harmlessly less than a hundred meters away. Relieved, Logan turned his head looking for the enemy fighter. Spotting the offending aircraft several miles to the east and heading for the deck, he put his fighter into a dive and selected an AIM 9M all aspect missile. To his left, he momentarily caught a glimpse of an F-16 going down in flames, unknown if it was a friend or foe.

Logan's quarry was already at Mach 1.1 running for his life. But the block fifty Model that Logan was flying was far superior than the block thirty models that Turkey had purchased in the late 90s. Closing in on the enemy plane, Logan's HUD came alive. The enemy aircraft now filled the square and indicated a lock. Logan pressed the button shooting off his missile. The Turkish pilot, anticipating the missile, pulled up and hit his flare and chaff dispenser. The missile flew harmlessly by, going for the decoys instead. At the same time the Turkish pilot turned to fight. However, Logan had expected the move and was waiting. The enemy pilot who was coming in on a head on pass was expecting an easy kill. When Logan's plane filled his gun sight, the pilot squeezed the trigger. Logan kicked the rudder to the left, at the same time putting his plane into a dive and passed harmlessly underneath the deadly stream of 20mm shells. Looping his plane, he rolled up behind the enemy fighter. It was now Logan's turn. The Turkish F-16 rapidly filled his gun sight and he squeezed the trigger, sending a stream of 20mm cannon shells into the enemy plane's engine. Seriously damaged, the enemy plane veered out of control and fire-balled into the ground. Logan didn't see a chute.

"Good shooting, Falcon leader." Momentarily surprised, Logan looked to his left and saw Wendy Barnes's fighter. He cursed himself for his inattentiveness which could have cost him his life and at the same time thanked God that she was okay.

"Thanks, for covering my rear; let's join the rest of the flight." Within a few minutes, Logan had rejoined the rest of the formation. Except for some minor shell damage to one of the other fighters, everyone had survived the encounter.

"Falcon leader to Tiger Shark, can you make the field."

"Roger Falcon leader, I just have some control damage, but I'll make it," replied Major Waslowski, his acting executive officer.

"Good work, gentlemen, oh, and ladies. Keep your heads up, we don't need any surprises."

Fifteen minutes later, the 526th had reached their destination, Piges airfield. Two Hellenic air force F-16s would remain orbiting the air field to provide CAP for the American planes until they got refueled and rearmed.

"Falcon leader to all birds, we're going to make our entry look good, overhead recovery." Logan knew that at the most, they would be lucky to get fifteen minutes notice of an impending air raid. It was every pilot's nightmare to get pounced while coming in for a landing. Besides being impressive to those on the ground, an overhead recovery was the standard landing pattern for fighters returning from a mission. It offered the least exposure time to vulnerable landing aircraft. The first three fighters approached the runway at echelon formation. The lead plane pitched out as it crossed the threshold and the others followed at five second intervals, seven hundred meters apart.

After landing at the field, the planes were quickly directed to air craft shelters by the base's ground control. Logan parked his plane outside the shelter where he had been instructed to taxi to. He was met there by his own crew chief and a Hellenic air force ground crew that would refuel and rearm his plane. Shutting down his engine, he popped his canopy and climbed out of the cockpit, drenched in sweat. Even before he had completely exited the plane, the Greeks had connected a tow bar to the front wheel and began pulling the plane into the shelter.

"It seems that they run a very efficient operation here, Cindy."

"They have to, sir. The enemy is only minutes away."

"I guess you're right. I'm sure the Turks know by now that this air field has been activated,"

"So, has everyone gotten a place to stay, Cindy?"

"I don't know, sir. We only arrived little more than an hour ago."

Logan heard the sound of an approaching vehicle and turned. A Mercedes 4x4 jeep stopped in front of the shelter and two men wearing Hellenic Air Force uniforms stepped out.

"Excuse me, Cindy, this must be the official welcoming committee,"

The older of the two men, sporting Colonel's insignia, walked up to Logan with a beaming smile and offered his handshake.

"Welcome to Greece. I'm Colonel Sardis, the Base Commander and this is my executive officer Lieutenant Colonel Kazas who will be serving as your liaison officer," he said in heavy accented English.

"Welcome to Piges, Colonel," said Kazas with a perfect American accent, as he offered his handshake.   He noticed Logan's surprised look. "I was born and raised in New York City. My family immigrated back to Greece in the early 1990s. I always wanted to fly, so I decided to join the Greek Air Force. I've been back to the States several times to attend training classes."

"Well that explains your American accent," answered Logan, as he shook the man's hand.

"Colonel Logan, on behalf of the Hellenic Air Force and Government, I would like to thank you and your men for the timely interception and destruction of the enemy raiding force. Their destruction saved countless lives," said Colonel Sardis.

"That's why we are here, sir."

"Our air force is still recovering from yesterday's surprise attack.   Many of our bases were hit by missiles carrying chemical munitions. We lost scores of pilots and personnel to those attacks. We need time to mobilize and restructure. What pilots we have left are barely holding their own. Our losses have been very heavy. We can continue the conversation later. I am sure, Colonel Logan, you would like to freshen up a bit after your long flight,"

"That sounds like a good idea," he replied, following the two men to the waiting jeep.

Istanbul Turkey
19 May 1900hrs

General Kemal stood silently watching the grim spectacle of the rescue crews searching for bodies in the still smoldering rubble, that only until recently had been the defense ministry. Most of the four story structure had collapsed after being struck in an early morning cruise missile attack on the city. He had spent much of the day shuttling back and forth from his new headquarters at Kesan, trying to coordinate the rescue efforts at the bombed out ministry. As the rescue teams carefully shifted through the debris, every now and then, there would be a cry as another body was found and pulled out of the rubble. The casualty toll in the attack had been heavy. More than seventy personnel had been pulled out dead from the rubble and another twenty had been pulled out injured. Thirty were still unaccounted for. This blow had been particularly serious because amongst the dead and missing were several senior officers, vital for the war effort. Many of these men had been his lifelong friends.

"Come sir, it's time to leave for Kesan," said his aid, Colonel Azoglou.

"Yes, Ahmet, there is nothing more that we can do here."

"The country and the Revolution were very fortunate today, sir. It must have been divine Providence that saved you. If the attack had occurred an hour later, you would have been inside the ministry, attending the morning briefing."

"That is very true, my friend. But we have been careless. I should have anticipated this type of reaction and attack from the Americans. Our carelessness has cost us dearly. My fourth Army Commander is dead, along with much of his staff and there are two members from the Revolutionary committee still among the missing."

"Don't blame yourself, sir." The two men's conversation was momentarily interrupted when a motor cycle stopped in front of them. The rider, an air force courier, handed the General a sealed envelope. Opening it, Kemal read its contents. The General's expression quickly changed from one of concern to one of anger and frustration.

"Is it bad news?" asked Colonel Azoglou.

"The air force is reporting that a strike package on its way to hit targets in Thessaloniki, was intercepted by what they believe to have been a flight of USAF F-16s. Most of our strike force was lost."

"Americans, sir?"

Kemal handed the message to his aid. Colonel Azoglou quickly read the message's contents. "But how is it possible that the Americans have reacted so rapidly. Where did these planes come from?"

"They must have stripped their bases in Europe of remaining planes to help bolster the Greeks!" said Kemal, visibly agitated by the sudden turn of events.

"It has to be only a token force, at the most a squadron, sir."

"In the name of the Prophet, I swear the Americans will pay dearly for their involvement! I want their airbase found and destroyed as soon as possible. I want no survivors! We will teach the Americans a lesson and demonstrate to the Greeks that nothing can save them."

"Not to worry sir, our forces will crush the Greeks, regardless of what the Americans do. Their air force is in disarray after the chemical attacks on their bases. Our resupply effort to Limnos will soon get under way and our tanks are almost to Kommotini. The city will fall within hours. The Infidels are in full retreat. They can't possibly hope to hold out much longer." said Colonel Azoglou.

"You are right, Ahmet. Victory is within our grasp. Our eternal enemies, the Greeks, will soon be defeated and at our mercy. Their fate will be to once again become a vassal state in our new Ottoman Empire! After we are victorious, the rest of the faithful will flock to our banner. Nothing will stop us. We will control the oil, the life blood of the West. They too will be at our mercy. There will be an Islamic empire once again that will stretch from Persia to the Atlantic under the Ottoman sultanate! But first, we must ensure the total destruction of the Greek military and the American air expeditionary force."

- Title: Operation Medina™: The Crusade
- Author: George Mavro
- Price: $27.95
- Publisher: TotalRecall Publications, Inc.
- Format: HARDCOVER, 6.14" x 9.21"
- Number of pages: 320
- 13-digit ISBN: 978-1-59095-747-9
- Publication: 2011

The second book of the series Operation Medina, Crusade, opens up with the Greeks retreating on all fronts from the Turkish onslaught. The U.S. has dispatched an expeditionary force consisting of a fighter squadron and a small USAF Security Force to assist the Greeks.

As the Americans join the fight against the Turks, they begin to exact a heavy toll on the enemy. The Greeks manage to stabilize their Albanian and Macedonian fronts, yet are unable to halt the Turks, who continue to push them back. As the tide of battle begins to turn against General Kemal, he plans a final act of madness. A daring plan is formulated involving a simultaneous attack from both air and land to stop the madman from carrying out his deadly scheme. If the plan fails, the Americans will use the only other alternative left to stop him, a B-2 bomber with a nuclear payload which could lead to a nuclear showdown with other Islamic states. With the odds stacked highly against them, the allies must find a way to stop Kemal and avert a nuclear holocaust.